Three
Albert
Terrace

M. S. CLARY

Matador
Unit E2 Airfield Business Park,
Harrison Road, Market Harborough,
Leicestershire. LE16 7UL
Tel: 0116 2792299
Email: books@troubador.co.uk
Web: www.troubador.co.uk/matador
Twitter: @matadorbooks

ISBN 978 1803132 556

British Library Cataloguing in Publication Data.
A catalogue record for this book is available from the British Library.

Printed and bound in the UK by TJ Books Limited, Padstow, Cornwall
Typeset in 11pt Minion Pro by Troubador Publishing Ltd, Leicester, UK

Matador is an imprint of Troubador Publishing Ltd

With grateful thanks to everyone who
helped me find my way to Albert Terrace
(you know who you are!)

Preface

'The waitress brings the drinks straight away. Mine's hidden under a ton of ice, bits of orange peel and a lettuce. I prod around with the straw but a chunk of ice flips onto the floor. I should grab a napkin, pick it up, but it's too far away, out of reach. The guy I'm with keeps talking, hasn't noticed, so I carry on nodding, trying to look cool.'

'So you've made it up with Simon?'

'All the while in my peripheral vision, I see this ice cube. I'm wondering, should I say something? And soon the ice is melting into a puddle. I can't stop looking. What if there's an accident, someone breaks a leg, bangs their head? What if it's fatal...?'

'So how is Simon these days?'

I love Adele, but she can be difficult at times, doesn't always seem to cotton on.

'Who I was with is not the point,' I say.

'What is the point then?'

'Well, I suppose what I'm trying to say is, who would be responsible?'

'Is this a quiz?'

She has this annoying habit of twisting her hair round her finger. Perhaps she thinks it makes her look younger. Perhaps I find it annoying because my hair isn't the sort you can twist.

'I'm trying to describe how I was faced with a dilemma.'

'But, Hanna, it's only hypothetical, so does it matter whose fault it was?'

'Suppose the fault was mine?'

There, I'd said it. Out Loud. What had been worrying me for days. I couldn't bring myself to walk past the Blue Banana in case they'd been closed down.

'I think you're taking it too seriously. Food gets dropped in restaurants all the time.'

'Yes, but if I was responsible and did nothing, that makes me responsible for any repercussions doesn't it?'

'But you don't know there were any repercussions. Unless there's something you're not telling me?'

We were both silent for a while.

'Anyway,' she says. 'Did you enjoy the meal?'

Part One

1

I'm due to meet Angela Marriott at three. Records show I've introduced her to twenty-eight properties in the past two and a half months. We're on first name terms now. We're here to view one of the new apartments by the river. I'm sure she's seen two already, if not three. They're conversions on the site of an old factory. Mostly they get bought up as an investment, or by rich folks to rent out to other rich folks who never stay long because they're in transition; a divorce maybe, or short-term work contract. It's very quiet here. You seldom see anybody and most of the properties appear empty. One or two owners have put out shiny painted tables and chairs on the balcony, but I've never seen anybody sitting there.

I let myself in, open the blinds and switch on the lights. Ten past three and Angela still hasn't arrived. We're four floors up, it's overcast outside, so it doesn't make a lot of difference. I wish I'd bought some flowers. Actually, Angela has done this to me more than once. Telephoned at the last minute to say something has come up or not turned up at all. She's going through a separation and there is always some crisis brewing about who is getting custody of this or that. I think they sorted out the cat, but I forgot to remind her there's a clause preventing pet ownership at Riverside Apartments. Mr Marriott (Jim) went out to Dubai a year ago and doesn't seem to be coming back. I'll give her until three twenty, then I'm off.

The previous occupant of this place took his own life eight months ago but it's only just recently been listed. The owner was advised to wait a bit longer but he seemed determined to crack on. Somebody told me the police were investigating. I can't remember if it was an overdose or whether he hanged himself. I look round but can't see any obvious spots for a hanging, though people who are determined can be very inventive. Must have had it planned well in advance. Would be weird though, cooking your supper every night, looking at a beam and thinking, that's the one.

I'm wondering how Adele is getting on at Albert Terrace. That house has been on the market for two years. It's what the agency optimistically call a fixer-upper. I've offered to buy her a drink if she ever manages to sell it. I'm a bit worried about Adele. She didn't make her quota last month.

Right, Angela, your time's up. Her mobile's switched off, but I send a text anyway. I pull the blinds and turn off the lamps. As I walk to the car a slight drizzle starts up. I encounter nobody.

2

It's Simon's weekend to have Sam. He phones to ask if we can all meet up.

'You're not working, are you Hanna?' He says. 'You know she really likes to see you.'

I remind him of the day she threw my green bean salad into the river.

'Well, you know what she's like about anything with air miles.'

'Hmm…'

'Well, what about a trip to London, a museum, or perhaps a movie?'

I picture Sam's face at the thought of a museum. I ponder the likelihood of Sam and me sitting through the same movie. Early on, one bright Saturday morning, we bonded in Superdrug over the eye shadows, but it wasn't a theme that helped us move forward. She's always fiddling with her phone and if I ask what she's doing, she ignores me.

'Afterwards we can eat at that place you like – you know, where you dropped the ice cube.'

He hasn't asked what sort of day I've had or called me gorgeous. And I'd rather not be reminded of the ice cube.

Simon and I met in a bar one lunchtime just after he and Annie separated. We had too much to say to each other, too much to drink and I slept with him the same afternoon. I know, I know, first date, but at the time I didn't realise we were having a date.

'Her mother and I had words,' he says.

'So, what's new?' I say.

According to Simon, Annie is either a mad bitch or, in extremis, a fucking mad cow. But today she's just got 'issues'. There was obviously something between them once. I'd like to get to the nub, hear some detail, but he never quite says and perhaps I don't really want to know. 'She's a busy woman,' he said once, 'writing poems to Bruce Springsteen.' He was being sarcastic, but she did once get one published.

'Are we on for Saturday, then? I could pick you up at four.'

I tell him I'll have to look at my diary but I know I'll probably say yes.

*

A few weeks ago, Adele asks me if I was going away for Christmas. Are you joking? I said. The commission I've earned recently would hardly buy a couple of nights in Chipping Norton, though if I get a bite at Riverside, I'll be laughing. I wonder how Adele can afford thoughts of holidays based on her recent sales. It's early, 9.30 a.m. on a chilly autumn morning and the office is quiet.

'So how did it go at Albert Terrace? Didn't you have another viewing yesterday?'

Adele is blowing her nose, the manoeuvre taking longer than might be expected.

'Oh, OK I suppose.'

'Are they interested?'

'You never know, do you.'

She's acting skittery, opening her desk drawers as if looking for something then, finding nothing, closing them again. It's like she's drunk too much coffee. Something's on her mind.

'Well you must have some idea. Did they say anything about a second viewing?'

'Not exactly.' She's twisting her hair round her finger again. One day I'm going to ask her to stop.

'You never told me if you and Simon are getting back together,' she says.

'You never know, do you.'

We can both play that game. I open up my inbox. Nothing from the Marriott woman about Riverside. I remind myself to phone her later. A heavy silence in the office is broken by another forceful nasal blast from Adele. I pass over the box of tissues and say, 'Is something up?'

'You never said how things are going between you and Simon.'

'There's nothing to tell and why do you keep changing the subject?'

I think she's going to ignore me, then suddenly she blurts out, 'I'm fine! Leave it. Bugger Albert Terrace! If you really want to know, I never went. I missed the appointment. I forgot. So shoot me. Tell Charlie. Tell him to fucking fire me, if you like.'

The outburst comes from nowhere. I turn to look out of the window. A strong breeze is blowing a clutch of browning leaves along the street. There's something strange about her manner. She's hardly looked in my direction all the while we've been talking, and she doesn't often swear. I feel troubled at the thought of her risking her job.

'It's not the end of the world, Adele,' I say. 'If it comes to anything, tell Charlie you were unwell. He'll understand.'

'You know he's only waiting for a chance to fire me.' She spits out the words.

It's true. Adele hasn't had a sale in months and, to Charlie, missing an appointment is worse than homicide.

'Well, it's not exactly a crime,' I say. 'It's only one appointment. If there's a complaint, I'll say you asked me to cover for you and I forgot.'

'What if I missed more than one?' she says, which strikes me as a strange response.

'I'll say I double-booked or went to the wrong address. We'll think of something. Nobody died.'

Silence descends over the office. A silence that creeps out from the four corners of the room, drifts past the computers and over the filing cabinets.

'You'd do that for me?' asks Adele, eventually.

'It's no big deal. I'll alter my diary, make it look official. I'll do it now. If Angela Marriott puts in for Riverside, Charlie won't even notice.' I don't believe this for one minute, but the thought is comforting.

It occurs to me it's odd there hasn't already been a complaint from an angry client left standing in the cold outside the Albert Terrace property. Perhaps she never made any appointments. But why not? I'm baffled. The phone rings and there's no opportunity to say more. We make an effort to get back to work.

Later, Adele brings me a cup of coffee, asks me to tell Charlie she feels unwell, and goes home early.

Next morning, there's no sign of her. Charlie comes in much later than usual. Wants me in his office asap. He's got this kind of floppy hair, dirty-blond, that needs a trim but something in his manner tells me this isn't the moment to offer advice. He doesn't bother asking me to sit, but I sit anyway. I think I know there's trouble coming.

'Pity Adele's not here yet,' he starts off. 'Do you know anything about what happened at Albert Terrace yesterday?'

I'm about to break in with my apologies on Adele's behalf when Charlie says, 'The police have been in touch, asking if we saw anything funny.'

The police? I don't know what to make of this, so I shake my head and say nothing.

'Well,' says Charlie. 'I told them Adele would have let me know if she'd seen anything fishy but I had to ask. Has she said anything to you?'

Cautiously I ask, 'Has something happened?'

'Too right,' answers Charlie. He leans back and his jacket falls open to expose a red checked shirt stretched tight across his belly.

'They've found a body.'

A body? Does he mean a dead body? Such concepts are completely out of place in this office. Here we talk of charming properties, cheeky offers, and new bathrooms.

'Adele asked me to keep the appointment for her,' I say, 'but in the end I couldn't make it. I was going to ring the client and apologise.'

'Oh, you'd never have got near the place. The postman noticed a broken window and spoke to a neighbour. Neighbour called the police. Police broke in and found this body. A woman. Blood everywhere.'

Completely shocked, I sit back in my chair and try to think. Even Adele would have noticed a dead body.

'Why did the police want to speak to us?' It's a feeble question but I'm playing for time, giving myself a chance to think. Fortune Estates 'For Sale' sign has been anchored outside the house for months. Some wag had painted in Mis-Fortune. Charlie ignores the question anyway.

'Do you know anything about the other visits she made before yesterday?' He is puffing a bit.

'Cancelled, I think she said.'

'What? All of them?'

'You know how it is. People drive past. Don't like the look from the outside.' Why am I saying all this?

'Hmm. Well, you'd both better check your diaries for dates. We need to get everything ship shape before Billy Boy comes calling.' I catch his tone and nod. 'We'll all do our best to help.' He's having difficulty catching his breath. 'Tell me the minute Adele comes in.'

I've got Adele on speed-dial. I try her three or four times during the day, but get no reply.

3

Police Officer Morgan stands by the office window, feet wide apart.

'So you've never been to number three Albert Terrace on any occasion?'

I've offered him a chair but he says he prefers to remain standing, so I, too, feel obliged to stay on my feet.

'That's right. I should have gone there last Friday afternoon to cover for a colleague.' Officer Morgan doesn't react. He's thumbing backwards through a small notebook.

'A statement by Ms Adele Stevens, your colleague here at Fortune Estates, claims differently.'

'Oh?' I haven't heard anything more from Adele. She's been off work for two days and hasn't responded to my texts. I wonder when the police spoke to her. I look past him as rain begins to splash across the window, quickly turning to hailstones. I'm wondering where I've left my umbrella. Wondering where this is going.

'In her statement, she gave me a list of the dates you visited on her behalf over the past six weeks.'

Six Weeks! Is Adele mad? I should have anticipated this, got my story straight.

Officer Morgan straightens, preparing to ask further questions. I notice the sharp crease in the sleeve of his white shirt. I wonder who ironed it for him. Perhaps there is a nice wife at home with the children or perhaps he does his own, maybe he sends out to the laundry...

'Well?' he asks.

'I will have to look at my notes, officer, and let you know.'

That should satisfy him. Give me a chance to speak to Adele. Get this mess sorted. I need to sit down.

'Please, won't you sit down,' I say.

Officer Morgan doesn't reply. A useful fact gleaned from TV dramas is that lying to the law, even an accidental lie, is always a bad idea. It worries me. It's as though I've already been found guilty of something. But of what? Lying obviously, but...

'So, can I take it you are familiar with three Albert Terrace?' He is writing in his little notebook.

'Well, yes, of course I am. Technically, it wasn't really one of my listings.'

'But you agreed to take on viewings to help out your colleague?'

'Yes, in a way.'

'So when was the last time you went to three Albert Terrace?'

'Well, as I said, I should have gone a few days ago but...'

'No, the last time you visited the property.' He emphasises the *last*. 'Precise dates will help with our inquiries.'

I cast about wildly and pull a phantom out of the air. 'Oh, perhaps about three weeks ago. I'll have to look it up.'

A silence fills the room. The lie sits between us on the wood-look laminate like a troublesome spider. He's closed his notebook, tucked it away. I would like to snatch it out of the top pocket of that too-white shirt. I should have tried to distract him. Should have crossed my legs slowly, even though I despise that sort of thing. At least offered him a cup of tea.

'Have you found out yet who the person was?' I say, not quite knowing what words to use. 'The one who was found there?'

'The deceased has yet to be identified but we will keep you informed.' A formal response, what else did I expect?

A message comes in for him on his radio. I hear a scratchy, distorted voice at the other end but can make no sense of it. It seems he's being called away somewhere. He's picked up his jacket and is making for the door.

'Would you like a cup of tea?'

'I would appreciate it if you could phone those dates to me asap Mrs… err,' looking at his notes, 'Ms. Summers. And if anything else occurs to you, let me know. No matter how small.'

He hands me his card and walks out of the room, ignoring my offer of a hot beverage.

I don't understand why I haven't heard anything from Adele. I've sent several texts but she hasn't got back to me. When I asked Charlie if he knew anything, he just said women's problems' in that infuriating way of his. I smiled in agreement then felt a complete traitor. I realise I need to speak to her urgently. Tell her I want some answers. I tell Charlie I'm leaving early to do a viewing that's just come up.

It takes me over twenty minutes to drive across town in heavy traffic. There are no lights on in the ground floor flat where she's lived alone since her mother died. I ring the bell twice, wait for the no-reply that comes. I peer through the frosted glass front door and rap sharply several times. There's no response and it's obvious she's not at home. A neighbour passes, stops, and glances at me curiously.

'I'm looking for Adele Stevens.' I say.

'Hardly ever see her,' he replies, going inside, slamming his own front door.

I can't get over the feeling that I made a mess of my interview with P.O. Morgan. Trying to be helpful and appear innocent of any wrong-doing, I gave the exact opposite impression. I try texting Adele again, but am not surprised when there is no reply. I cannot imagine where she could be.

4

The Terry's have asked to view Croft Avenue today. They want to downsize, but say everything I show them is too small. On the way across town, I make a detour and veer off towards Albert Terrace. It's out of my way but I'm curious to see whatever there is to see. I keep to twenty mph and try not to look as though I'm rubbernecking, but apart from a strip of yellow tape across the gatepost you wouldn't think anything exceptional had happened.

Jo and Graham Terry are already waiting outside number eleven. I can tell from their expressions they are not impressed. It's a newish estate, built for young couples with jobs and a joint mortgage who enjoy the smell of barbecue every summer weekend and with a rated primary school next door. However, I smile cheerfully, extend my hand and we go inside. I had forgotten to let the owners know we were coming and we have to step around a rusting scooter and a half eaten apple on the garden path.

We take precisely four and a half minutes from front gate to back gate and back out on the street again. I try to help them look past the biscuit crumbs on the Ikea throws, and suggest they come back to the office later in the week to review their needs. They will need to review their budget too, but I think they know that already.

On the way back to the office I make another detour past Albert Terrace. I don't know what I think might have changed in an hour. There's been nothing new about the body in the local paper so I guess the police are still looking at missing persons.

It's quiet with Charlie out somewhere and Adele still away. I take a look in her desk drawer but apart from a half-finished packet of Haribos it's empty. The lower drawer seems to be stuck. Back at the office, I catch up on emails, look out of the window, file my nails. I see only two other clients who've been searching for properties on the internet, I hand them details, and then it's five o'clock. It's already turning dark as I get ready to leave.

5

Charlie has made an appointment for me to see a Mr James Batley. 'Loaded,' says Charlie. 'Try to interest him in the place up by the golf course.'

I'm a bit baffled and must show it, because Charlie goes on to tell me a large four-bedroom property in that location is coming in any day now. He taps his nose in a way that says it's hush-hush at the moment. I wonder how I'm going to interest a buyer in a property with no details that isn't even on the market yet. 'Just show him what we've already got in his price range, but keep his interest – tell him we've got a beauty coming in any day soon. He'll be the first to hear about it.'

Mr Batley is a man of medium height in his mid-forties. Charlie said he works in financial services, lives in London during the week and is looking for a rural retreat to use at weekends. No mention of a partner or family, but that doesn't mean anything. He's wearing a rather tired looking tweed jacket over a nondescript check shirt, and cords that have gone a bit shiny around the seat and the knees. No tie, of course. It must be his idea of off-duty wear for people living outside the M25. Perhaps he's too high-powered to be bothered with such considerations. My experience as a negotiator for Fortune Estates has taught me never to be surprised by anything, especially first impressions. He sits across from me, one leg propped onto his other knee, looking at the brochures I've put in front of him. He leafs through without comment.

'And have you got a house to sell, Mr Batley, in London?' What I'm really asking is, have you got cash in hand, or are you just wasting our time.

'No.' This tells me something, but not a lot.

'Will you need to raise a mortgage?'

'That depends.'

'How soon do you need to move?' I ask.

He floats a hand in the air as if to say what business is it of mine. I give him a bright smile. Perhaps this is the moment to tempt him with the house up by the golf course.

'Do you play golf?' I ask.

'Why do you ask?'

'Well, we have a property coming onto our list that might suit you.'

'I doubt it. I'm not much for outdoor sports.'

He looks straight at me as he says this. Is he making a rather crude pass? I close down my friendly smile, pick up my reading glasses and put on a serious voice.

'The nice thing about a house near a golf course is that it's usually got good views.'

He shoves the brochures aside. 'Is this all you can show me?' He's looking round the office, his eyes fall on Adele's empty desk. 'How many of you work here?' It's an odd question, so I pretend not to hear.

'I think I've got most of your details,' I say, 'I'll let you know about the house I was telling you about, and if anything new comes in, I'll send it straight through to you.'

I wonder what made Charlie so confident that James Batley is such a catch. He has shown no interest in anything I've suggested. He hasn't really said what he's looking for. I give him a brief nod and stand up. James Batley remains in his chair, looking round the office.

'Well, if there's nothing more I can help you with today...'

'There is one thing.'

'Oh?'

At this point, the doorbell goes and a young couple enter. I've seen them in here before, they were probably Adele's clients before she... well, before she... I can't even explain her absence to myself. It's been four days now.

'I'll be with you in a moment,' I say to them, indicating a seat.

'You were saying, Mr Batley?'

'No matter.' He's walking to the door. I turn my attention to the young couple who are leafing through the brochures left by Batley, exclaiming over the prices. I hear the door slam. I don't expect to hear from him again.

6

In the end, we don't go to London. Sam has spots and is spending the day with her mother. The forecast isn't good, so we decide on the cinema anyway. It's a moody piece about a father who may or may not have abused his children. Russian, I think. Subtitles. The film leaves us both feeling a bit flat. We decide to go for a pizza. It's that sort of night.

'Car's playing up again. I've got to book it in.'

'Shame,' I say.

'How about you?' he asks. 'Any developments on the murder?'

'None. Let's not talk about it.'

'OK. Sold any houses lately?'

'It's a slow time of year. But there's a few coming through the pipeline.'

The conversation lags. I desperately want to talk to him about Adele, but the restaurant is full and noisy. Not the right time or place. And what to say, anyway? We fall into what might be called a companionable silence, but feels more like we've run out of things to talk about.

'How's your pizza?' I ask.

'Same as last time.'

I raise my glass of Trebbiano. 'Cheers.' Simon takes a sip of mineral water. 'Does it bother you, this glass of wine?' I say.

'You know it doesn't, not at all.'

Simon recently celebrated his fifth birthday. In AA terms, that's five years since he stopped drinking.

'How's your pizza?' he asks.

'I should have had the one I had last time.'

Shrieks come from a nearby table as a waiter brings desserts.

'You seem quiet today,' I say.

'Just tired. That's all.'

'Me too. Maybe we should call it a night. What about next weekend?'

'I'll see what's happening with Sam.'

'Of course,' I reply and try to smile.

Simon pays and we get up to leave. As we squeeze past the tables, someone catches my arm. It's Rob, sitting at a table on his own.

'What did you think of the film?' he asks. I stand there awkwardly. I would have introduced Simon, but he's walked on.

'Oh, a bit harrowing.' I wouldn't have thought it would be Rob's sort of thing. 'Well, good to see you,' I say.

'See you Thursday,' he says.

'Who was that?' asks Simon.

'Someone from the book group,' I reply. 'I would have introduced you, but...'

I drive Simon home. I'm glad he doesn't suggest coming in. I'm not in the mood and would have had to make some excuse. I check my phone again but there's still nothing from Adele. I decide to write a note to drop through her door.

> *Where the hell are you? You've landed me in it. For fuck's sake, why don't you ring, text or something?*

I read it through, screw it up and start again.

> *Dear Adele. I'm very worried. I came by your place but there was no sign of you. The police have been to the office and want a formal statement. What shall I tell them about the dates I'm supposed to have visited Albert Terrace? I need to talk to you urgently. Are you coming back to work soon? Please get in touch. Love Hanna.*

I try to read it over, but can't read my own hand-writing. I ball it and start over.

> *Adele. What's going on? Very worried. Hanna.*

I'll drop it through her letterbox in the morning. No. Why wait until tomorrow.

I bang on the door anyway, not expecting any reply. I push the note through the letterbox. It shuts tight with a firm snap. My hands and feet are freezing. Once home, I make a hot water bottle and look out my fleecy pyjamas. The ones auntie Jean gave me last Christmas with the pink puppies. The ones Simon's never seen.

7

It's two in the morning when my land line rings. I was in a deep sleep, dreaming about the Terrys, showing them a house on a hill with a hundred rooms. Too small, says Jo Terry. Too small, echoes her husband. I pick up and it's Adele. She got my note. I don't know whether to feel relieved or angry.

'Is it too late to talk?' she asks.

'Well,' I say, 'I'm ready to listen.'

'I feel dreadful,' she says.

'What's going on, Adele?'

She stays silent. Questions flounder around in my head, like fish in jelly. Like what were you doing all those times you were supposed to be showing Albert Terrace?. And with who, I think, but don't say, despite starting to seethe inside.

'It was Luk's idea,' she says at last.

'Who is Luk?'

'You know, the one I told you about.'

She has never told me anything but I let it pass.

'I suppose he's married,' I say. It's just a guess, but it hits the spot.

'Yes, he's Romanian. From Romania.'

'Where is his wife?' I'd like a cigarette, though I haven't smoked for years. Funny how the urge never quite goes away.

'In Romania.'

'With the two kids no doubt.' I reply.

'Actually, there are three…'

'It's none of my business what you do, Adele, but you've made it my business now. I lied to the police for you. I deserve to know what's going on.'

After a silence which seems endless, I wonder if she's hung up, but she's suddenly talking again, her voice so quiet I can hardly hear.

'You know when my mother was ill in hospital last year? Luk used to come in to clean her room.'

Brilliant. I suppose he was a brain surgeon back in Romania, I think, but don't say.

'He was kind, you know, about my mother, and so thorough. Worked long days, started at six, didn't finish till eight. Sometimes worked all night.'

'I'm surprised he found time to chat you up,' I say. Even to my own ears, I sound nasty.

'He was sharing a studio flat with five others, all Eastern European, all working shifts.'

'What does any of this have to do with Albert Terrace?' I ask. But the penny has already dropped. 'That's where you used to meet, I suppose?'

'Not always.'

I'm puzzled. 'So what do you mean the idea was Luk's?'

Adele doesn't answer. I hear her blow her nose. She doesn't have to answer.

I already know the answer.

'You let him have a key, didn't you?'

'I've been so stupid, Hanna.'

There's another long silence.

'Albert Terrace has been empty for months. Nobody's interested. It was only meant to be for a night or two. He told me he owed a mate a favour...' Her voice trails away. She blows heavily on her nose again. 'But it went on until...'

'Until they found a body,' I say. What else is there to say? 'So, he must know something about all this.'

'I don't know what he knows. I haven't heard from him... he... '

'Why did you have to involve me?' I say. I know I sound angry and don't expect any reply and none is forthcoming. 'The police are asking me questions, Adele. It's hideous.'

She's blowing her nose again but this time it sounds more like a sob. 'Luk doesn't answer his phone.'

Of course he doesn't, the bastard. 'What a bastard,' I say. 'This man has done you no favours, Adele. You must go to the police, tell them everything you've told me. You haven't done anything wrong. You've committed no crime.'

We both know withholding information and perverting the course of justice are both serious crimes. And once Charlie finds out about the key she'll automatically get the sack. No references. No question.

'It's late,' she says finally, 'I'm too tired to talk anymore. I'll see you tomorrow.' She rings off before I have a chance to confirm that she means she will be in the office tomorrow, back to normal.

At 4 am Madame Bovary lies on the floor under my bed, pages unturned, a half empty mug of cold tea keeping her company. Outside it's dark. Only the occasional passing lorry on the motorway lets you know the world is still turning.

8

I must have slept eventually because the alarm wakes me. I get up in a rush. I need to be at Park Street at 9.30 to give a valuation to a couple about to divorce and split assets. I shower, would like to wash my hair but there's no time. An ache hovers over my left eye, as though I've got a morning hangover but without the night before.

The Doctors Elliott come to the door together. Neither smile but I hope the brightness I'm affecting will make up for it. It is, as expected from the address, a substantial house with large rooms. The faded soft furnishings only serve to enhance their surroundings. Dr Trevor excuses himself and disappears, leaving Dr Janice to show me round. She points out where they have made improvements; a fancy wood-burner with a steel chimney in the centre of one room. It's a pity they took out the old fireplace I think, but don't say. In the kitchen, marble tiles shine like glass and clitter-clatter under our feet. I take measurements, make notes. The garden is huge. Their man comes once a week to keep it up, a hard worker, she tells me. Polish.

Upstairs there are five bedrooms. All appear empty and unused. The smell of fresh paint lingers. The doctors' current sleeping arrangements are not obvious. Perhaps one of them has already moved out. She shows me the three en-suites, a family bathroom and a powder room downstairs. No family photos, no pet hairs. No sign of Dr Trevor. Perhaps that's been an on-going problem for Dr Janice, too.

She suggests coffee and I'm grateful for the offer and chance to sit in her conservatory, away from the kitchen with its granite slabs, an indifferent witness to a wrecked marriage. I wonder how long they have been together, what went wrong. I hope Dr Janice isn't going to tell me. I'd like to cry but for whom I'm not sure. I take out my laptop and bring up our website. Let's talk figures, I say, trying for another bright smile.

I get back to the office a little before lunch-time. Charlie wants to hear about Park Street and I tell him I've estimated it conservatively at a little under nine hundred thousand. This cheers him. Is it suitable for James Batley, he asks, and I tell him I'll send on the details. There's no sign of Adele and Charlie asks if I know where she is. I look over at her empty desk and tell him, honestly, I haven't seen her for several days. But I don't mention last night's phone call.

It's strange and disquieting to see her empty desk. I wonder if she will start looking for another job. I think how much I'd miss her if she left. I sit at my desk and eat a lonely tuna sandwich, thinking of the money I could save by making my own. Charlie tells me Mrs Marriott wants to arrange another viewing at Riverside Apartments. I try her number with a sigh, but have to leave a message. She rings back almost straight away and asks if we could go this afternoon. Given our history, I'm not optimistic, but agree to meet there at four o'clock.

The office is quiet without anybody here. I half-heartedly change a photo or two around in the window and spray a bit of Pledge on the desks. The potted palm seems to be rallying. I haven't heard from Simon either. I wonder if I should ring or wait until I hear from him. There are a number of calls to the office phone but, after the first couple, I let the answering machine pick up. Charlie is out somewhere, probably having a haircut or buying a shirt for his boyfriend. I try Adele's mobile but my message goes straight to voicemail.

At three thirty I make my way over to Riverside. Angela shows up fifteen minutes late looking preoccupied. There's no sun today and the heavy skies cast shadows over the rooms. For the third time, we walk through the empty apartment. We lean over the balcony and peer down into the murky water. I wonder why anybody would choose to hang themselves here when they could just jump into the river. Maybe it was fear of heights. Maybe that was the problem. I wonder if Angela knows what happened here. Perhaps she's visited secretly behind my back and quizzed the neighbours. Asked questions in the local pub. It's what buyers do. There's a faint but persistent smell of creeping mould, the sort of smell you get in empty properties near water. I'll bring some air-freshener next time. 'I'm still not sure,' Angela says at last. 'Have you got anything new on your books?' In other words, she's saying Riverside is not for her and probably never will be. 'I don't think anything suitable has come in since we last checked,' I reply. 'Within your budget,' I add.

She looks disappointed. This woman will never be satisfied. 'It's such a big decision,' she says.

I nod in agreement. I once had great expectations of Angela Marriott. She was willing to look at everything I suggested and was a cash buyer. Now I know I got it wrong. She's just making the most of the full-on attention she's getting for the half hour I've allotted her.

'I read about that body they discovered in Albert Terrace. Who was it, do you know?

'No, I don't,' I reply, truthfully.

'Doesn't Fortune Estates manage that property?' She asks, her tone sharp.

I pretend not to hear; open a cupboard door, shine my torch and make as though I'm looking for something.

'Well,' I say, 'unless there's anything else you'd like to see here?'

'Poor woman. I wouldn't want to be the person buying that place. Bad karma.'

She's talking about Albert Terrace. I wonder how many more questions I'll be asked about it over the next few weeks. She follows me to the door.

'Will you let me know if anything new comes in? You know what I'm looking for.'

'Of course,' I say.

The rain that threatened hasn't started but there's a chill in the air. I need to talk to someone. I decide if I don't hear anything from Simon, I'll call him at home tonight.

On the way home I pick up a pizza and put it in the microwave as soon as I get in. I've had no time to shop and there's nothing in the freezer. After the first few slices I feel guilty and push the greasy stodge away. I'm thinking I should go down to the supermarket and buy a piece of salmon when Simon rings. I'm relieved. He asks how things are and what I've been doing. The problem is I can't tell him the things that really press on my mind, especially not over the phone. Things like Adele, the police, the body, so there isn't a lot I can say. But it doesn't matter, he's worried about Sam, 'She's a woman now,' he says, and starts on about the worries fathers have when daughters enter their teens. 'She'll be fine.' I say, in a routine way.

I think back to my own teens, finding my way around the new school, the unflattering uniform a size too large, trying to make new friends. 'She'll be fine.' I say again. What I'd really like would be if Simon suggested the two of us doing something together. Just us. Something that doesn't have to include Sam. But he doesn't, so I suggest it myself.

'What about if we do something one evening,' I say, 'it will take your mind off things.'

'Where would you like to go?'

I would like him to suggest somewhere we might go, some place colourful, sexy and wild, but he doesn't. There is a long silence

'Why did you ring?' I ask.

'I was wondering about the body,' he says. 'Is there any news?'

'Is that why you rang? To talk about a murder?'

'So it was a murder,' he says, quickly jumping in. 'I knew you'd know something.'

'Didn't it say that in the paper?' I ask.

'It just said dead woman found in an empty property. You must have heard something.'

'No, not really,' I say. 'When you decide what you want to do, let me know.' I put the phone down and glance at the left over pizza. It suddenly looks more inviting.

Someone once asked what do women want and I would like to say, ask Gustave. I've just got to the part where she persuades her husband to perform an operation he feels ill-equipped to deal with. My sympathies used to be with his wife, tired of her boring husband, longing for her freedom. Now I realise that poor Dr B had a lot to put up with.

I read a few pages, but can't get engaged. I've got two more chapters to get through before book club. I turn on the TV and tune in to Crimestoppers. Later, stuffed with cheese, I dream Adele is in a field being interviewed by P.O. Morgan. There is a small blood stain on his white shirt. I know nothing about it, she says, over and over, nothing at all.

9

Only three of us tonight. Pam never misses and is always several chapters ahead of everybody. She talks a lot about motivation and feminism in the nineteenth century. She's a retired teacher, so can't help herself. It's still raining when we leave and I'm fumbling for my keys when I hear a click and Rob is behind me holding a large umbrella. He's not much taller than me, so I have to duck.

'Fancy a beer?' He asks.

'Do I look like a beer drinker?'

'Or a glass of wine? We could always go for coffee.'

I say, 'Coffee would be good.' Then remember coffee after eight pm doesn't suit me anymore.

He's unlocking the chain on his bike, so I hold the umbrella as we walk the few yards to the pub. Inside, there's a smell of stale ale. The sort of place where people stare as you go in, then ignore you for the rest of the night. I wonder what I'm doing here.

'How are you enjoying Madame B?' he asks when we're sitting at a corner table, my hands around a glass of warm white. He's wiping foam away from his beard (neat and closely trimmed). A packet of crisps sits between us.

'I'm enjoying it, actually,' I say. 'What about you?'

'Not a lot,' he says. 'It's more a woman's thing, isn't it?'

I remember Rob told us he's a writer himself. He once pitched us the idea of *Saturn Triple X*, a sci-fi thriller he probably self-published, but it was out-voted.

'Why do you come, then?' I ask.

'To meet people like you,' he says.

He's looking around as he says it, so I can't think he's flirting. Outside the book club, we've hardly spoken. I try to see past the height factor. It's not so noticeable while we're sitting down. I wish Simon would pass by and accidentally glimpse us through the window. Outside it's raining hard. I wonder where Rob lives and ask if he has far to cycle home.

'Not far. Off the Main Road. Albert Terrace,' he replies.

He picks up something in my expression. 'Yes. The body in the bath or the airing cupboard, next to a blunt instrument,' he goes on. 'The police are there a lot. They even came to my door for a statement. To ask if I'd seen anything funny.'

'And had you?'

'Just people coming and going at all hours. I hardly saw anyone in the daytime. As I told the police, I like to write at night when it's quiet.'

I would like to change the subject, but don't want him side-tracked onto interplanetary warfare.

'Although once I did see a couple arguing in the street.'

'Oh?' This is where I should declare my own interest, but somehow don't.

'A fight?'

'There was a lot of shouting.'

'Did you tell the police?'

'I didn't want to get involved. Want another drink?'

'No thanks. I'd better make a move.'

'Your car's parked over the road isn't it? Red Clio?'

I pick up my bag and make for the door.

'See you,' says Rob. He's up out of his seat. I think he's standing up for me, but he's making his way back to the bar.

'See you,' I echo.

10

I sleep badly again. I'm wondering if I should see the doctor, ask for some pills. I struggle to the car and get to the office to find Charlie already there, pacing.

'That policeman Morgan's coming in again this morning. I've told him we've said all we know. He wants to know when Adele will be in. Do you know anything?'

I look over at her empty desk and wonder if I'll ever see her again.

'I haven't got anything new to tell him,' I say. 'What time is he coming?'

'Who knows. He said late morning. Didn't want to tie himself down. I'm hoping they've identified the woman, then he won't need to bother us again.'

It's unlikely the police will ever stop bothering us, I think, but don't say. Was it Charlie or the police who had to notify the owner, I wonder. What would have been the correct procedure? I'll look at the file later and find out who owns the ugly little property where ugly things have happened. I offer to make Charlie a coffee but he shakes his head. I make one anyway, sit at my desk, turn on the computer. Charlie is on his mobile, talking to his boyfriend. What about a memory foam? I hear him say. They are looking for a new bed and I overhear a plan to go late night shopping at John Lewis. There is small disagreement about the number of pocket springs most desirable in a mattress. Charlie tells me he has to pop out for a couple of hours and asks me to take care of things in the meantime. He doesn't say where he's going. It's extraordinary how our days carry on, just like normal, as though nothing has happened.

I pick some brown leaves off the rubber plant on the window-sill. Adele always did the watering. I try her mobile for the hundredth time but it's still turned off. I try to concentrate on my work. Try to search for something new to show Angela Marriott. Look through my list for someone with a big enough budget to warrant contacting about Park Street. I discover that the owner of Albert Terrace lives abroad. I think about what Rob said last night. How he knew I drive a red Clio. I suppose writers notice things like that, even sci-fi writers. I wish I'd noticed more about what was going on under my nose. I wonder what I shall say to P.O. Morgan.

A couple come in to make enquiries. They've seen Riverside Apartments online and think it could suit them. The young woman is five months pregnant. I remind them it's on the fourth floor. It's not right for them, but I don't say because they need to find out for themselves. Clients often fall for the complete opposite to what they think they want. I offer coffee, but they decide to go out instead to talk it over so I give them some other details to take with them. My teeth ache with smiling. The morning drags. I stay at my desk until one o'clock. Then, feeling famished, put the closed sign on the door. No sign of Police Officer Morgan.

Driving home through darkened streets last night, I made out two Santas abseiling from chimney pots and some shops already lit for Christmas even though it's only the end of October. Soon people will be bragging about their holidays on the ski slopes. My own plans will no doubt follow the pattern of the past three years and depend on Simon's frantic last chance arguments with Sam's mother. Last year I gave Sam a photo frame. I hoped she might like a picture of the three of us together, but I've seen it at Simon's place, still in its box. Since Mum passed away, Dad usually spends Christmas with his sister, Auntie Jean.

At lunch-time, I put all thought aside and go next door to buy a sandwich. Tuna's finished so I opt for brie and sun-dried tomatoes. The cheese smells off. Reminds me to do some shopping later.

When I get back to the office Charlie is there and tells me that PO Morgan isn't coming to see us today after all. Something has come up. I wonder what it means and don't know whether to feel troubled or relieved.

11

It's after seven when I get home. The rain has stopped but it's turned chilly and the stars are out. It's a relief to get indoors and hear the heating click on. I'm putting away my groceries and realise I have forgotten to buy milk when the doorbell rings. It startles me because I'm not expecting anybody. I peer through the blind and see a police car. My armpits start to prickle. The doorbell rings again. They've already seen my light so there's no point pretending to be out. I open it to see Officer Morgan standing there with a woman in a grey suit.

'May we come in for a word, Hanna?'

I widen the door and allow them to step inside.

'We just want to ask you a few questions,' says the woman who introduces herself as Detective Inspector Naomi Reynolds.

'I've just got back from work.' I say, as I move yesterday's newspaper and a couple of *Marie Claire* off the sofa. Naomi sits, but Morgan remains standing. Perhaps he's got piles, I think.

'Have there been some developments?' I ask. I need to know, but don't want to hear. Neither replies anyway.

Naomi's skirt is stretched a little tightly and exposes her plump knees but she makes no attempt to adjust it.

'Can you tell us when you last spoke to your colleague, Ms Adele Stevens?'

A thud comes from the upstairs flat. I'm glad of the interruption as we all look up.

'That's my neighbour,' I say. 'She's elderly. Wants to move to a bungalow.'

Naomi interrupts smoothly. 'I gather from what Adele told Officer Morgan you were friends as well as colleagues. When did you last hear from her?'

I continue to look at the ceiling as if it might provide an answer. I turn my attention to the floor, but my thoughts are still blank. Both officers are watching me and waiting. Both calm and expressionless. I struggle to calculate back. I haven't seen Adele now for over a week. The last time we spoke was on the phone, the night she told me she had given her boyfriend the key to number three. What was his name? Luk? I remember being angry with her. Remember telling her to go to the police. The thought still makes me angry.

'We've been trying to locate her, Hanna,' says Naomi. 'Her neighbour tells us she's not been seen at her address for six days.'

Six days. Such a precise number. Had the neighbour seen me on her doorstep, too? The night I delivered the note?

'Have you received any texts, emails, phone calls? Has there been any contact at all?'

The thermostat clicks off noisily and silence takes over. The room is warm, but my hands seem to be trembling.

'No, nothing.' I say. I clasp my fingers firmly together in my lap, in an attempt to get them under control. Officer Morgan looks at his notebook and writes something down.

'Your employer, Charles Porter, says she had no holidays booked. Would she normally fail to turn up at work or be away from home for several days without letting anybody know?'

With a shock, I see where this is going. I realise I should have been more worried.

'Did she have any family, a boyfriend, somebody who might know her whereabouts?'

Is this a trick question? Do they already know about Luk and about the key? Is Adele a suspect? The thought is ridiculous. I think I've got the trembling under control, but wonder if it will start up somewhere else if I loosen the grip on my fingers.

'We didn't talk much about that sort of thing.' I say.

Naomi writes something down. Morgan has received a call on his radio and is talking briefly into it. A confused crackle breaks into the silence.

'If you do hear anything, we need to know. And anything you can remember, no matter how insignificant.' Naomi is standing up.

I think they've finished, but Morgan goes on. 'We'd like the dates you visited Albert Terrace. Soon as possible. We may need you to come down to the station for that.'

I sink down on the sofa, into the imprint left by Detective Inspector Naomi Reynold's sturdy thighs. Until now, it had never occurred to me to be worried about Adele's silence over the past days. But isn't that what they implied? And now they want me to go to the station to make a formal statement. I feel nauseous at the thought of going over it all again.

There's a sharp ring at the doorbell and I open it to find Mrs Baxter from upstairs. 'I saw the police car, dear, and wondered if anything was wrong?'

'No, Mrs Baxter, there's nothing wrong. I'd ask you in but...'

She's looking past me as if trying to picture what's taken place.

'I lost my purse and somebody found it. They just brought it back.'

I am becoming an expert at telling lies.

'Oh, fancy them sending two policemen for that. I wondered if there had been trouble in the flats, you know, a break-in or something.'

'No. Don't worry, nothing like that.'

'Oh, well that's good to hear. If you get any news about my flat, let me know, will you dear? You haven't sent many people lately.'

I feel weak. My legs might collapse under me any minute.

'Do you think we should reduce the price?' She asks.

'I'm back in the office in the morning, Mrs Baxter, and I'll look into it then.'

I think I need to sit down. 'I haven't eaten yet.'

'Oh, you young people. Always on a diet. I always used to say to my Julie...'

Her voice keeps going, but I am drifting away. I'm standing on Adele's doorstep on a bright summer morning, and she is running out to meet me. She's wearing a pair of shorts, high-waisted and flared, a perfect cut for her. Where's your car, she says. Is it still the Clio? She's laughing as she says it. Where are we going, I ask. Why to meet Luk of course, she says...

'Well dear,' Mrs Baxter breaks in, 'I'll look forward to hearing from you tomorrow.' She turns and walks slowly away up the stairs.

I pick up the phone and dial Simon's number. It rings seven times before he picks up.

'Oh, Hanna!'

'I'm wondering if we can meet. Something's happened. I need to talk to someone – well, to you.'

'OK. What, now? Do you want to talk now?'

He sounds a little guarded. I wonder if he's got somebody with him. Not Sam, surely. Not on a school night.

'Can you talk now?' I ask.

'Well, I suppose. I'm OK to talk if you want. Is it about the weekend?'

I try to remember whether it's a weekend with Sam or not.

'Sam's going on a school outing to London,' he offers.

'Is someone there with you?'

'Oh, just Claire from work. You know the problem with my car. She gave me a lift home. We're just having a coffee.'

Nice, I think. 'I'd better call you some other time,' I say.

'But I'm on for the weekend, if you like,' he says again. 'Think about what you want to do and let's talk again tomorrow.'

I try to remember Claire. Is she the fifty-five year old chain smoker in Records, or the twenty-three year old PA with the hair extensions? I don't understand why he didn't ring me for a lift home. Then I could have been out when the police called. Perhaps Claire lives nearer. I feel oppressed by my own thoughts. I suppose this is why people have a cat. I heat up a tin of soup and decide on another early night. As I pick up my book, I wonder what Emma Bovary would have done. But she doesn't give anything away.

12

I sleep badly again, wake at six and wish I could go back to sleep forever. Driving to work, some impulse takes me out of my way down Albert Terrace. I'm surprised to see the yellow tape has been removed from the gate at number three and there is no sign that anything ever happened there. Apart from an elderly dog walker there's nobody about. I wonder which house is Rob's. The front gardens are mostly scruffy. Even the bins look abandoned.

I am the first to open up the office. When Charlie comes in I start to tell him about the visit from the police last night, but he interrupts. Wants me to arrange an interview with a prospective house seller asap.

'She's got a little gem,' he says, 'the one I told you about, up by the golf course, Braids Crescent. Should sell quickly.'

I wait for the chance to tell him about the visit from the police. I want to talk about Adele. I want to know if he's worried about her absence. Perhaps the word is disappearance. The thought is shocking. Charlie vanishes into his office and spends the rest of the morning on the phone. I wonder if the murder at Albert Terrace has affected business. Perhaps that's why he seems so preoccupied.

The morning drags. The young couple with the pregnancy never came back with more enquiries about Riverside. I have their number but hold back from calling. I telephone the owner of Braids Crescent, a Mrs Caswell, but she's out. I decide not to leave a message but plan to speak to her later.

Simon phones while I'm making coffee. 'Want to go to that exhibition Saturday?' He asks.

It means a trip to London. I'd rather just hang out here, go for a walk, go for a meal, go back to his place, just talk.

'Maybe,' I reply.

Then I remember Sam's going to London on a school trip. Is this his covert attempt to keep an eye on her, maybe bump into her accidentally, surprise her? Why do I feel I'm being manipulated? I wonder how Simon got to work this morning. Did Claire drop by to offer her 'assistance' again?

'Did you get your car sorted?' I ask

'It's in the garage for a day or two. Electrics. It won't be ready by the weekend. We could go up on the train, though.'

'Do you want me to pick you up later,' I ask, 'after work?'

'No. don't worry,' he says, 'Claire can give me a lift.'

'It's no trouble,' I say.

'Don't worry,' he says. 'Any developments about that body?'

'Nothing new.' My default response.

'There was something in last night's paper,' he says. 'Did you see it?'

'No.'

'Said she remains unidentified, police checking for missing persons. It may be difficult if there are no official documents.'

'What does that mean?'

'Well, dental records, nobody reported missing who answers the description, that sort of thing.'

I remain silent. I want to talk but don't know where to start. Can't bear the thought of hearing myself say the words.

'Simon,' I start.

'Hanna, Have you spoken to Mrs Caswell yet?' Charlie calls out.

'I've got to go, Simon.'

'Let's speak tomorrow then,' he says and rings off.

13

The Hollies is detached, brick, and fifties built. Zoe Caswell is younger than I'd expected with curls, red-lipstick and a pale mole that sits prettily on her freckled cheek. 'Inside, Banquo!' she says, firmly shutting the kitchen door on a noisy woolly black dog of uncertain parentage. Mrs Caswell, 'call me Zoe', offers tea. I thank her and suggest we might look around first. The sitting room does have a good view of the golf course

'Do you play?' I ask.

'No but my husband did. That's why we bought the house really, for the view and for the golf.'

Past tense, I notice.

'Gerald was a lot older than me, though we were together nearly twenty years.'

I run the metal tape along the walls as she talks.

'I'd like to sell the carpets and curtains, all in,' she says.

I nod and make a note of a brown stain on the ceiling. I don't ask why she is moving, but she wants to tell me anyway.

'That's from the bathroom. We had a leak. It started with a dripping tap and, in the end, we put in a new bathroom – you'll see. Just before Gerald died. Heart,' she says, tapping her left breast.

'I'm sorry,' I say. What else is there to say.

The kitchen is a square, well used, friendly space which also looks out over the golf course. I see one or two figures teeing off in the distance. I'm not sure what's happened to Banquo.

'Lovely view,' I say again.

She's putting the kettle on and setting out quality bone china on a tray. Wedgwood Bianca. Aunty Jean has the same set. I think she plans to leave it to me.

We go upstairs to measure the three bedrooms.

'I want to sell the carpets in here too,' she gestures.

I make a note. They are all well-worn, with good rugs on top.

'But not the rugs,' she says. 'I'll take those with me.'

I wonder where she is planning to move to but don't ask. It will all come out when she's ready. We linger slightly longer in the renovated bathroom. Italian sea-green tiles, contemporary shower cubicle, and a bidet. Sticks in a jar send out a whiff of tobacco leaf. Shame Gerald didn't live to enjoy it, I think.

How lovely,' I say, 'very tasteful.'

We finish the tour in the garden, which contains a summerhouse, and a low hedge, escallonia, I think, not holly. Sharp and prickly. I wonder if it was gardening that led to Gerald's heart troubles.

'You'll be sorry to leave it, won't you?' I say, as Zoe pours a fresh pot of Earl Grey; leaf-tea, a strainer – milk or lemon?

'I don't want to be here any longer without Gerald,' is all she says, dropping her eyelids. The pale mole moves bravely downwards, as though in agreement.

'No, of course not. Will you be staying in the area?' I ask.

'I haven't decided yet. It rather depends on…' what it depends on remains vague. I wonder if she's already got a lover.

'Properties like yours are selling for about the 950,000 mark,' I tell her and give her a brochure with our terms for single agency instruction. 'It's a lovely family home,' I say. She leans back in her chair and sips her tea.

'I should have asked if you'd like a biscuit. I've gotten out of the habit of having them in the house now that Gerald…' I hear a bark and realise I'd forgotten about the dog. 'Oh, the gardener took him for a walk.' A young, skinny guy in a brown check shirt and jeans waves at us through the window. 'Such a hard worker, he's from…' I wonder if she knows where he's from. 'Such a relief for Gerald when we found him. Well, for us both,' she adds.

I wonder what extra services a good-looking young gardener might offer a lonely, attractive widow on a damp November afternoon. 'Well,' I say, 'I think I've got all I need at the moment. We'll send the photographer to take photos.' Charlie was right about this one. James Batley pops into my thoughts.

'How long will it take to sell?' she asks.

How long is a dog's leg? 'Oh, sure to go quickly,' I reply. 'We've always got clients looking for this superior type of property. I'll notify them as soon as you've confirmed with us and spoken to your solicitor.'

Zoe tosses back her curls and holds out her hand. It feels like the start of a love affair. 'I'll be in touch very soon,' I say. Somewhere inside, Banquo, sensing change, gives a solitary bark.

*

Later, I get a call from Dr Janice at Park Street. She and Dr Trevor want to know when they can expect some viewings. I am startled to think I have done so little. Charlie had the brochures printed up over a week ago. I look through my list and pick out some likely clients. A number live outside the county so I email and advise them of this unique and exciting opportunity just available. While I'm at it, I look at Mrs Baxter's file. It has been lingering on for months. I need to do something about Riverside Apartments, too.

I remember an enquiry from a Mr Sellers and contact him about Mrs Baxter's flat, the one above me in my apartment block. He's a divorced man, he tells me, trying to plan for a new life. I doubt Mrs Baxter's place will meet up to his expectations, but he likes the price, and it's already been reduced.

I ask Charlie if he's got any news. We both know what news we're talking about.

Later, he comes over and says, 'Detective Inspector Naomi what's-her-name is on the phone and wants to speak to you.'

Naomi is friendly. 'I take it you haven't heard from your colleague, Adele Stevens?'

'Nothing yet,' I say, trying to sound breezy, as if the

question is just an innocent inquiry about the availability of bananas.

'We need to make an appointment for your statement,' she counters.

'Well,' I say, 'I'll have to speak to my boss.' Perhaps Charlie will say I can't go under any circumstances, ever, client confidentiality, or something.

'I've already spoken to him. Can you come to the station tomorrow afternoon at 3 pm?'

'I do have quite a lot on at the moment,' I say.

'It shouldn't take long. Bring your diary with you.'

This is about the dates. They want the dates I visited Albert Terrace. Even though I never once visited Albert Terrace. My thoughts race back to Adele. Where are you, Adele? I stare out of the window at the heavy sky. We haven't seen a glimpse of sun for nearly a week. The plant on the sill has dropped another leaf. Soon Charlie will be bringing in the poinsettias.

'All right,' I say. What else can I say. 'See you at three o'clock tomorrow.'

Then I have this brilliant idea. I'll have to tell her I lost my diary. Tell her I can only be approximate. Then it's not so bad. It's not exactly a lie, is it?

I struggle through the rest of the day. No one gets back to me about the Doctors' place on Park Street, and at the moment I only have Mr Sellers booked in the day after tomorrow. At least I'll be able to meet him upstairs before coming to the office. I must remember to let Mrs Baxter know.

14

'So you've lost your diary, Hanna?'

'Yes, that's right.'

'So you are unable to be specific about the dates you went to Albert Terrace.'

'No. Yes.'

'These days a lot of people keep details like that on their phone. Is that something you ever do?

'No. I prefer to use a paper diary.'

'We would be particularly interested to have the names of clients you accompanied to the property.'

'Sorry?' How could I not have thought about that? Of course they would ask me that.

'Is it possible you might have a record of it elsewhere – emails or phone calls for example? Did any client make an offer, for instance, or want a second viewing? Did any of the clients' behaviour strike you as suspicious?'

'Not really.'

'Not really?. You don't sound too sure.'

'I think I would remember something like that.'

'Something like what?' Her voice drones on, monotonous, cajoling.

'I wish I could tell you more,' I say, 'but we see so many clients, so many properties.'

'Surely something must have stuck in your memory, can you remember anything at all about the viewings you undertook on behalf of your colleague? Wouldn't you have some emails on your computer relating to visits?'

'Sorry. I only wish I could be more helpful.'

Naomi's tone changes, sounding more crisp. She's wearing another grey skirt today, with a white blouse. Her jacket's hung over the chair behind her. I wonder what her salary is. Where she lives. She's not writing anything down but I don't know if that's good or bad. 'The neighbours have told us they saw a number of different people coming and going at three Albert Terrace. Would you like to comment on that?'

'No. I don't know anything about that.'

'What I'm trying to establish, Hanna, is do you believe anybody other than the agency held a key to the property?'

'How do you mean…?' I falter.

'Well, for example, did anybody from the agency give out a key to the property?'

'Why would they do that?'

She smiles and crosses her legs. She's wearing solid, crepe soled shoes. Running faster than you shoes. No matter how fast you run, I can…

'Do you know a Mr Robert Green?'

'No.'

'Mr Green says he knows you. He lives in Albert Terrace, a couple of doors away from number three.'

She means Rob. 'Oh, yes.'

'From the photos he's been shown, he says he can't recall

seeing you in Albert Terrace although he does remember seeing a person with a key resembling your colleague, Adele Stevens.'

What a worm, I think. He told me he hadn't spoken to the police. My face feels hot. I wish I hadn't accepted her offer of a mug of coffee.

'Well, he couldn't have been looking out of his window all the time could he?'

'No. Quite. I'm just trying to establish who visited the property and how often. You see, Mr Green says he saw a number of people coming and going from the property.'

'Then why aren't you talking to him about it?'

I instantly regret that remark. Naomi's no longer smiling. She's uncrossed her legs. Her skirt is not so short today. The black tights are more flattering. All the while she's probably making similar judgements about me. Am I coming across as earnest and truthful, professional, a trying to help as much as she can sort of person?

'We will, of course, be interviewing a number of people in the course of this enquiry, Hanna,' she says calmly. 'We are still looking into the identity of the woman's body found at the property. Just one other thing, you say you've had no communication recently from your colleague, Adele Stevens?'

At last a question I can answer honestly. 'No. I say.'

'And this would be unusual?' I nod even though Naomi is not looking at me, and carries on asking questions. 'Are you at all concerned about her whereabouts? Was she seeing someone? Did she have a boyfriend? Was she sleeping with somebody? Did you ever meet him? Where did he work? Did he have friends?'

She's good, I think. Naomi is very good. She's followed me through the maze and trapped me at the heart.

'I don't feel well,' I say. 'I can't sit here any longer.' I stand up.

Naomi leaps out of her seat and opens a door. 'A glass of water for Ms Summers, please,' she calls out. 'Sit there for a few minutes Hanna. We don't want you passing out. We'll continue this interview another day.'

I ring Charlie and tell him I'm unable to get back to the office today. It's nearly five o'clock anyway and I feel exhausted. I can't stop my teeth from chattering all the way home. I have to drag myself upstairs to let Mrs Baxter know about tomorrow morning's viewing.

'Thank you dear. I'll have a good tidy up,' she says.

Simon has left a message. Says shall I come over tonight?

I phone and tell him about my early start with Mr Sellers tomorrow and say let's leave it until the weekend. I don't tell him I've been at the police station all afternoon. He would question me about it, and I'd be forced to prevaricate all over again. My diary lies on the kitchen table. I remember it's supposed to be lost. I ought to destroy it. But how? Perhaps I could bury it. But where? It's quite bulky, with several notes and dates and nothing connected to Albert Terrace. That's the problem. All the same, I give myself a small pat on the back for being so quick to tell Naomi it was lost.

15

Next morning, the sun shines out from a clear cold sky. It lifts my spirits, and I feel the urge to take a bit more trouble. Feel I should make an effort. I try out some dark blue eye-liner and put on my new Baby-Kisses bra. I go upstairs to Mrs Baxter's and together we wait for the arrival of Mr Sellers. He's a short man, slightly balding. Tells me again he is divorced, they've settled their finances, and he's basically a cash buyer and fancy free. I think he gives me a wink as he says this. I resist any temptation to wink back.

Mrs Baxter has tidied up, but the overall impression is dismal. Knick-knacks everywhere, old photos, cushions not exactly grubby, but not quite clean either. It's worse in the bathroom. Everything pink, a candlewick mat covers the toilet seat. I can't imagine where she bought it or when. Mr Sellers takes his time looking round, but to my surprise, seems to like what he sees. I sit down on one of Mrs Baxter's flat cushions and let them get on with it. The wire from my bra is digging, giving me a sharp pain in the ribs. Mrs Baxter asks if we'd like a cup of tea. I say no thanks, but Mr Sellers says yes please.

This delays us for another half hour, while Mr Sellers tells us again about his divorce. 'She got tired of me, that's all. What could I do about it? She's seeing another man now, met on the internet. I think she'll live to regret it, but it's freed me to start a new life of my own.'

I think he gives me another wink as he says this, but perhaps it's a wandering eye-lid he can't control.

'Well,' I say brightly, 'I'm sure you'd like to think things over, Mr Sellers.' I hope Mrs Baxter hasn't told him I live in the flat downstairs. Or said anything about the police visit.

'Oh, I'm a man who likes to take his time,' he replies. 'Over everything.' The eye-lid wanders again. 'I take it you can keep a dog in these flats?' He asks.

'I'm not sure,' I say, 'I'll look into it.' Actually, I'm sure you can't, but I write it down anyway. Dogs don't live forever.

'It's not a big dog,' he says, 'but I couldn't move anywhere that's not dog friendly. It's handy here for the park,' he says. 'I think Bobby would like it here.'

At last we make ready to leave. Mr Sellers says he'll be in touch soon and we shake hands. I pop downstairs and change Baby-Kisses for something more functional. I check myself in the mirror, see the eye-liner has smudged, and wipe it off with a tissue.

I've already decided to drive to Adele's house on my way into the office. If nothing else, I can leave her another note. As I get close I see a police car parked outside and her front door ajar. I don't stop. I have to face facts. I no longer believe Adele is to be found at home, or indeed anywhere at all.

My thoughts are increasingly turning to Luk, the boyfriend. Didn't Adele say he worked as a cleaner at the hospital where her mother died? That would be Whitefriars on the Great Barns Road. Luk must know something about the body, even if he's only heard or read about it. Perhaps the police know about him and have already interviewed him. On my way back to the office I think of a plan. I ask Charlie if he wants me to cover any of Adele's outstanding clients while she's still away. He doesn't say a lot but gives me a list. 'Don't neglect your own work,' he says. I ignore any addresses that aren't in the direction of Great Barns Road. I phone one at random and speak to a Mr Jones and arrange an immediate visit.

16

The fog is lifting and the hospital looms, ten storeys of glass and brick, attached to an older annex. I weave through a maze of terraced houses, slowing occasionally to allow a car or ambulance to pass.

Mr Jones doesn't smile as he answers the door. 'Nasty day,' I say.

'It's about time someone got in touch,' he says. 'The other one's lost interest.' He means Adele, of course. 'My wife is at work. She's a nurse at Whitefriars. The hospital. I expect you know it?'

He nods towards a chair. My invitation to sit. As I look around the front room, I am at a loss to know why this property wasn't sold months ago. Medical staff are always looking for places to live in this area. I assure Mr Jones we've had a busy summer with sales but I will give his house priority; refresh the brochure, take some new pictures. The daffodils in the current one are a dead give-away to the length of time the house has been on the market. I feel an unexpected flash of anger towards Adele. What had she been doing all this time?

Mr Jones grumbles on. Tells me he, too, works at the

hospital but mainly nights. He's a porter. He and Mrs Jones hardly see each other. They want to move up to Middlesborough to be near his elderly mother. She's ailing. It's a familiar story.

I'd like to come right out with it. Do you know a cleaner called Luk? How can I get in touch with him? Mr Jones is looking past me, barely bothering to stifle a yawn. But I need to tread cautiously. I assure him the agency are fully committed to selling his house and promise to get back to him very soon. As he sees me out he says he's seen Fortune Estates is in the news and are we closing down. I pretend not to hear and give him a cheery wave.

The next contact I try is a Mr Turner, but all I get is an unobtainable signal on his mobile. Mr and Mrs Sands aren't home either, but I am able to leave a message. I go back to the office and tell myself that I now have a legitimate reason to look at Adele's computer to see what she's been up to. However, Charlie tells me the police have already taken it away. I should have realised and wonder when they'll come back for mine.

17

I buy an egg salad for lunch. Before I even hang up my coat, Charlie's out of his office. He's locked the door and turned the sign to CLOSED. On this late November morning the lights are already on inside, fluorescent, glaring and cold.

'I think you'd better sit down,' he says. 'I've got some news.'

'Oh,' I say,' has someone put in an offer for Riverside?' I know what he wants to say has nothing to do with Riverside, but something, anything, makes me want to put off hearing what it is. 'I was at Mrs Baxter's this morning,' I say, 'a cash buyer seems keen.' He pulls up a chair, the one from Adele's desk. I glance towards the door, willing somebody to enter. But they won't because the sign says closed.

'I've heard from the police,' he says.

'Oh? What do they want?'

'There's been a development.'

'Oh?'

'With the body,' he says.

'That's good, then,' I say.

'They've been in touch with Adele's relatives.'

'Adele's relatives?' I've only ever heard her mention one. A cousin who lives somewhere up near Cambridge. Surely she's not the murderer, I want to say. I try to suppress a nervous laugh. I remember the police car I saw parked outside Adele's house this morning.

'Is the cousin helping with the search, then?'

'Not directly. But the cousin has been asked to give DNA.'

A silence follows. There's a strange ringing in my ears. I look at Charlie, hoping he will stop talking soon, turn the door sign to OPEN, and suggest we get back to work.

'Don't you see,' he goes on, 'they want to know if it's a match.'

'A match?'

'They must think it's a possible match with the body.'

I'm desperately trying to hold myself together. My thoughts are flying round the room, resting on a filing cabinet, soaring up to the strip light. They flutter over Adele's desk like a grey damp mist.

'I can't believe it either, but it must be what they think.'

'What do they think?' But I know the answer already.

'They must believe the body is Adele,' he says.

I want to stand, but I'm afraid I'll fall down. 'How can that be?' I ask. I can smell the sickly egg wrap in its greasy bag and think I might throw up right here on the floor.

'The description fits, she's been missing since it was discovered and now they're checking up on DNA. They must think it's her.'

I am trying to calculate backwards. When did I last speak to Adele? It was surely the night she told me about Luk. I remember telling her how stupid she'd been. Were those really our last words? But the body had already been found by then, hadn't it? I reach into my bag for my diary but then remember it's at home, hidden in the oven. Somebody is looking through the window at us. It's a man with a bicycle. He catches my eye and points at his watch.

'But it couldn't be Adele,' I blurt out, 'I...' But I don't finish the sentence. I would have to contradict myself, contradict the statement I'd given to the police. Admit I'd spoken to her *after* the body had been discovered.

Charlie reaches out and touches my hand. 'Of course, it's yet to be confirmed but this is a terrible shock for both of us. I think we should close the office for the afternoon.'

It's growing dark outside. I stare at the window, seeing only our reflections in the darkened glass. The man with the bicycle has disappeared.

'The police will probably want us tomorrow for more statements. I'll fend off any appointments here. You should go home, get some rest.'

'Yes, I'd like to go home,' I say automatically.

'Are you OK driving?' he asks. 'What about a taxi, or shall I call somebody, Simon perhaps?'

'I'd just like to go home,' I say again.

'Well, I'll stay on here for an hour or so.'

I tell Charlie not to worry, it's going to be alright, but I'm talking to myself. I collect my coat, pick up the greasy bag containing what should have been my lunch and walk outside, throwing it into the nearest bin. The chill wind makes my eyes water.

I stumble to the car, almost dropping the keys as I open the door. Four thirty in the afternoon, yet it's dark as midnight. I'm angry with Adele, but now I feel afraid for her too. Do the police really think she's dead? I immediately push away the thought. Surely, she can't be. But where is she?

I'm dazzled by lights from oncoming cars and hear an immediate rebuke from a driver's horn when I veer slightly out of lane. I should have said something to Charlie. Perhaps I should say something to the police. But until I hear directly from Adele, wouldn't I just be making trouble for her? The police will find out for themselves when the DNA fails to match. I manoeuvre back in lane, cut my speed and I'm made instantly aware of headlights flaring up aggressively close behind.

I wonder why they haven't already traced Adele's last call to me. But perhaps if Adele is missing, so is her phone. Maybe they will want to check my phone. Perhaps I should have got rid of it. But can't they trace records anyway? Thinking about everything I have to think about is overwhelming.

Somehow I manage to get myself home and collapse on the bed without bothering to undress. Almost immediately there's a knock at the door and my first wild thought is that Adele's come back to put everything right. Then I hear a discrete cough and recognise it's Mrs Baxter from upstairs. I keep very still until I hear her footsteps move away.

Through the night, I doze on and off, but Luk appears at every turn of the pillow. He's got a gold tooth and a lazy smile. Sometimes he wears a surgeon's mask. Why won't you tell us, I say. Meet me at Whitefriars, he says. Emma will operate. Meet me today, I say. Sorry, I have windows to clean, and with a flash of gold he's gone, only to return later in a clown's hat.

It's a relief when morning comes. It's barely light outside and a thick fog lies over the trees. I dress in a hurry and call Charlie on his mobile before eight.

'Charlie,' I say, 'I don't want to stay home. I'd rather come into the office.'

'There's no need.'

'We must keep things as normal as we can,' I shout. Charlie says nothing. It's as though the fight has gone out of him.

'I'll be at the office later,' he says. 'We can talk about it then.'

I've never seen Charlie so distracted. His face looks grey and his tie mismatched with his shirt. I wonder why Ed, his boyfriend, didn't tell him. I wonder if he talks the situation over with him. I realise how little he talks about his life outside the office. I wish I could reassure him the body couldn't possibly be Adele's. I tell him about my visit to Mr Jones at Great Barns Road, and how I'm going to refresh the brochure, but he hardly looks up.

18

I have several missed calls from Simon.

'I've been trying your number for ages. Were you switched off?'

'I've been busy, Simon.' I try to remember when we last spoke.

'Is something the matter,' I ask.

'Nothing's the matter,' he says. 'Just wanted to see how you are. Have there been any breakthroughs?'

'No.' I reply. I can't bear to think about it, never mind talk about it. 'I can't talk about it now,' I say. 'Did you ring for any particular reason?'

'Well, only that it would be nice to see you. What are you doing tonight?' I'm still thinking, when he says, 'Shall I come over to yours? I'll bring take-away and a bottle and we'll have a night in. You usually like that prawn thing don't you?' He doesn't wait for a reply. 'I'll come straight from work – see you around six-thirty,' he says and rings off.

The flat looks a bit of a tip. I pick up two pairs of discarded trousers, a jacket and some knickers from the bathroom floor. I didn't used to be so untidy. What have I been doing to let things go like this? It's only half past five.

I run the bath, toss in some Oils of the Orient and soak myself until my skin turns pink and the mirrors mist up. Part of me wishes Simon wasn't coming. Not that I don't want to see him, it's just that I feel so exhausted. However, I make an effort with my black palazzos and the vest thing he likes. My hand isn't steady enough for eye-liner, and after two attempts I wipe it off. I turn up the thermostat and cover my bare arms with a cardi.

The kitchen looks decent enough and I go into the living room to wait. There's a knock at the door and I wonder why he hasn't used his key. Then I hear Mrs Baxter's cough and it's too late to pretend to be out.

'Hello dear. I'm glad I caught you.'

'How are you, Mrs Baxter?'

She's peering past me and obviously expects to be invited in. 'How nice you look this evening dear. Are you off out somewhere?'

'I'm expecting a visitor, as it happens.'

'I won't keep you very long. It's just to let you know that the gentleman you sent over wants to have another look at my flat.'

She means Mr Sellers. 'I hope you told him that he'll have to make the appointment with the agency.'

'Well, I wasn't sure what the procedure is.'

Of course not I think. 'He'll have to go through the proper channels,' I repeat.

'Perhaps you'd have a word with him yourself, dear.'

I don't need to respond as we both hear Simon's footsteps on the stairs. He's carrying a supermarket bag for life and a bunch of yellow chrysanthemums, its leaves already dry and drooping.

'Oh how lovely,' croaks Mrs Baxter.

Simon squeezes past and plants a kiss on my cheek.

'I'd better let you go, dear.'

'That's a nasty cough you've got there, Mrs B.' Says Simon, then, turning to me, 'Better get this food inside.'

I close the door and follow him into the kitchen. He's already turned on the oven and is holding my diary in his hands. 'What's all this then.? Hiding the evidence?' If he only knew.

'It got soaked in that downpour.'

'Well, it's dry now.'

He twists the screw-top and pours me a large glass of Trebbiano. 'Not the best to go with Indian, but I know you like it.' He helps himself to tap water, and we raise our glasses.

'You're looking tired,' he says.

'Thanks,' I say.

We eat dinner on our laps.

'I've missed you,' he says at last.

'I've missed you too,' I say. And realise it's the truth.

'Another glass?'

I shake my head. 'I think an early night would suit us both. Don't you?'

He pulls me to my feet and holds me close. I rest my head against the softness of his Cotton Traders blue check shirt. I'd like to stay there forever.

'I'll sort all this out later,' he says, nodding at the empty cartons and discarded lids. He leads me towards the bedroom, removes his belt and goes to unzip my palazzos.

'Bit hot in here, isn't it?' he says.

'Hang on,' I say.

I go back to the kitchen to check the thermostat and notice the yellow flowers still in their paper sheath. 'I'll just put these in water,' I call out. When I get back to the bedroom, Simon's lying on his back, his head turned away, breathing evenly. I climb in beside him, taking care not to disturb him and pull up the quilt.

Next morning I find the note he's left. *Sorry darling, I'll make it up to you next time. Meant to discuss Christmas xxx*

I have a wild thought. Perhaps we could go away somewhere nobody has ever heard of. Somewhere with a sandy beach. Somewhere where we would never have to think about a thermostat. We could lie under a palm tree all day. And never come back.

19

The person who's constantly in my thoughts now is Luk. I remind Charlie I'm working on another brochure for New Barns Road and need to take a photo of the garden. But really, I want to talk to Mrs Jones.

I ask Charlie if he's had any news from the police about the DNA. He shakes his head. Poor man, he still thinks Adele is dead. How I'd love to just tip him a nod and a wink. Say, don't worry, Charlie, I know it's not her. But of course, I can't. It would only raise suspicions. We're sure to hear soon, anyway.

Charlie's talking on the phone, and I can tell from his voice it's not good news. 'The Drs Elliott want us to take their house off the market,' he says. 'They're angry. There have been no viewings. Why haven't we sent anybody?' He goes on, 'and I had a call from Zoe Caswell yesterday asking if we're still open for business!'

There isn't a lot I can say.

'What I don't understand,' he says 'is why Adele didn't realise something fishy was going on at Albert Terrace. That girl seems to have walked about with her eyes closed. We've no record of her ever going there, and now they think she was murdered there.'

'No, Charlie. Let's not think that. Adele will turn up and there will be a proper explanation for everything.'

'Well, she won't be coming back to work for me, that's for sure,' he spits out. His words don't surprise me. More the bitterness in the way he expresses them.

Later that morning, I phone the Jones's and I'm relieved when Mrs Jones answers. She's off duty today and invites me to go over this afternoon.

The rain that threatened earlier didn't materialise, but it's grey and there's a biting wind. I wander around the small garden, taking photos of brown earth, bare trees and shrubs. It won't make for a great look. Mrs Jones offers a cup of coffee. After one or two sympathetic enquiries after her mother-in-law's health, I ask about her shift work, and she tells me the strain it presents to her and Mr Jones.

I take my time with the coffee, then say, 'I know someone who works at Whitefriars, actually. He's a cleaner, called Luk, sorry I don't know his second name.'

'Oh,' Mrs Jones looks puzzled but only for a second. 'I think I know who you mean. Bulgarian or something, wasn't he?'

I note the past tense, but plough on, smiling. 'Romanian, I believe. Do you see much of him?'

'Well, he left Whitefriars a few weeks ago. Quite suddenly.'

'Why was that?'

'I really couldn't say.'

'Do you know where he went,' I ask. 'I mean where he's working now?'

She shakes her head. 'I heard the police came to see him though. Perhaps it was something to do with his passport. But I'd have thought Staff Recruitment would have checked that out before offering him a job.'

I've finished my coffee. Mrs Jones isn't going to offer me another cup but I want to keep the subject going for as long as possible. 'Did you ever meet any of his friends, a girlfriend even? Do you have any idea where he was living?'

Mrs Jones looks startled and looks away out of the window. 'I'm sorry I don't know anything more about him,' she says firmly. 'Now then, Ms… have you got all you need now, about the house I mean?'

I collect my belongings and say goodbye.

'I hope we'll get some interest soon,' she says. 'My husband's losing patience. He's heard you're closing down after that business with the murder, but I've told him you wouldn't be going to all this trouble if you were.'

I stand up and offer Mrs Jones my hand. 'I'll be back in touch with the new brochure as soon as possible, and if you think of anything…' But Mrs Jones has closed the front door behind me.

When I get back to the office, Charlie says, 'You've had a visitor. A young man, but not Simon. Not a policeman either.'

The attempt at a joke falls flat. He hands me a piece of paper with a hand-written note.

Missed you at Book Club, Coming Tonight? Rob.

With a start I remember tonight is Book Club. It's true. I missed the last session. I haven't done any reading either. But mostly, I wonder why he's gone to such trouble to contact me.

As the afternoon drags on, I look through my listings to see if I can breathe a little life into them. Riverside Apartments has been on hold for too long. I put my head round Charlie's door and ask if he can suggest anyone who might be interested. I ask him if he wants to me contact the Elliotts and offer some financial inducement to keep them on the books. Ditto Zoe Caswell at the Golf Course, who seems to be wavering too. I need to check my records as I can't remember if I sent James Batley the details. There's Croft Avenue too, which puts me in mind of the Terrys. Charlie says enquiries are down, we must do what we can.

'I think I'll send the Terrys the details of Park Avenue,' I say. 'It's way over their budget, but you never know.' At least they won't say it's too small.

Charlie responds with barely a shrug. 'Worth a try,' is all he says.

I'm getting worried about Charlie. I'm sure he's worn that shirt two days running. He asks if I've heard anything from Mr Sellers.

'Mrs Baxter says he wants to arrange another viewing,' I tell him.

'Well, you know what to do,' is all he says. I ring Mr Sellers and leave a message. The phones are curiously silent all day.

I leave work early as I want to speak to Mrs Baxter. Make sure she understands the proper procedures. I hear laughter as I climb the approach to her flat. I'm taken aback when Mr Sellers opens the door.

'We were just talking about you,' he says.

'Oh? Did we have you booked in for a viewing today?'

'Oh, this isn't a viewing. I've dropped by to see Elaine, not her flat.' He laughs as he speaks and looks past me with a wink. But this time I think it really is a wink.

'I'm glad you like the flat, Mr Sellers, but if you want to view, you really must make an appointment through the agency.'

'Yes, yes, I know all that. You won't want to lose your commission, will you?'

I give him a false smile. 'Is Mrs Baxter here?'

'Oh, yes, she's in the kitchen. She's cooking me a lovely dinner. It's a long time since I had a proper home cooked dinner.'

Mrs Baxter comes to the door, wiping her hands on a tea-towel. 'Hello, dear, I'm a bit busy at the moment.' Then she gives me a wink. It must be catching. Soon, I'll be doing it.

'I've told Mr Sellers he must get in touch with me if he wants to put in an offer.' That should show them.

'I'm cooking chops, dear,' says Mrs Baxter, turning back towards the kitchen. She's wearing something sparkly, with dangly earrings that twinkle in the hall light.

'I told her I'd set the table and I've brought a bottle,' joins in Mr Sellers.

It's obvious they want me to leave. I go downstairs and shut my front door. I take off my jacket and Rob's note falls out. I'm still wondering whether to go tonight or not. It might take my mind off things.

I'm in the bedroom wondering what to wear, when there's a knock at the door. Thinking it must be either Mr Sellers or Mrs Baxter, I hastily grab my dressing gown and go to answer it. D.I. Naomi Reynolds is standing in my hallway.

20

'Can I come in?' she asks. 'This won't take long.'

I gesture towards a chair, but she remains standing. Perhaps it means she's not planning to stay long. My legs are wobbly and I would like to sit down, but don't want to give her an advantage, so remain standing. Naomi's wearing a navy two-piece tonight. It looks very formal. I feel foolish in my dressing gown. I wish I could go back to the bedroom and smarten myself up.

'It's about the unidentified victim,' she says. 'You will be relieved to hear we've proven it's not your colleague and friend, Adele.'

She's telling me something I already know, but I pretend to look relieved. 'We've had the DNA checked, there's no match with her cousin. It's definitely not Adele,' she repeats.

'Who is it then?' I ask. I think that's what she's expecting me to say.

'That's something we're still working on. We've no clear idea yet. That's why we need to talk to Adele. To see whether she can help us with our enquiries.'

Help us with our enquiries. Isn't that what they say when they arrest you? Naomi is looking at me. She, the all-seeing one, can't fail to see my legs shaking under the thin beige towelling, my breath coming too fast, and my lying eyes looking anywhere except into hers.

'Have you had any communication with her? Is there anyone you can think of who might know her whereabouts?'

This is the moment I shall tell her about Luk. Tell her about my attempts to trace him; about the couple I've tracked down who work at the hospital. I force myself to meet her gaze but after a few seconds have to look away. I glance around the room and my eyes come to rest on Simon's chrysanthemums. The petals tinged with brown. I think back to last night. I'm very aware of the stale smell of curry. It's then I spot the diary.

Naomi's got her notebook out. 'Shall we have some more light?' She asks.

I switch on the reading lamp, glad to have something to do.

'Let's sit down,' she says. 'This is a shock for you Hanna.'

Naomi takes the sofa and I sit opposite her, directly under the lamp. I feel its heat piercing my head like a spotlight. Once again I am aware of how clever Naomi is. Whatever made me think I could fool her.

'I'd like you to think very carefully about what Adele said to you the last time you spoke,' she says. 'Any little thing at all would help us.'

Did she grow up wanting to be a policewoman, I wonder. Did she have an encounter at a tender age, or was it the uniform?

'I've already told you everything.' I say.

I try to avoid looking in the direction of the diary. It seems to be advertising itself, as though it has a flashlight attached. She could get up at any moment, walk across, pick it up and that would be the end of everything. But Naomi's gaze is fixed on me.

'You must miss your friend,' she says. 'Yet you don't appear to be very worried about her.'

'Yes, yes, of course I am,' I say 'I've never stopped worrying.' I raise my hand to my head in an effort to make it look as though I'm thinking. But there's nothing I can share with Naomi.

'We've searched through her computer files. But we found nothing that helps us with our enquiries.' That phrase again.

'Were you planning to go out this evening?' she asks, taking me off guard. 'Or were you having an early night?'

'Oh, Book Club,' I say. 'I was thinking of going to my Book Club.'

'Was Adele a member of the Book Club?'

I smile at the thought. 'Oh, no. Not Adele.'

'Well, as I say, whatever you can think of, no matter how small.' She's standing up getting ready to go.

'Lovely colour,' she says. 'The chrysanthemums.' This is the moment she's going to say, Oh I see you found your diary. But she doesn't seem to notice it. 'We'll let you know of any further developments.'

She's walks briskly to the door and it slams behind her. I go back to the sitting room and pick up the diary. The oven is still the best place until I've thought of something better. From my window, I watch her walk to her car. The wind has blown away any last lingering leaves from the trees. Like their bare branches, I feel as if I've been completely exposed.

21

I don't go to Book Club, and sleep badly after Naomi's visit. I feel pressure from all sides. Charlie's going to be furious about Mrs Baxter's flat slipping away from us, right under my nose. But mainly it's the visit from DI Reynolds that troubles me. Did I do enough to allay her suspicions? I think probably not. She's already interviewed me twice. If she wants to see me again, I think it will be under caution.

I dress quickly, deciding to wear my red jacket today. The colour helps to give me a confidence I don't really feel. Charlie always says how good it looks. Simon too. I'm thinking Simon and I still haven't made plans for Christmas.

When I get to the office, Charlie isn't there. No message either. I open up my computer and try to plan the day. There should be plenty of work to follow up, but Adele and Luk just won't go away.

Zoe Caswell may have been wavering, but she's very cheerful on the phone. I hear Banquo barking in the background. "Have you got some news?' She asks. Of course I haven't, but I flannel her a bit and she says why don't you come round this morning, we could have a chat about it. I'm glad to have something to do.

Zoe is wearing black today, as befits a widow in mourning. She makes us both a coffee and we sit down once again in the room that overlooks her garden and the golf course. Lovely view, I say again as we look out of the rain splattered windows. Yes, that's what we thought when we bought the house. You will be sad to leave it, I say. Well, it's got so many memories now and since my husband passed away. This is the same conversation we had last time. She finishes her coffee and runs her hand through her blonde curls. So, what developments, she asks, reasonably.

I look past her and see a man go by the window. Her eyes follow my gaze. 'Oh yes, Marek. He's just tidying up for the winter.' I wonder what Marek is finding to do here in the garden in early December. No borders to attend to, no leaves to sweep. He gives a thumbs up as he passes and Zoe gives a little wave.

'Where did you say he comes from?' I ask.

Zoe looks confused, and doesn't answer. 'Oh, Marek? He's very thorough. As well as good looking.' She laughs and tosses her curls again. The tiny mole had gone a little pink. There's definitely something going on here.

'I'd hoped to be out before Christmas but I haven't had any viewings. I'm wondering if there's any reason?' She's put down her coffee cup and is looking at me closely. 'Is the agency in difficulty? I couldn't help reading about the body they found.'

'Oh, that hasn't affected business at all,' I lie. 'The police are looking into all that. In fact, we're busier than ever.'

'That's good,' she says and leans back in her chair.

Marek walks past again and looks at us both through the window. I take out my notebook and try to look busy.

'Can I expect some viewings soon?' she asks.

From my records, I note that I had sent James Batley the details, but there was no record of any reply. 'I will definitely make it my priority. Of course this isn't the easiest time of year to be selling,' I add.

'No, I suppose not,' she says.

'Things will pick up in the new year.'

'Well, I look forward to hearing from you again soon,' she says, leading the way to the front door. I have no other option but to follow her. The dog barks somewhere in the house and a door slams.

'Tell me, Mrs Caswell, Zoe, how did you find your gardener?'

She looks surprised. 'I can't quite remember. I think he was recommended. Yes that's right, somebody recommended him. You know how it is.'

She looks towards the closed kitchen door. I have the distinct impression that Marek is behind it, listening. I'm wrong, because as I make my way down the front path, I see him. It's as if he's waiting for me.

'Good morning,' I say brightly, letting my red jacket do its work. 'Nice day for gardening.' He doesn't reply but I press on. 'Lovely garden,' I gesture. 'Have you worked here long?'

'Eight month,' he says.

'Big garden,' I say. He nods. 'I was wondering where you come from.' He appears not to understand. 'Where is home?'

'Romania,' he replies.

'Not Poland, then?' I say.

He laughs. He's got very good teeth. 'Only plumbers from Poland,' he says.

'Your English, very good,' I say. He looks away. 'How did you learn to speak such good English?'

He appears not to understand and I'm about to repeat myself when, looking me straight in the eye, he says, 'Mrs Caswell help me.'

'That's nice,' I say.

'And club. I go to club.'

'That's nice,' I say again. 'I know someone from Romania. He's called Luk. Have you ever met anybody called Luk? At the club?'

'Now then, Marek, we mustn't delay Miss Summers.' Without warning, Zoe has crept up on us. Marek takes his cue, picks up a hoe and saunters slowly away.

'Was there something else?' asks Zoe.

'No,' I say, and shake my head.

'Goodbye, then,' she says, 'hope to hear from you soon.'

I go back to the office and contact one or two names on my list. Neither looks particularly promising. I send another email to James Batley. We haven't had many new enquiries lately, and I don't understand why Charlie isn't more worried. Perhaps he is. Later, when I take off my jacket, I see a brown stain on the cuff that wasn't there before. It resembles a tear-drop, an indelible reminder of my coffee with Zoe this morning.

It's already turning dark outside, as if the day is half over. Still no sign of Charlie. I'm wondering if I should ring him when I hear the door open. I look up to see Rob.

'Hello there,' he says. 'I hope you don't mind.'

'It's alright, Rob. I'm not that busy, as it happens.'

'All that publicity stuff can't be good for business.'

I can't be bothered to correct him. I'm beginning to think it's true anyway.

'What brings you here?' I ask.

'I left a note for you yesterday.'

'Yes, Book Club. To tell the truth, Rob...'

'Don't worry, you didn't miss much. Actually it's not what I've come about.'

'Oh?' I hope he's not going to ask me along to a late night moon-watch.

'I want some advice.'

'Oh?'

'It's about Albert Terrace.'

His words, unexpected, drop to the floor and scatter like stones. He's looking at me closely.

'What about it?' I try to stay cool.

'I don't want to make trouble. For anybody.'

'O.K.' I reply cautiously.

'It's about your colleague, Adele Stevens.'

'Adele? What about her?' I look at him in silence. I seem to be holding my breath while still breathing. 'Go on then,' I say.

'I saw her, saw her go into the house. Let herself in with a key. Well, she would have a key, wouldn't she. Actually, I saw her there more than once. On a couple of occasions, there was a man with her.'

'So? She was trying to show the house, trying to sell it.' I already know what he's going to tell me.

'Yes, but the thing is, the last time I saw her was the day the body was discovered.'

'So?'

'She must have seen it.'

There is a silence while we both ponder the implication of this.

'Have you seen her since?' I ask, hoping to catch him out.

He breathes a deep sigh, 'No, I never saw her again after that. I didn't want to get involved, but now I wonder if I should say something… to the police.'

My mouth has gone dry, but I manage to ask, 'Why didn't you say something before?'

At this point the phone rings. I'm glad of the interruption. 'Hello, Charlie,' I say.

'Sorry about today, Hanna. Have had an almighty migraine. Sick like you've never seen.'

'Sorry, Charlie.' I say, I've never heard of Charlie getting migraines.

'Must be something I ate or picked up a bug. Is everything OK? At your end?'

'Of course,' I reply. 'No problems. Don't worry. Are you likely to be back tomorrow?'

'Well, I would have been but I've got to go down to the police station again tomorrow morning. They want to go over my statement again. I can't remember what I said to them in the first place.'

'Don't worry, Charlie. It will be fine. See you when you get here.'

I put the phone down, scribble a note to myself and turn to face Rob. But it's as though he's disappeared down his own black hole. I didn't even hear the door close.

22

Later that afternoon, Simon texts. Wants to know when we can meet. What do I want to do? As always, he pushes any decision making back to me. It's a month since I had my low-lights done and Sinead did my nails. Diva is still in place, but the cuticles are showing obvious signs of new growth. The dark red gel suggests a more glamorous life than the one I'm living. What is it I want, I ask myself. Private villa on a private island? The sound of the ocean so close I can hear the crash of waves as they hit the shore. Lazy wicker chairs on a veranda always lightly dusted with sand? A maid to dust them. A closet sweetly stocked with classy beach and bed-wear. I think I just want to run away. I text back: Whenever you like! Will phone tonight, is his reply. I make a mental note to book an appointment with Sinead.

Later, Simon tells me his ex has a new dog. It's a rescue animal from Spain, highly strung. Sam always wanted a dog, growing up, he says. It's her Christmas present. He sounds quite excited. He hasn't called his ex a fucking deranged cow for some time now. Are his feelings towards her changing?

'We've been talking about Christmas,' he says.

'Christmas is always a difficult time for a fractured family,' I venture, sounding more like his therapist than his lover.

'Oh, I think we've got over all that.'

'So what's this dog all about?' I ask.

'Like I say, Sam always wanted dog, but Annie never liked animals.'

'So what's changed all of a sudden? It's your turn to have Sam this year, isn't it?'

Simon doesn't appear to see any element of manipulation in his ex-wife's unexpected canine conversion.

'Sam doesn't know yet. It's a surprise. For Christmas.'

'Does that mean Annie wants Sam with her over Christmas?'

'Possibly.'

'So we're free to do something ourselves? Maybe plan a little trip?'

'Well, it's complicated.'

Of course it is.

'What she's suggesting is I take Sam over on Christmas Eve, she introduces the dog – it's called Trixie by the way – it's in kennels at the moment. I, we, take her for a walk Christmas morning, then Sam, me and Trixie come back to mine for the rest of the holiday. With you, of course.'

Great, I think.

'Great,' I say.

*

It looks like Christmas is here, already. Along the main road, an avenue of trees strung with coloured lights blow around in the wind. Shop windows bright and gaudy, Chris Rea driving home for Christmas, it all makes me want to cry. I realise I have done nothing. Have felt stuck. Made no lists. Bought no presents. I know I should phone Dad, if only to verify his plans.

All thoughts bring me back to Adele. Is she somewhere planning Christmas? Or is it too late for that? Will there ever be an answer? The thought makes me choke.

Next morning, still no sign of Charlie. I'm anxious to know how he got on at the police station. His mobile is turned off. I try his home number, but there's no reply. Waiting around in the office reminds me of Rob's unexpected visit yesterday. So he'd seen Adele at the house. So he'd worked out it was around the time the body was discovered. Why was he telling me, and not the police? Could have been mistaken? He could have seen anybody, assumed it was Adele. Adele had stupidly given Luk a key. Luk could have had it copied. Could have given it to anybody. The more I think about it, the more I realise Luk literally holds the key to everything. My visit to the Jones's and my polite questions have led nowhere. I turn on my computer, locate the Whitefriars website, and dial the number.

'I'd like to speak to the housekeeping department, please.'

'What name?'

'I want to speak to the person in charge.'

'Hold on.'

There is a short delay, then suddenly a man's is saying, 'Peter Ford here. How can I help you?'

'I'd like to speak to Luk, please?'

'Who?'

'Luk. He's one of your cleaning staff.'

'Surname?'

How many Luks could they possibly have? 'Do you have someone on your staff called Luk?' I say. 'I'd like to speak to him.'

'I can't give out personal information over the phone, I'm afraid.'

'I'm only asking to speak to him. Does he still work for you?'

'Sorry miss, what did you say your name was? I'll make a note of your number.'

What else had I expected? Had I really thought Luk would come to the phone? I pause for a couple of seconds before hearing myself answer, 'It's Stevens, Adele Stevens. Perhaps you could pass on a message for me? Just tell Luk that Adele Stevens called. He'll know what it's about.' I give him my number, and hang up.

I feel strangely calm after leaving the message. It's unlikely to reach him so what is there to lose. If by some chance Peter Ford does manage to pass on the message, I'll deal with that when the time comes. It's Luk who should be worried, not me.

I peer into Charlie's office. It's very tidy. It's always tidy, but today there is a lack of anything that suggests any work in progress. There has definitely been a falling off of new inquiries. It could be the time of year, but…

The main office feels cheerless. The overhead lights throw a harsh glow. I might suggest buying a couple of side-lights. I don't know why we didn't think of it before. Charlie hasn't bought the poinsettias this year and I don't think he will now. I remember there is a box of Christmas decorations somewhere in the basement. Charlie might think lights and tinsel tasteless in the circumstances. Adele always used to take care of that sort of thing. All thoughts lead back to Adele. But I no longer think she will turn up unexpectedly with some funny story to explain her absence. I wish I had managed to speak to the cousin who gave the DNA. I missed my chance there. I suppose I could try to locate her, but I'm not sure how and I don't want to draw any more attention to myself. The office is deathly quiet. Outside trees bend in the brisk wind. A passer-by attempts, but fails, to keep an umbrella up.

It can't hurt to go down to the basement to look for the decorations. The light bulb blew months ago and it's never been fixed. I use the light on my phone to make my way down the stairs. I don't remember the last time anybody came down here. It smells musty. It's only used for keeping boxes of files and documents that pre-date the internet. The idea is that one day we'll update everything and put it on line, but that day hasn't come yet.

I can't immediately locate the decorations. I hear the door-bell, signifying someone has entered upstairs. 'Charlie, is that you?' I call out. But there's no reply. As I'm hurrying back to the stairs, I stumble and knock my shin on a broken chair. It's painful. Probably bleeding and I need to get a wet towel. I've dropped my phone somewhere and the light's gone out. 'Is that you, Charlie?' I call again, but there's no reply. I fumble around in the dark and shout out, 'I'll be with you in a minute.' I find the phone, relieved to see the light come on, and make my way back upstairs.

There's nobody there. I'm sure I didn't imagine it, but the office is empty. A strong wind can sometimes blow the door open, perhaps that's what happened. I look briefly into Charlie's office but there's no sign of him or anybody else. I decide not to bother any more with the basement and go back to my desk. It's then I see the note. It's been typed and reads:

Dear Hanna
Can you meet me at the office tonight at nine?
Please come. I'll explain everything.
Adele

At last! Thank God. I am so grateful to hear from her. So thankful, I don't bother to ask myself why the mystery, why she didn't just wait to see me. Perhaps she asked someone else to leave the note. Perhaps Luk did get my message after all. Perhaps Luk brought the note. Whatever's going on between them, it doesn't matter. I'm so relieved to hear from her. It makes up for everything. Adele will explain everything later.

I don't know how to fill in the hours, but somehow, I do. I close the office early and leave a note for Charlie in case he stops by. I take the long route home, passing Riverside Apartments. I play a bit of Leonard Cohen. He's one of Simon's favourites, but I seldom listen unless he's in the car with me. Adele gave me Abba for my birthday last year, but the CD keeps skipping, so I switch it off. I glance up at Riverside and wonder if it's my imagination or is the light on in one of the windows? Surely I couldn't have left it on – it's a couple of weeks since I showed it to anybody. I slow down and sit for a moment. But I must have imagined it, because when I look again, the light's gone. I resolve to email anyone who's shown interest in the flat, and invite them to an open day. We'll re-advertise, but it will have to wait until the New Year now.

I drive home and let myself into the flat. There's no sign of anybody upstairs at Mrs Baxter's. I wonder how things are going between her and Mr Sellers. I'll try to speak to her over the weekend and ask if he's still interested in buying her flat.

I change into some comfortable clothes, turn on the TV and go to make a cheese sandwich. I slice into the cheese but see it has mould spots and have to throw it out. I'm reminded of the need to go shopping. I must have dozed off because when I come to the news is over and there's a wildlife programme showing about otters. It's still only seven o'clock.

I wonder what Adele will say. How I'll be able to make any sense of what she does say. Part of me is still angry with her, the way she involved me in the murder. Well, not exactly involved me, but the way I was given no choice but to keep telling lies to the police. But Adele surely will have had good reason to "disappear" the way she did. I keep glancing at the clock, wondering why she wanted such a late meeting.

I get to the office just before nine and see the lights already on. Peering through the glass door I fumble for my key.

23

'Charlie,' I say. 'Whatever are you doing here?'

'I might ask you the same.'

'I, er… are you here alone?'

Charlie looks surprised. 'Yes, why?'

I hold back from telling him why I'm here. I'll wait to see if he, too, has had a message from Adele.

'How did you get on at the police station?' I ask.

'Well, they asked me to go over the same old stuff. Then told me I could go.'

Any minute I think we're going to hear Adele come through the door. She'll rush in, toss her hair and throw her arms round us both. I can almost smell her shampoo. Pomegranate and Passion Fruit, she used to say, with a laugh.

'I've got something to tell you, Hanna. Something I think you should know.'

'Yes?' This is it, I think. I'm disappointed Adele hadn't wanted to see me on my own. But perhaps this will be better.

'Sit down, Hanna. I didn't expect to see you here tonight, but now is as good a time as ever.'

'What is it?' I lean forward, pretending ignorance of what he is about to tell me.

'The police are going to put out an appeal on TV. Ask people to come forward with information.'

'Oh. Well, that's good, isn't it?' Perhaps this is why Adele has chosen this moment to re surface.

'Well, it's good for the investigation, not so good for us. You must have noticed how business has fallen off.'

I say nothing. I don't want to admit it. To say it makes it real.

'The thing is, it's going to be difficult for us. The police say we're likely to be approached by nutters. Get hoax phone calls, that sort of thing. Some of our clients might be harassed by cranks.'

'Surely not,' I say. My thoughts are racing. He's not going to close us down is he? Move us to different premises? What will happen to my job? I can't say it, though. It sounds too self-serving. Cars occasionally swish past on the road outside, their lights reflecting in the glass windows.

'These are difficult times,' he says, turning away. He turns back and asks, 'What brings you here at this time of night?'

I'm still taking in his news, and I've momentarily forgotten why I'm here. 'Oh, I forgot something. Forgot to lock the basement door.' What a stupid thing to say. He just looks at me so I add, 'I was looking for the decorations – you know, for Christmas.'

'Don't bother. Pick up a couple of new things from the market.'

I glance at the office clock. Twenty past nine. She should have been here by now. I try to make small talk.

'Are you looking forward to Christmas?'

'We were planning to go away. Now I'm not sure. We'll see.' He looks at his watch. 'Anyway, it's late. It's time we both went home.'

It's clear to me now that Adele is not going to show up. 'Will you be in tomorrow?' I ask. 'Is there anything you want me to do?'

'Just carry on as normal for the time being. I know it's not easy.'

I nod again.

'See you tomorrow,' he says.

'Goodnight,' I say, standing up. I've been dismissed.

There's no sign of anybody outside. I take a hard look down the street. It's obvious Charlie knew nothing about Adele's attempt to meet me tonight. She must have seen us both through the window and, for reasons of her own, decided not to come. Or was she planning to come at all?

A horn blares at me as I pull out. I'm accelerating fast, too fast, as I join the traffic on the main road.

24

The following night, I haven't been home long when Dad phones. 'Your Aunt Jean has had a fall,' he says. 'Broken her hip.'

'How did she do it?' I ask.

'Running for a bus,' he says. 'You know your Aunt Jean.'

Indeed, I do know my Aunt Jean. 'What will happen?' I ask.

'Well she's in hospital for the time being. Living alone, as she does, they thought it for the best. How she'll manage when she's discharged is another matter. I'll do what I can, of course.'

I think of Dad. Overall, in good health for a man of seventy-six, but taking on the care of his older sister is another matter.

'What can I do to help?'

'Well, she's in the best place at the moment,' he says. 'It's painful of course, but she's still got her marbles,' he adds.

My thoughts race ahead to Christmas, less than two weeks away. 'Dad, what will you do about…'

'Oh, don't worry about me. I'll visit Jean if she's still in hospital. The couple next door have asked me in for Christmas dinner. You don't have to worry about me.'

But I do worry. And feel guilty. I've been so pre-occupied with work and the police investigation, I've allowed other responsibilities to slide. Simon and I haven't decided on Christmas plans. I don't feel guilty about that because I know I'll be last in a queue behind his ex-wife, his Sam and the new dog.

'As long as you're OK, Dad,' I venture.

'I'm more than OK,' he says. 'Don't you worry about me. How are things at work?'

'OK,' I say, 'it's always quiet at this time of year. I was going to ask what you want for Christmas – a new duvet perhaps? Some slippers?' With all that's going on, I sound ridiculous.

'Don't worry about me,' he repeats. 'I could do with some new socks though.'

I tell him I'll try to come up to visit him and Aunt Jean soon.

'Yes, I'll look forward to it.'

I worry about him, living on his own.

As if he hears me thinking, 'Don't worry, Hanna, I'll be fine,' he says. 'Just you take care of yourself.'

After he rings off, I sit for a while going over the day's events. Dad didn't ask me about Albert Terrace, so it must have gone off the radar in his part of the country. Some other crime will have caught the headlines. The TV programme they're planning will definitely bring it all back to the surface again. But that's good, isn't it? If it helps to resolve the murder? Thoughts revolve in my head like flashing disco lights, illuminating nothing. The dance floor is empty. My thoughts now are only for Adele. Is she in trouble, just waiting somewhere nearby, waiting for a chance to come forward? But what could be preventing her. The thing that had been nagging at me finally surfaces. I have to confront the thought that the note probably came from somebody else. Someone who knows my name, and where to find me. Somebody who knew about Adele's connection to Albert Terrace.

25

Adele's body is found on Boxing Day. A 10-year-old child veers off the path on her new bike and wobbles into some bushes. Her fall is broken by a covering of rotted leaves that had been piled over the body. In fact, it is quite likely that the child wasn't even aware she had fallen onto a body, although the ensuing fuss when her father called 999 made up for it.

Simon and I didn't manage Christmas together after all. With Annie, Sam and the dog making their demands, we decided it would be best to plan something for New Year instead. Simon expresses some surprise when I suggest it, but he doesn't disagree. It's a good opportunity for me to go up to see Dad. He seems to be holding up well, quite cheerful actually, as though taking care of Aunt Jean's has given him some purpose. It makes me aware of how lonely he must sometimes be, though he would never admit it.

'Lovely socks,' he says as he opens my present on Christmas morning. 'Just the right colour too,' he says as he gazes at the bargain pack of navy blues.

'I got you this to go with them,' I say, throwing him a navy fleece, and this too he cries as he opens up a knitted woolly hat.

'You shouldn't waste your money on me you know. I don't need anything much. I have got my pension, you know.'

'You're a difficult man to please.'

'Yes, your mother always said that. And I got you this,' he says, handing me an M&S voucher for £50, which reminds me I still haven't spent the one he gave me last year.

The neighbours seem happy to have us in to share their Christmas lunch. Make a big effort with the food, the tree and crackers on the table. Dad and I bring red wine and chocolates. Their son works abroad for a humanitarian aid charity and couldn't get home, though I don't suppose we are much of a substitute.

Next day I'm getting ready to drive home.

Dad is cooking breakfast. 'Hey,' he shouts up the stairs, 'they've found a body. Down your way. Fairview Park. That's near you, isn't it?'

We both watch as they give a brief outline of the discovery. The person has not been named, says the newswoman in a serious voice, before moving on to a more seasonal topic and adopting a brighter tone. But I know. Straight away, *I know*.

'Some family is going to have a nasty shock,' says Dad, turning off the TV.

I say nothing. We'd planned a walk before I leave, but the day has turned cold and wet, so it's not difficult to tell Dad I'm leaving earlier than expected.

'You go. I don't want you driving too late in this weather,' he says.

I keep the car radio on all the way home. They only mention the body once more, and repeat that the identity isn't yet known. But I know. The rain turns to sleet for most of the journey. I search for news bulletins which reveal nothing new. It feels false to tune in to music or DJ banter and eventually I turn it off, my thoughts dulled by the monotonous swish of the wiper blades.

I haven't been home long when I get a call from Naomi. She apologises for calling me on a bank holiday, but there has been a development. Could she come over to discuss it with me? Tomorrow?

26

D.I. Naomi arrives at four o'clock the following afternoon. By then, they have released the identity of the body discovered in Fairview Park. Believed to be… Simon has heard it on the news, rings, and asks if I want him to come over. I am relieved at the thought of having him here. He's dismayed the police wanted to interview me and suggests I contact a solicitor. I am almost wondering myself. But I haven't been charged with anything, have I? And who would I call? What would I say to a solicitor anyway?

The D.I. doesn't caution me, which I am half expecting, which shows my state of mind that day. She tells me she is sorry to bring bad news. They had been able to identify Adele almost immediately, she says. Adele was already a misper and there is a positive DNA match with her cousin, Rosemary.

Naomi has no objection to Simon sitting in on the interview, although she shuts him up quickly if he tries to say anything. She's figured out that what has happened is nothing to do with him. I must have been in shock. I can only answer in monosyllables, which is probably a good thing.

'I'm sorry to bring you bad news, Hanna.'

'Yes.'

'We were also able to recognise her by a photograph of the two of you together.'

'Oh.'

'We found it when we searched Adele's house.'

At this point she holds out a photograph. It was a selfie Adele took of us in the office a year ago when my hair was longer. Adele with Hanna she's written on the back. She must have really liked the picture to have gone to the trouble of getting it printed.

'Do you remember where that photograph was taken, or when?'

'No,' I say.

It seems best to say as little as possible. I'm imagining strangers rummaging through Adele's things. The thought is sickening. I have the strange notion that it won't be long before the same latex-covered fingers will be crawling through my own cupboards. Naomi reaches out and takes the photograph back. It's as though the subject is closed, but she produces another.

'What about this one, then? Do you recognise anybody in this photograph?'

Adele is sitting next to man on a garden bench smiling up into his eyes. The photo is indistinct, dark and smudgy, as though taken from a distance, though it's definitely her.

'Well? asks Naomi.

'No,' I say. 'Only Adele.'

'And the man she is with? You haven't seen him before?'

'I don't think so.' I shake my head.

'I've asked you before, but this might jog your memory. She never spoke about a man she was close to?'

I shake my head again. 'No. Never.' My voice comes out as a whisper.

'We're trying to build up a picture of her life. So take your time, Hanna. This could be important to our enquiries.'

I make no reply. What reply could I make. I think I put my head in my hands. Blotting out the room, wishing I was somewhere else. Anywhere else.

'I know this is a difficult time for you, Hanna, but I have to ask you again. Can you remember the last time you either saw, or spoke to Adele?'

'Only what I've already told you.'

'Can you tell me where you have been for the past two days?'

'With my father.'

'Can you give me his address?'

At this point, I think I shout at her, something like why are you asking me this over and over, because I remember Simon taking hold of my hand and saying something like, 'You know she's gone over all this before. Nothing's changed. Can't you see how distraught she is?' Naomi takes no notice of him, but I feel comforted by his interruption.

'Have you found your diary yet, Hanna?'

I had forgotten all about the diary. 'Not yet. I'll keep looking.'

'Let us know when it turns up,' she says getting ready to leave. 'Try to think back to your last communication with Adele. Any little thing will be helpful.'

I can't work out why she came at all. Just to show me a couple of photos I could barely bring myself to look at? Does she really think I'm involved? Does she think I'll crack up? Reveal something new? I feel so drained, I no longer care. And what will Dad think when the police turn up on his doorstep. I should ring him and warn him. Tell him not to worry. I hold on to the thought that I have done nothing wrong, well nothing that could connect me to all this horror.

I would have liked to ask Naomi what *she* knows of Adele's last movements. Does *she* know about Luk? Is Luk the man in the photograph? I doubt it would take her long to find out. Perhaps she knows already. It's hurtful to realise I know so little about this chapter of Adele's life. Was this the time to tell Naomi everything I knew? Nothing could hurt Adele now. But some weird internal voice is telling me to keep my mouth shut. I probably shouldn't have listened to it.

'So, you were hiding the evidence,' says Simon when she's gone.

'What do you mean?' But I know what he means.

'In the oven.'

'No. I had mis-placed it, that's all. You know, how sometimes you can't find your keys then they turn up in the fridge.'

'That's not what happened, though, is it?'

I try to figure out an explanation to give him, but fail.

'Is there's something you ought to be telling me?' he says. 'Where's the diary now?'

I don't tell him I shredded it at the office one quiet afternoon and later took the bin-liner full of strips to a recycling centre across town.

'Don't you trust me?' I say.

'It's never very clever to lie to the police.'

'I was worried Charlie would see how slack I'd been with my appointments.'

'It wasn't Charlie you were worried about though, was it?' He's raised his voice and I'm afraid Mrs Baxter will hear us.

'You make me sound like a criminal,' I whisper.

'Well, what am I supposed to think? You're being so weird…'

I burst into tears when he says this. He pulls me towards him and says no more about the police visit. That night we hold each other close and have the best sex we've had in a long time. We cling to each other as though clinging to life itself and after it is over, we weep.

27

Simon has to go back to work next morning. The cardboard box industry takes quite a hit at Christmas. The Agency is officially closed between Christmas and New Year, but I have a hunch Charlie will be there, and he answers the phone.

'I was going to call you, Hanna. It's dreadful news. I've just heard they've identified Adele.'

'The police were here yesterday. Have they been to see you?'

'No, not yet. Why did they want to talk to you?'

'I've no idea. They only wanted to show me some photos. They keep going over the same old ground.'

'So, did they say what they thought had happened to Adele?'

'No, nothing.' It occurred to me in a flash I should have asked. My lack of curiosity will count against me.

'It's such a horrible business. Who could possibly want to hurt Adele?'

'It could have been random,' I say. 'You know, wrong person, wrong place.' Neither of us believes this.

We both fall silent. Trying to collect our thoughts, wondering what to say. I think back to the events of the past few weeks. Starting with the discovery of the body at Albert Terrace. Adele's late night confession about her affair with Luk. The fact she'd given him a key to the empty property. Was it Luk in the photo Naomi had shown me? But something about him had looked familiar. I feel my face go hot, and feel angry with her all over again. Why, why, why had she been so stupid?

'I suppose there will be a post mortem,' says Charlie.

'Yes.'

'Then it will be the coroner's court. That should throw up something.'

Silence descended again. Neither of us knows what to say, yet neither of us wants to hang up.

'We open up the office again on the second, don't we?'

'Well, that's the plan. I wonder if we should stay closed a bit longer.'

'It's up to you, Charlie.'

'The police haven't returned our computers yet. I can't imagine they'll keep them much longer. I don't know how long they'll keep...' The sentence is left hanging. He means Adele's body.

'Surely we can get hold of a couple of computers.' I realise the futility of my words straight away but Charlie doesn't seem to notice.

'You're right. I'll get on with it.'

There's another awkward silence that neither of us knows how to break. Then, 'Would you like to come over one evening – you and Simon?'

I am surprised by the invitation. It's never been offered before. 'That's nice of you,' I say. 'When do you have in mind?'

'What about New Year's Eve? Ed and I are having a quiet evening at home. Especially this year.'

'I'll speak to Simon. But thank you.'

The flat feels freezing. I take a long, hot shower and put on a warm sweater. I turn up the thermostat, and turn on the TV. Adele's discovery isn't mentioned again and I don't know whether to feel grateful or sad.

Simon hasn't said he's coming over again tonight, but part of me thinks he will. Especially after last night. I stretch and feel a pleasantly familiar lurch deep down in my stomach. I catch sight of myself in the mirror and smile. I change the sheets and hum a little tune as I replace the burnt-out candles.

He rings late in the afternoon and says he's promised to take Sam ice-skating. With all that's been going on, he couldn't let her down. No, course not, I understand. I am about to tell him about Charlie's invitation for New Year's Eve, but he goes on to tell me about Christmas and the new dog. Sam has changed its name to Lady Gaga, as she has such delicate little legs and paws. Lady Gaga isn't keen on walking too far. I wonder if Simon will suggest me going with them to the ice rink, but it either doesn't occur to him or he thinks it unlikely I'll want to go in the circumstances. Later, I phone Dad and tell him that my friend and work-mate has died.

'It was her then, found in that park?'

''fraid so, Dad.'

'Terrible shock for you.'

'Yes.'

'Do they know what happened?'

'No. Not yet. How are you, Dad?'

'I've spent the afternoon at the hospital. Auntie Jean's caught an infection.'

'Is it bad?'

'Not great. But you know your Auntie Jean. She'll rally.'

'Yes. By the way, the police might get in touch with you to confirm where I was over Christmas.'

'They already have.'

'It's nothing to worry about, Dad.'

'I'm not worried.'

I'd like to say more, but don't want to burden Dad with my worries.

'I'll call you again soon. Let you know how things are.'

'I'll let you know about Auntie Jean if there are any changes. Look after yourself. Sorry about your friend.'

'Thanks, Dad. Goodnight, kiss kiss.'

I put the phone down, and wonder what I'm going to do for the rest of the day.

28

I am now convincing myself that Luk was the man with Adele in the photo. Who else could it have been? I wish I'd looked at it more closely but didn't want to give anything away. My feeble attempts to track him down had come to nothing. He could be the murderer, or at the very least hold the clue to both killings because in my mind they are definitely linked. I sit down with a jolt. Who did I think I was? Some kind of Miss Marple, an amateur sleuth who could outwit the police and solve a crime? I had to face a bitter fact. I had attempted to keep Adele out of trouble but, by saying nothing, I may have unwittingly brought about her death. The thought is hideous. I want to scream. I lean back on the couch and put a cushion over my face. Perhaps now is the time to tell Detective Inspector Naomi all I know. I would have to eventually, if she hasn't already worked these things out for herself. The bell rings and I open the door to find a young woman standing there.

'Can you spare a few minutes, Hanna? You don't mind me calling you Hanna?'

She's got heavily highlighted hair, thick and untidy, bundled up on top of her head. She's smiling and has placed a fashionably-booted foot casually against the door.

'No,' I say, too late.

The woman is introducing herself, 'Sarah Fielding, freelance journalist,' she says holding out her card.

Charlie deals with all press enquiries and has told me under no circumstances to talk to anybody about Adele and her disappearance, especially the press. This is also what the police have advised. She places a hand on the door as I attempt to close it. She's a strong girl and I have to let go. 'I gather you worked with Adele,' she's saying. It must be a terrible shock for you. I'd like to write an article on her disappearance, from your angle. The thing is, it keeps your friend in the public's eye and may just prompt...'

'No. No.' I say. 'I can't say anything. Please go away.'

But Sarah Fielding is used to this kind of thing. She knows how to inveigle her way into an interview, knows just what to say to persuade a reluctant witness that it's in their best interest to talk to her. It's a slow news time between Christmas and New Year and a body found locally, possibly connected to another murdered woman, is a big story, just what's needed to sell to a magazine.

'I'm not attached to any newspaper, so I can get your side of the angles and present it in a sympathetic and professional way.'

I don't understand what she's talking about. I've hovered with the door ajar for too long. Should have slammed it shut at the first sight of the woman's smiling face. She seems to have more teeth than the average mouth.

'How did you find out where I live?' I ask. Charlie wouldn't have given out her address. Neither would P.O. Morgan or Naomi.

'Oh, we have our ways,' she says with another big smile. 'If you let me come in for a few moments, I can explain and it will be more private.'

We both look around, having heard footsteps coming down the stair. It's sure to be Mrs Baxter.

'Only for a minute,' I hear myself saying. 'And no photographs.'

'Of course not.'

Apart from anything else, my hair looks a mess. I widen the door and she steps inside.

'Nice flat, Hanna.'

Sarah sits down without being asked, and says, 'You look tired, Hanna, all in. You like me to make you a coffee?'

The situation is developing rather too quickly, but I feel grateful for the kindly words. Glad someone, even a stranger, has voiced them.

'The past week must have been a terrible shock for you.'

I sit down opposite Sarah and nod. I really I do feel all in. It can't hurt to sit with her for a few minutes. I don't have to tell her anything, after all. I'm still holding her card.

'I write articles for higher class women's magazines,' she's saying. 'Where readers want to read a sympathetic true account of what it's like for a woman caught up in a nightmare situation.'

She doesn't say what the magazines are and I can only picture the papery publications that look like comics you see at supermarket check-outs.

'This is just an exploratory chat, Hanna, just to introduce myself and to get your thoughts.'

My thoughts, thinks Hanna. I can only think how

furious Charlie will be when he hears about this. I have to be careful what I say.

Sarah has produced two cups of coffee and thoughtfully provided some sugar. I don't usually take sugar but as I stir it in with the teaspoon, also thoughtfully provided, I suddenly feel my resolve slip away.

'Nice place,' says Sarah, looking around again. 'So how long have you lived here?'

I sit back and hear myself answer. Her questions soon move along swiftly to my job and my connections to Adele. Sarah has a soft voice and the more I hear her softly persistent words telling me about the difficulty of losing a friend and the chaos surrounding a murder, the more my thoughts start to wander. I finish my coffee, hoping I've not said anything too personal or incriminating, but I need to think carefully before saying any more. Sarah is looking at me, with a sympathetic look, her head on one side and I don't think she is finished with me yet.

'Of course, this is confidential today, Hanna,' she's saying. 'Nothing can be published without your written consent.'

I stand, collect the coffee cups, and move towards the kitchen.

'Sorry, but you'll have to go now,' I say. 'I have an appointment.'

'Of course,' says Sarah, standing up.

I think she must be disappointed not to finalise anything today, but she's trying not to show it.

'Can I come back to see you again? I think readers would be fascinated to hear more about your story.'

'Maybe,' I say. 'I'll let you know.' With that, I gather the strength to show her to the front door.

'Thank you, Hanna, I'll be in touch.'

I'm still holding her card in my hand. It has dawned on me, if she could trace me to my address so easily, perhaps she could find Luk.

*

Five minutes later, my thoughts are interrupted by another ring at the doorbell. Mrs Baxter is standing there holding a supermarket bottle and a plate covered in cling film.

'These are for you, dear. I saw you had visitors. Did you have a nice Christmas with your father?'

'Yes, thank you Mrs Baxter.'

'I've brought you some Christmas pudding. Jack – Mr Sellers – and I couldn't finish it. Your appetite goes a bit when you…'

She obviously wants to know who it is has only just left. I want to get her off the doorstep. To stop intruding. She would have seen the police car yesterday and would have kept up with the local news.

'I saw that police woman here again yesterday. She is a police woman, isn't she, plain clothes? And her this morning…'

There was no way out of this one, but I was determined not to let her into the flat.

'So sad to hear about that poor girl. Worked with you, didn't she? Reminded me of my Julie… '

'Mrs Baxter, thank you for the wine and the pudding, but I really can't talk to anybody at the moment.'

'Don't worry, dear, I understand.'

I start to close the door.

'By the way, there's been a man here over the past few days. Looking for you. I told him you were away, but then I wished I hadn't.'

'Why?'

'Well, you can't be too careful.' I ignore the fact that she hasn't been careful at all. I think of the note left on my desk supposedly from Adele. I no longer think it was from her. But someone wanted to talk to me, someone who knew where I worked and possibly where I lived. After she leaves, I bolt the doors and windows. Then feel as though I've locked myself into a prison.

29

I have to get out. Even if only for a walk, go window shopping, sit in a cafe, walk the streets, anything. Minutes later I meet Rob in the street outside the flat, fastening the lock on his bicycle.

'What are you doing here? Are you looking for me?'

'Yes. Were you away?'

'I've been staying with my father.'

'Terrible news about your friend.'

How any times was I going to hear this. 'Yes.' I say flatly. I wonder why he's come to the flat, and what he wants.

'I expect the police have been to see you?'

Why would he say that? 'What do you want, Rob? I was just on my way out.'

'Have you got time for a coffee?'

For some reason, I agree. We walk down the street to a Costa. It's dead after the holidays, people sick of food and drink, now getting ready for New Year. We sit down on the deep armchairs by the window.

'Why did you want to get in touch with me?'

'Oh, nothing really. I knew you'd be upset... about Adele.'

I don't like the way he uses her name. It's too familiar. After all, he didn't know her; had never spoken to her, so he said. I'm wishing I hadn't accepted his invitation to coffee. I don't even think I like him very much. I order a cappuccino and he asks for an americano, cold milk on the side. I think he picks up on my thoughts because he changes the subject.

'Are you coming back to Book Club in the new year?'

'I don't know.'

I don't ask Rob if he plans to go back to Book Club, because I don't care. The waitress brings our coffees. Mine is served in a paper cup the size of a small bucket. I take a sip, but it's too bitter, too hot to drink. I lean back against the brown faux leather cushion.

'I've got a spare copy of...' He names the title of a book but I'm not really listening. 'I could drop it off if you like...'

'That's alright, Rob. I'll find a copy for myself when I've decided.' Actually, I've already decided. I'm not going back. What is more, I regret coming here with him. I think I've led him on. He probably thinks so too. I want to finish my coffee and go.

'How did you know where I live, Rob?'

'Well, you told me, didn't you?'

I don't remember, but suppose I must have done. It was careless. It was probably Rob who Mrs Baxter saw on the stairs, the man who was asking for me.

'Did you come to my flat before... speak to my neighbour?'

He looks surprised. 'No, I spent Christmas with my brother near Reading. We don't get on. I came back early.'

I try a sip of coffee. It's still scalding hot and has a

burnt taste. I notice Rob has barely started on his. I make a decision.

'Look Rob, I'm sorry, but I have to go.' I rapidly think up an excuse. 'These past few days have been difficult.'

'Of course,' he replies. 'I hope you do come back to Book Club. It's not the same when you're not there.'

'Must go, Rob,' I say and fumble for some coins in my bag.

'Oh, this is on me,' he says.

I don't want to have any further dealings with him. Don't want to be obligated to him in any way. I leave some coins on the table.

'Goodbye,' I say, pushing my arms through my coat sleeves. 'Must go.'

'Happy New Year,' he calls out.

30

I make an appointment with Sinead and try to look satisfied as she reapplies Diva to my broken nails. After she's finished it looks as though the tips have been dipped in blood.

'Have we been under stress lately?' She asks.

Sinead can see the colour is a mistake. 'It's lovely,' I say and give her too large a tip. 'Happy New Year.'

On the way home I pass Veronica's Secrets and buy myself another pair of black trousers. I think I've lost weight. Veronica persuades me into a black top scattered with sequins. It's rather low cut, but being black somehow makes it all right. What doesn't feel right is doing stuff like this. But I desperately need to do normal stuff. I tell myself I need to look smart for Charlie's do. I haven't heard anything from the police since Naomi's visit. Thoughts about whether I should contact the journalist, Sarah, keep intruding.

It's New Year's Eve. Its 9 p.m. I'm ready and waiting when I get a text from Simon.

Lady Gaga Dead. Sam distraught. Annie freaking.
Can't leave house. So sorry. Happy New Year xxx

I feel so let down I can't be bothered to reply and call a taxi.

I've never been to Charlie's place before. Only met Ed once when he dropped something off at the office. Their house is detached, square, modern, like I would have imagined if I'd thought about it at all. The kitchen-diner floor tiles are black, shiny as a mirror, with little diamond insets which glitter under the recessed lights. In my new black outfit it's as though I've disappeared. Shadows flicker on walls painted in clever shades of white. Candles of differing heights give out an unidentifiable scent.

'Mulberry,' says Ed as I lean over, 'with Fig. Let me take your coat.' He kisses me on both cheeks and hands me a glass of fizz.

Both men are dressed alike in dark denim and close-fitting D&G shirts. Ed has the beginnings of a beard. I'm glad to see Charlie looking more like himself. He's lost some weight too. They probably wish they hadn't invited me, especially now Simon isn't here. I tell Charlie he's ill. It's less humiliating than saying I've been bumped for a dog. Charlie offers a bowl of some strange-looking fruits. Like Gogi's he says, but more anti-oxidant. I turn down the offer of more and become aware of some monotonous drone in the background.

'Do you like Philip Glass?' asks Ed. 'Not everybody does. I can change it if you like.'

The three of us stand awkwardly together, surely all

thinking the same thing but none wanting to be the first to voice it.

'Let's raise a glass to Adele,' says Ed, at last taking the initiative. I wonder if he ever met her.

'And hope they find the bastard quickly,' echoes Charlie.

We all take a sip. Then another. Soon the bottle is empty.

'To Adele,' we chorus.

I turn to Ed and ask 'Did you ever meet her?'

'Only once. Charlie used to talk about her, of course.'

I wonder what sort of things Charlie might have said about Adele. How often she cropped up in conversations over an aperitif while something intricate was simmering on the stove. There's a ring at the doorbell and Ed, smiling an 'excuse me,' goes to answer it. My glass is already empty. I help myself to a refill and wander through to the next room where a table is generously set with fancy bought-in food. There is so much choice, I wonder how many more guests are expected. I wonder who takes the lead in domestic matters. Probably not Charlie. Ed is the younger by about ten years. I hear laughter coming from the kitchen, then Charlie is standing beside me holding a bottle. He asks me about Christmas, and how I've been coping.

'I'm OK,' I mumble, not knowing what to answer, not knowing how I've coped.

'You're looking good, anyway,' says Charlie. 'Like the top. Is it new?'

I ask Charlie if the police have been to see him, but his answers are vague so I press him.

'There's no point. I'm not saying anything more.'

'What do you mean?'

'To tell the truth, I feel guilty. But I can't tell them that.'

'Why guilty?'

'If I said, they'd only misinterpret—'

He picks up a glass and fills it from the bottle he's holding.

'Not bad this merlot, what do you think?'

'Charlie, misinterpret what?'

'Ed chose it.'

'Charlie!'

'Well, it's nothing really, and this is just office stuff, between ourselves.'

'Go on,' I urge.

Charlie takes a slurp of wine and tops up my glass which, mysteriously, is already almost empty. I look across at the food and tell myself I should eat something.

'The thing is, Hanna, the last time I saw Adele…'

I almost dread to hear what's coming but keep my eyes trained on his face.

'The last time I saw Adele at the office,' he repeats, 'I had to bawl her out. Ed will tell you… well, her work had got… I don't know if I should say this…'

'Sloppy?' I fill in.

'You'd noticed?' I can tell he's relieved to hear me say it.

'I know she was struggling to fill her quota,' I add.

'How could she expect to? Missed appointments, I'd had complaints. I had to say something. I asked her if she was ill.'

'And was she?'

'No. That's what's so odd. She didn't really have an explanation. I knew her mother died last year, so I didn't want to get too heavy, but she didn't even try to explain.'

'So, what did you do?'

'What could I do? She wasn't pulling her weight. I told her she'd have to improve, otherwise… I wondered if she was having boyfriend trouble.'

'And was she?'

'Well, it wasn't any of my business, was it?'

'No, but you asked her anyway?'

'I just said is everything all right at home?'

'And?'

'She burst into tears. It was so unlike her. From that I took it she was going through some sort of break up. Did she ever mention a boyfriend to you?'

This is the moment I should confide in Charlie. I long for the relief that would come from sharing the stuff I'd kept buried.

'No,' I say. She didn't.'

'You'd be the one to know if she did.' He's looking at me intently, his remark feels like a challenge. He suspects I know more than I'm saying.

'I think she may have met someone,' I say cautiously.

'Did she tell you who he was? Was he giving her some kind of grief?'

I shake my head, not knowing what to say in reply.

'Do you think the police know about the boyfriend?' Charlie persists. 'Perhaps we should say something.'

'Charlie, I need to eat something.'

'Did she tell you his name?'

I am so close to telling him about my last telephone conversation with Adele, my ears are ringing and my legs feel weak. I'm about to speak when loud laughter comes from the kitchen and Ed appears in the room with a group of chattering, brightly-dressed guests who crowd round the food table. The doorbell sounds again and Charlie hands me a plate. We know we have to stop talking about Adele.

Everyone waits around until midnight and, when it comes, we raise our glasses to a new year. I know I've drunk too much. My heels are pinching and I'd like to kick off my shoes and lie down. I drift to a nearby sofa.

A voice nearby soothes, 'Put your feet up, sweetheart, close your eyes. You're with friends.'

I feel my eyes close, but I'm sure it's only for a second. When I open them, the room is empty. Soft rock is playing quietly in the background, but there's no sign of Ed or Charlie. I hear raised voices coming from upstairs, like some sort of row. I put on my shoes and make my way to the hall, find my coat and call for a taxi. The party-goers are out tonight, but luckily, I don't have long to wait.

31

A week later, the police release Adele's body. It seems they have gathered all the forensics they need. I can only imagine what that means and the thought is horrific.

The funeral takes place on a chilly January morning and is organised by her cousin, Rosemary Styles. 'She's very efficient,' says Charlie, 'and she wants us there.' Of course we'll be there. Where else would we be? The crematorium is a stone's throw from Whitefriars hospital. There are only a few people in the chapel and I half expect to see Luk at the back, standing tall, holding a white handkerchief, ready to confess all.

Rosemary introduces herself and when I say how sorry I am, she gives me a closed-lipped smile. 'I didn't see her very often,' she says. 'She wasn't very good at keeping in touch.' Then neither were you, I think, but don't say. She moves quickly away to speak to a sprinkling of others. 'I must talk to Adele's neighbours,' she says. As she keeps her dark glasses on throughout, it's hard to gauge her feelings.

The short service is led by a celebrant who had clearly never met Adele and I wonder why nobody asked Charlie or me to contribute a few words.

Even when the organ plays 'Abide with Me', I can't manage to shed a tear, though my eyes are very watery. When at last the wicker casket glides discretely away behind a curtain, I have to turn away.

I walk between Charlie and Ed out into the cold air, where P.O. Morgan and D.I. Naomi are pretending to look at the floral tributes.

'I keep wondering if her boyfriend will show his face,' whispers Charlie. 'Perhaps the police will pick him up.'

We've not exchanged any more words about him since the party, yet the conversation feels unfinished. Charlie has organised an impressive display of white roses set in green moss and ivy. From us all at Fortunes, it reads. We miss you. Adele would have liked those, I think.

'Sad day,' says a voice somewhere behind me. I recognise Rob.

'I didn't see you inside,' I say.

'Wanted to come, but barely knew her – didn't seem right,' he replies.

He's not dressed for a funeral, just wearing his usual anorak and old jeans. There is an awkward silence. It's obvious we have nothing to talk about and giving a slight wave, he walks away to collect his bicycle.

I notice Charlie deep in conversation with P.O. Morgan and D.I. Naomi. I wonder if he's telling them about Adele having boyfriend problems. I dread they'll try to talk to me, but next time I look, they've gone. Charlie comes over and takes my arm.

'What did they want?' I ask. 'Why were they here?'

'It's procedure. It's expected.'

'What did you tell them?'

'I've got nothing more to tell them. You know that.'

'Nothing about the boyfriend, then?'

He's looking at me strangely.

'Well, we both know you know more about that.'

Despite the chill, I feel my face redden and look away as Ed approaches.

Again, I walk between them to the local pub where Rosemary has laid on sandwiches. I feel very hungry all of a sudden and try to talk to an elderly man who tells me he was Adele's next door neighbour. I wonder if he's the same man I spoke to the day I tried to see her but he doesn't seem to recognise me.

'Terrible business,' he says. 'All those police questions. Wonder what will happen to her house.'

Rosemary leaves early, still wearing her dark glasses. 'Stamford,' she explains. 'Long journey.'

Ed drives Charlie and me back to the office. None of us talk much but I think we find comfort in the silence of being together.

Part Two

Three months later

32

One day in late spring, I'm in the supermarket downtown and I look over to see Simon standing by the bread counter. I don't think he sees me. In fact, I have to look twice to be sure it's Simon. In that split second, I can't decide whether to go over and speak or whether to turn away. I haven't seen or heard anything from him since New Year. I half expect to see Sam sulking nearby, fiddling with her phone. However, when I look back at Simon, because it's definitely Simon, a woman is approaching him waving a packet of cheese. He nods and she tosses it into his trolley. She reaches past him and picks out a loaf –it looks like sourdough – and throws it in with the cheese. After that, they move along to the deli section, just outside my range of vision.

I decide to follow at a discreet distance. I couldn't tell you why. At one point, they have a disagreement about a cleaning product. I hear him say Sam won't use the shower if it's been cleaned with parabens. His voice is exactly the same, so familiar, it's as though he's talking to me. I could almost run up and show them the gel we used to buy. But of course, I don't. The woman says nothing, puts it back on the shelf. Her hair is long and hangs down either side of her face. She pushes it away, as though it's too heavy for her head. They're definitely extensions. It occurs to me this must be Claire, so-helpful Claire, always ready with her offer of a lift home and the loan of a box-set. Is Claire helping Simon with his shopping now? Or is this something more intimate?

I follow them as they walk down each aisle in turn. They don't look round, but just in case, I keep a distance, stooping down, peering closely at the shelves to avoid being seen. Claire appears to be holding a list. They're in the drinks section now, and she has picked up some wine. She seems to favour red. I count as they place five bottles into the trolley, then a bottle of whisky. It's not a good idea for a recovering alcoholic to have all that booze in the house. Perhaps Simon's started drinking again. I feel I should say something. Their trolley is laden, but they toss in several packets of nuts and crisps. Then I get it. They're planning a party. Simon and I were together three years. We never had a party. Didn't know enough people to invite to a party.

I dawdle by the cakes as if trying to decide between chocolate and coffee. For the good of my waistline I choose neither. They are at the check-out now. Simon pays with cash. He and the girl at the till share a word or two and he smiles. It's just as though he's smiling at me. If he made a half turn, he would surely see me. Would come over, talk over old times, forget about Claire, ask me to the party.

I watch them wheel their purchases through the car park and stow them in the boot of a dark blue Volkswagen. Simon is holding the keys, so he must have bought a new car. It hurts to think I will never sit beside him in the passenger seat, my knees nudging up to his. Maybe it's

Claire's car, but it's Simon in the driver's seat and they are preparing to leave. It takes me no longer than a few seconds to decide to follow them.

I trail them slowly as they drive for about fifteen minutes. It's not difficult; Simon always was a cautious driver. They turn into a medium-sized estate of new-builds and stop outside a semi with a tidy paved front garden. Pots of pansies sit on the doorstep. I park in the residents-only space some way down on the opposite side of the street.

I watch them in my wing mirror as they unpack the groceries and carry them into the house. I try to angle the mirror to peer inside the front door, but it's too far away. There isn't much interaction between them. Perhaps, after all, this expedition is nothing more than one work colleague helping out another. Simon locks the car and they go inside and close the door. I sit there for a few minutes, thinking. Someone has driven up close and is hooting their horn at me. Wants my parking space. I drive slowly round the block, passing Claire's house once more, but there's no further sign of them.

33

Charlie has invited three applicants to come to the office to be interviewed for Adele's replacement, though this isn't officially what he calls it. Re-vitalising the team, he called it over a coffee-break. Expanding the business, he once said when we were re-organising the window photographs.

Adele's desk has been empty for nearly five months. Somehow it allowed me to believe she'd not gone far and any day might walk through the front door again. Laughing as she tells us of a new development planned for a flood plain, or a couple she's just left, arguing over the size of a downstairs loo. Reaching down into her desk drawer I see her take out a crumpled bag of Haribos, or offer us a soft mint from her bag. We don't take her up on the gesture, but smile as we turn back to our work.

Mrs Rayner is due at ten o'clock. She arrives early, is anxious and inexperienced. She has three children of school age, she tells us hesitantly, and works part time in a cafe. They want her to do overtime and shifts, but she refuses. She needs to be home for the children. I can see straight away this is a problem for Charlie who needs his negotiators to be free to fit in with weekend or evening appointments. She doesn't know it but she's ruled out in the first five minutes. We let her sit on for a bit though and the interview ends with her showing us photos of her family on her phone.

Ms Spring arrives on the dot of 11.30. A retired science teacher, she is dressed formally in a grey wool jacket and skirt. To put her at her ease, Charlie asks silly questions about litmus paper and explosions, but she doesn't seem to find it funny. Lack of necessary experience, says Charlie shortly after she's gone.

The third applicant, Jason Fairbrother, fails to turn up. Charlie says he'll have to re-advertise. Later that afternoon Jason Fairbrother calls the office. Charlie says he had a genuine excuse for missing his appointment but doesn't share it with me and arranges another appointment for later in the week. I have an appointment that afternoon, I say, but he tells me not to change it. He'll deal with the interview himself.

A few weeks after this, I hear from Dad that Auntie Jean has died. 'Stroke,' said Dad. 'Major. Collapsed during Songs of Praise. I phoned her as usual and when I got no answer, I knew something had happened. Called the ambulance, but she had already gone.'

'So sorry, Dad. I'll come up. I'll come tomorrow.'

'Merciful really. She'd never have coped on her own.'

'Shall I come up tomorrow?'

'I'll let you know when the funeral's planned. I'll need help clearing the bungalow.'

'Of course. How are you, Dad?'

'Don't you go worrying about me. You've got enough on your plate.'

I wasn't sure what he thinks might be on my plate, but I agree with him that it is rather a lot.

I worry about Dad. He is Auntie Jean's only surviving relative apart from me and will have to deal with the formalities.

'She made a will,' said Dad. 'Left her house to a cat sanctuary. They won't get much, only a few years left on the lease.'

I explain to Charlie what's happened and say I shall be away for a few days. He's fine about it. Tells me to take as long as I need. He and Jason can manage.

Dad and I do the clearing out together a couple of days before the funeral. Everything was left very tidy, as though she knew she would soon be leaving. Dad tells me to take the hand painted table I'd always admired and a few other pieces, including the Wedgwood Bianca. He will keep them until I'm ready to collect them. Her wardrobe is sparse, consists entirely of navy blue trousers, cardigans and sensible shoes. I take them all to the charity shop. There is one decent silver necklace, which I keep. I ask Dad, but he doesn't know where it came from. I hope she had a lover once and that it was a gift from him. Or maybe her. Papers and books have already been set aside, bequeathed to the college library where she taught. We call in house clearance for the rest.

One or two neighbours come to the door to offer their condolences. She seems to have been well respected, although I get the impression she kept her distance. One neighbour offers to take on Persia, her elderly cat. Another neighbour asks for some flowers from her garden. Our memories are enough to remember her by, say the others.

The funeral takes place one sunny Saturday morning. A few of Auntie's academic colleagues attend and some of her former students, all getting on in years. I recognise Dad's next door neighbours from Christmas. Dad looks down into his lap most of the time, but at one point, he reaches for my hand and squeezes it. It feels cold to the touch. A wavery soprano voice sings out loudly when the organ plays Abide with Me. Tears come to my eyes at this point, not only for Auntie Jean, but because it brings back memories of Adele. They are the tears I couldn't shed for her. It's shocking we've heard no further developments in the murder investigation. Afterwards we go to a local hotel for refreshments. The academics sit together in a small knot, laugh loudly, drink sherry and nibble sausage rolls.

I tell Dad it will be best if a local agency and solicitor deal with the house sale. He is surprised Fortune Estates wouldn't want to take it on. I waffle on about a conflict of interest which he clearly doesn't believe. I have begun to wonder about Dad's health too. He seems frailer than I'd remembered and I tell myself I should try to get up to see him more often. It occurs to me that is why he hoped I'd handle the bungalow sale. The truth is, I have become very pre-occupied with what I call 'The Neighbourhood Watch'. I drive down Percival Street regularly looking out for a dark blue Volkswagen. We're into June already and the days are longer, but sunshine is unpredictable. The pansies have gone and, in their place, Claire has planted out scarlet geraniums and purple trailing lobelia. A harsh combination. Simon's blue Volkswagen is nearly always parked outside at weekends. However, during the week he's mostly parked outside his own flat, so it's obvious they haven't moved in together. I wonder how Sam has taken to the new arrangements. Do they stay at Claire's when it's Simon's weekend to have her? How does Sam get on with Claire? Does she prefer her to me, I'm really thinking. I wonder if she's got over Lady Gaga and if there's a replacement. I realise I should have made more effort with her. I wonder if she ever talks about me and what she says. In a funny sort of way, I miss her. I've started keeping a notebook with the dates Simon's Volkswagen is in Percival Street. I have already decided that if he were to see me, I'll act surprised and say I'm doing a valuation on a house nearby.

I must have got a little careless. One day I park too close and Simon opens the front door. I was sure he couldn't miss the red Clio, but he turns back into the house as though he's forgotten something. My heart starts thumping so hard, it could jump out of my chest. I put my foot down on the accelerator and drive off.

34

I've also been observing Jason, our new negotiator. I hated the idea of somebody else sitting at Adele's desk. But Charlie has shifted everything around, so the office looks different. He's hung a large canvas print of Jack the Dribbler's later work, probably Ed's idea. I wonder how much Charlie has told Jason about what happened and why we were recruiting. Jason's never asked me, so I guess he either knows everything or has heard nothing. He's got a decent telephone manner, takes accurate messages and asks sensible questions. He doesn't chatter too much either. He gets on well with Charlie, I notice.

One morning, I have an appointment at Zoe Caswell's house. A couple want to see it for the third time and I think they are likely to make an offer. Charlie suggests Jason go along with me for the experience. I feel rather irritated at first, prefer him to stay in the office, but what can I do about it. He turns up at the office punctually at 9.30, wearing his better suit and a red and grey striped tie. We drive together in the Clio. He asks a few bog-standard questions about the age of the car, how long I've had it, and obviously expects similar questions from me about his own mode of transport. Actually, I've noticed it's a clean but rather old Ford he keeps parked some distance from the office.

'What can you tell me about these people we're going to see?' He asks.

'The house has been on the market since last year,' I say. 'We had two offers but neither came to anything. It's a nice house, you'll see.'

For some reason, I'm reminded of James Batley, but can't remember if I ever sent him details. Anyway, it doesn't matter now.

I introduce Jason to Zoe. We use first names from the start these days, just like banks and dentists. Charlie says it creates a special bond. Business with the caring touch. I'm not so sure myself.

While waiting for the Saunders to arrive, (Jane and Mark) we wander outside into the sunshine. I notice how overgrown the garden looks. The grass could do with a cut and in the borders, shrubs are fighting the weeds.

'I'm sorry it's got a bit out of hand lately. My gardener left. Quite suddenly.' Zoe is wearing dark glasses this morning. She shields her eyes with her hand and looks in the direction of the golf course as if we might just see him teeing off in the distance.

'That would be Marek,' I say, to nobody really. 'Where is Banquo today?' I ask. 'Banquo is a lovely Labrador,' I explain to Jason. But as to the dog's whereabouts, Zoe makes no reply. Anyway, of course it's not our business.

Jason asks a few sensible questions about the house – how long it's been on the market, how many viewers, how long she's lived there etc. He's read the file and knows the answers and is only filling in an awkward gap, but still. Charlie will probably keep him on after his three months trial is up.

The Saunders arrive ten minutes after the appointed time. A couple in their early to mid-forties with a four-year-old child.

'She'll love the garden,' says Jane. 'Won't she, Mark?'

Mark looks serious. Mark needs to be serious. On the verge of making an offer. Doing his sums. I introduce them to Jason. Jason asks if they've come far and then sensibly shuts up. I give him the nod to follow us, then take the couple through the house for the third time. I'm pleased to see Jane carrying her notebook and measuring tape. She's serious too. In the end, hers will be the deciding vote. It's nearly always the woman's decision.

Zoe waits for us in the garden, reading a magazine. We have turned down her offer of coffee. The moment is too important to be distracted by cups of coffee. The recent sun has intensified the mole on her cheek. I wonder if she's ever thought of having it removed. She'll certainly have plenty of money for private surgery if today's sale goes through.

'Shame she's let the garden go,' says Mark, leaving Jane to check out the white goods in the kitchen.

'Well, it wouldn't take a lot to lick it back into shape,' says Jason.

'We could probably come to some arrangement,' I say.

At last, the couple have seen all they need to see and asked all the questions they will ever need to ask.

'Jane and I both like it,' says Mark. 'It feels right for us and Anthea. I will have to look into a couple of things today and I'll drop into your office in the morning. Eleven o'clock suit you?'

'Perfect,' I say.

Jason reaches out to shake their hands. 'Good to meet you,' he says. 'And good luck.'

I look around the shambles of a garden and estimate how much it will cost to employ someone for a day or so. I'm wondering what has happened to Marek. Maybe I was wrong about him and Zoe all along.

'See you tomorrow at eleven,' I say.

Zoe is already starting to make her way back into the house. I would like to share my thoughts on Zoe Caswell and her absent gardener with Jason, but wouldn't quite know what to say.

'Do you think they'll definitely finalise?' asks Jason.

'We'll find out tomorrow, won't we.'

35

I couldn't quite say why, but I found the visit to Zoe Caswell this morning unsettling. It brought back memories of the first time I visited. Her manner was so different this time. And what has happened to Marek and Banquo?. She could have arranged for a friend to take care of the dog while the Saunders were viewing. That would make sense. But what has happened to Marek?

Charlie hardly looks at me as he calls us both into his office. 'There's been a complaint,' he says. The Joneses up at White Barns Road. Remember them?'

'The name rings a bell,' I say.

'Mr Jones is very dissatisfied with the lack of proper service he's had from our agency. He's spoken to Challengers.'

Challengers is another agency, not exactly a rival but part of a national chain who frequently advertise on TV. Challengers told him we've seriously underestimated the value of his property. And did we know their fees are only 1.5% whereas ours are 2.25? In addition, Challengers have numerous existing clients desperate for his sort of property. That the house will sell straight away due to its proximity to the hospital.

'Well, they would say that, wouldn't they,' I say, raising my eyebrows conspiratorially at Jason, then at Charlie but neither seem to notice.

'When was the last viewing, Hanna?'

'I'll look at the file,' I say, starting out of my chair.

'Don't bother, I can tell you. It was before Christmas. At your suggestion I printed up new brochures and you took more photos.' He pushes the brochure across his desk. 'What happened to the photos?'

I look at the bumph he's pushed towards me. The daffodils tell a sad story. I am surprised to think it's over six months since I was there. I start to say something about it not being my listing then remember why I'd gone there in the first place.

'Would you like me to have a word with Mr Jones,' asks Jason, not looking at me. 'Fresh eyes and all that.'

'You can try,' replies Charlie. 'If the damage hasn't already been done.'

I remember back to those visits last winter. I'd questioned Mr and Mrs Jones separately about Luk, the hospital cleaner. When I hadn't made any headway, I hadn't given them any further thought.

'I could make another appointment,' I say.

Charlie ignores my offer, and brings up the details on his computer. 'Have a look at these Jason,' he says.

I feel as if I've been squashed. It's been an undeniably sticky meeting, but I am remembering unfinished business. My phone call to Whitefriars. Ask Luk to ring Adele Stevens, I'd said. Nobody ever had. Maybe Luk never got the message. Maybe he had left his job. Maybe he'd been spooked by the message. Not long after that, they found Adele's body.

144

I wait until Charlie leaves the office and Jason goes for lunch before I make the call.

'Whitefriars, Housekeeping.'

'I'd like to speak to Luk,' I say.

'Not here today,' she says. 'Is it urgent?'

'Can I leave a message?' I say.

'He's an agency worker,' she says. 'Call back in the morning, Best time 8.15.'

Agency worker. That could explain why nobody passed on my message. What can I say to him anyway? Do I really want to return to the dreadful events of last December? See it all spark up again? What if I were to contact DI Naomi and tell her everything I know. Let her look into it. But perhaps she already knows what I know, has already looked into it.

I leave a note on Charlie's desk to say I'm following up a couple of outstanding matters, which is true, and that I'll be in again tomorrow morning for the meeting with the Saunders. To settle my nerves, I decide to do another Neighbourhood Watch, though I wouldn't normally go on a weekday afternoon. As it happens, there's nothing to see, no sign of life, no cars parked outside. Nothing. Perhaps they're away on holiday. The thought is like a stab through the heart. Her geraniums could do with some attention, wilting in their pots. On the way home I pass the Garden Centre, stop to have a cup of tea, wander round looking at the knick-knacks. Before leaving, I buy a bottle of weed-killer.

That evening, just after six, there's a loud buzz of the doorbell. I rarely see Mrs Baxter these days, tied up as she seems to be, arranging her registry office wedding. 'You

145

will come, won't you dear, it's a small ceremony. We don't want any fuss. Bring that young man of yours, we haven't seen him for a while.'

I suppose I shall have to go, and I'll probably have to get used to calling her Mrs Sellers. I wonder if I should fix myself something to eat, but there's not much in the fridge and I can't really be bothered. Though there's nothing much on, I sink down in front of the TV. I might even doze off for a while, when I'm disturbed by another buzz at the door bell. The clock reads nearly 8 p.m. I'm thinking of ignoring it, but when a sharp buzz comes again, I drag myself over to answer it. P.O. Morgan stands on the doorstep.

'Hello, Ms. Summers. Can I come in?

I nod and allow him to walk past me into the sitting room.

'Has something happened?' I ask. 'Have you got some news?'

He stands looking around him. I remember the first time I met P.O. Morgan. It brings back a memory of his bright white shirt and its sleeves with sharp creases. I never did find out who did his ironing. This evening, despite the warm air, he keeps his jacket on.

'We've had a complaint.' Says P.O. Morgan.

'A complaint?' I echo. That's only the second one today I'd like to say, but don't. 'What sort of complaint?'

'Do you know a person called Claire Mitchell?' He asks.

'I don't think so. Why, who is she?'

'Ms Mitchell is a resident at 23 Percival Street.'

I frown, make it look like I'm thinking hard. 'No. No, sorry.'

'Ms Mitchell has made a complaint.'

'What about?' I ask.

'Stalking.' He replies.

I manage to control an urge to laugh, but he repeats 'Ms Mitchell claims she's being stalked. It's a serious claim. Are you the owner of a red Clio, TR20 DRY?'

'Yes, that's my car,' I say.

'Ms Claire Mitchell of 23 Percival Street has made a complaint that a person answering your description has been seen sitting in that car outside her property on a number of occasions.'

'How dreadful,' I say. I have to swallow the urge to laugh out loud.

P.O. Morgan produces a photograph. There's no denying it is my car with me in the driver's seat wearing a khaki hoodie. 'Do you deny this is you,' he says?

'Don't be ridiculous,' I say. Then, perhaps unwisely, I go on, 'I was asked to do a valuation in the area. But why that should concern this woman I can't imagine.'

'Could you tell me the address of a property where you carried out this valuation and the name of the owner?' He's opened up his notebook and is writing something down.

Of course I can't. Stupid man. Why doesn't he go away and start investigating real crimes? I connect the thought to Adele's murder and start to ask him what he's doing about that.

'Can you answer the question, please, Ms Summers?'

I shall have to think carefully here. 'Would you like a cup of tea? Officer Morgan.' I say. 'Or would you rather have coffee? I can make either. I can recommend the coffee since I treated myself to… '

'If we could just keep to the matter in hand, please. I have checked with Mr Charles Porter, your employer at

Fortune Estates, and he tells me the agency is not currently involved with either the valuation or sale of any property in Percival Street. So, can you explain why your car has been seen parked outside Ms Mitchell's house on twenty-seven occasions in the past three months? Some of these sighting after midnight. There are eye-witnesses to back up the claim.'

Could it really have been that many. I do a quick calculation. Three into twenty seven makes...

'Who are these witnesses?' I ask.

'Do you deny it?' He asks.

'I probably parked there for convenience, outside Ms, Ms.' I can't bring myself to say her name.

'Mitchell?'

'Yes, her. Her place. You know what parking is like round there...'

P.O. Morgan is writing something in his notebook. It's just like the notebook he used all those months ago. Fat lot of good all those notes came to. I'd like to snatch it out of his hand and tell him to stop wasting my time.

'Hanna, I have to ask you this. Did you recently purchase a container of GoWeeds weed-killer?

I remember the first lie I told him. How effortlessly one lie seemed to flow into another. But there was a reason at the time. I was trying to protect Adele.

'I don't remember,' I say. 'It's not against the law, is it?'

'Ms Mitchell found a half empty container of Go-Weeds in her refuse bin this afternoon. She claims she never purchased it. Doesn't believe in using chemicals. Do you know anything about it?'

P.O. Morgan is looking straight at me, waiting for an

answer. I can't think of what to say, so stay silent. But P.O. Morgan has more.

'The label showed it was purchased at the Bettergrow Garden Centre.'

I try to remember what I did with the bottle. I've no recollection of putting it in any wheelie bin.

'I only ask, because if you did make such a purchase, and CCTV cameras may be able to tell us one way or another, it seems an unusual purchase for somebody like yourself who doesn't have a garden.'

'I must sit down,' I say.

P.O. Morgan stays standing for a moment or two. He's clearly been practising his interview techniques. Probably picked them up from watching Naomi.

'How is Naomi these days?' I ask, but as he doesn't answer, I'm not sure if I get the words out.

'I understand you were once in a relationship with Ms. Mitchell's partner, Simon Fredericks?'

I feel my face start to redden. I'm glad I'm sitting down. He calls her Simon's partner. Scheming bitch is what I'd call her. A water cooler romance. A few seamless steps from discussing last night's TV and fancy a drink after work to sharing his bed and his box-sets. Inside I'm seething. I can't think what to say. Again, I say nothing.

'Come on now, Hanna.' P.O. Morgan sits down on the settee opposite and leans forward. He's so close he could almost put his hand on my knee. I think he'd like to, but understands the protocol.

'We know relationship issues can be difficult. Especially if you've been close.'

Close? Does he think this was a crime of passion? I know I should pull myself together, but can't seem to make the effort. I think I've started to cry.

'Harassment and criminal damage are offences we take very seriously, Hanna. At this stage we're just making enquiries, and you do not need to say anything. However, I may need to take a formal statement. I don't need to remind you if there is enough evidence to charge you, it could go to court.'

I'd like P.O. Morgan to reach over and take my hand, tell me not to worry, it's all just a silly misunderstanding, that he'll speak to Claire Mitchell himself and tell her it's her own fault for being such a stupid scheming bitch. But instead, he stands and puts his notebook away in the top pocket of his jacket.

'Meanwhile, I'd advise you to keep away from Percival Street,' he says, heading for the door.

36

I think I'll heed P.O. Morgan's advice and keep away from Percival Street for a while. Or maybe forever. I can't imagine why I started the Watch in the first place. I'll try to think what I did with the weed-killer. That would prove I had nothing to do with any dead plants. But I'm too fatigued to do anything at the moment. And surely I hadn't carried out the Watch as many as twenty-seven times? I'm nauseated at the thought.

I go to bed exhausted, but am unable to sleep. I pick up a magazine but I've read it before. I peer under the bed to look for something more recent and come across *Madame Bovary*. Poor Madame Bovary. Covered in dust and tea-stains. She too was betrayed by her lover. I wonder if the book club is still going and what they're dissecting now. I feel angry that the neighbourhood watch has come between me and my cultural pursuits.

I must have drifted off at last because at five am the light filters through the blind and wakes me. I get up and go to make a cup of tea. Then thinking it's too early to get up, I return to bed and fall asleep again. When I re-awake I find it's eleven thirty.

I am in a bit of a fog but at the same time something is pressing on my mind. It must be P.O. Morgan's visit, and my need to locate the weed-killer. However, a quick search in the cupboard under the sink fails to locate it.

I've had two missed calls from the office and a curt message from Charlie reminding me of my appointment with the Saunders. But I've obviously missed it now. Charlie will not be happy, but Jason will have been there to deal with them. It will be a good learning experience for him. I'll offer to split the commission.

Something else is pressing too. Whitefriars and Luk. What time did the woman say I should phone? I dial the number, but am advised to try later as the switchboard is experiencing an unprecedented number of calls. I feel exhausted after all this activity and want to go back to bed. I ring the office and leave a message for Charlie to say I'm unwell and will not be in to work today.

I go back to bed and sleep for hours. It's nearly three thirty when I wake. Perhaps I really am unwell. Mid-afternoon and the sun is bright. There are no further messages from the office. I take a shower and look for something cool to wear. I seem to have got behind with my washing and am forced to dig a t-shirt out of the laundry basket.

I walk the half mile to the shopping mall seeking the shady side of the street. It's cool and air conditioned inside. There aren't many shoppers around. I'm looking in the window of a fashion chain, wondering if the orange and lime pedal pushers on display are a little jeune fille for me when I feel a light tap on my shoulder.

'Long time no see.'

I don't recognise Rob straight away. He's wearing dark glasses and he's clipped his beard right back to the stubble. He looks almost handsome.

'Shouldn't you be at work at this time of day? Are you skiving?'

'I've got the afternoon off.'

'Business slow, then?'

'Up and down.'

'Fancy an iced coffee, or is it too early for something stronger?'

I don't want to go anywhere with him, but by delaying my response, he's been encouraged. He moves a little closer towards me and puts his hand on my arm.

'Come on. There's lot to talk over. It'll do you good.'

'Some other time, perhaps.' I step away, forcing him to remove his hand.

'You're looking peaky. Have you lost weight,' he asks?

'I've had a lot on, that's all.'

'Some other time, then,' I hear him say, as I walk away.

I'm just about to turn a corner, when I glance back and see Adele. She's standing where I was standing only a few seconds ago, looking at the same pair of orange and lime-green pedal-pushers. Of course. They'll suit her much better than me. She's so preoccupied she hasn't seen me.

I almost trip over as I hurry towards her. I think I've lost her when, through the shop window, I catch a glimpse of her carrying the trousers towards the changing room. I'm so glad she hasn't cut her hair. It's more curly than ever, longer and a bit straggly. The assistant hands her a top to try with the trousers.

I enter the shop and I'm greeted by a smiling young girl. I look over her head, tell her I'm looking for a friend. She carries on smiling, seems to share my excitement. I hasten to the changing room and wait outside, wishing I could see through the heavy curtain. Adele usually makes up her mind quickly, but this time she's taking forever. I'm so impatient, my heart's racing then, just as I'm about to call out her name and put my head round the curtain to surprise her, she comes out, wearing the trousers with a garish sleeveless top. She's standing in front of the mirror, turning this way and that, but it all looks too tight. Then in a loud, crude voice, nothing like Adele's, she asks for a bigger size. I turn away. Nobody notices me leave.

37

I make an effort to get to work early next day. There's no sign of Jason and Charlie's face is a blank. With a nod of his head he indicates he wants me in his office.

'What's going on, Hanna?' he asks.

I think I know what he means but don't want to admit it even to myself. 'Sorry about yesterday,' I say. 'I wasn't feeling well. Sorry to miss the Saunders.'

'Jason handled it,' he says. 'They made a good offer. But this isn't about the Saunders,' he replies. 'Are you ill?'

The question is so blunt, it shakes me. 'No. No, not really. I've been feeling tired lately, that's all.'

'Something's been affecting your work here for the past couple of months.'

'I'm sorry, Charlie. I'll try to make it up to you.'

'Adele's death affected us all. Horrific. And then your Aunt died, didn't she?'

I could say, well my aunt was nearly ninety and died of natural causes. Adele was brutally murdered, where is the connection, but I stay silent.

'Have you and Simon split up?'

Again, I'm surprised how blunt he is. It's a personal observation. Not the sort of territory he'd normally intrude upon. Maybe he's learned from the mistake he made with Adele. I can't think what to say.

'Is there anything you'd like to talk to me about?'

I glance around the office. The windows are open, allowing a light breeze to flutter the delicate leaves on the pot plants. One looks like an olive. It's new. How fresh and green it looks with tiny new shoots already emerging. Jason must have brought it and taken over the watering.

'The thing is, Hanna, your personal life is your own, nothing to do with me at all. But when it starts getting in the way of your commitments here, it becomes my business.'

I nod. A silence descends over the office. He's right of course. I wonder if he's going to sack me. 'Do you want me to leave?' I ask.

'No. No, of course not Hanna. I've always valued your work and you've been an asset to Fortune Estates, to me. But I want the old Hanna back. Not this imposter.'

He attempts a smile, trying to lighten the mood. I try, but my lips won't stretch.

'Why don't you to take a bit of time off. Rest. Have a break, a holiday if you like.'

He's looking out of the window. He too would like to be outside, far away from here. Sitting on a terrace somewhere with Ed, sipping a margherita, watching the sun go down. But instead he's waiting for my reply. I wonder again if this is his round-about way of getting rid of me.

'Take a few days off. You'll come back refreshed. And if you want to talk about anything, I'm always here, you know that.'

'Thank you, Charlie.'

I think the meeting is at an end. I go back to my desk

and open up my computer. There's nothing that can't be postponed for a few days. I wonder what I'm going to do with myself. Now I've decided to give up the Watch, I'll be at a loose end.

38

I had a letter from P.O. Morgan. Well, not him exactly, but I think he's the one behind it. It's a formal sort of letter, perhaps just a routine thing that gets sent out, but I'm touched to know he's thinking about me. It says I might qualify for counselling under some kind of victim support arrangement. It seems rather late in the day, but all I have to do is tick a box at the bottom of the letter and somebody will be in touch.

That's why I've been seeing this counsellor. Call me Beryl, she said at our first meeting. The first time we just talked about the weather which seemed all right to me, not too difficult. She's a middle-aged woman perhaps fifty-ish, and she's let her short hair go grey. She usually wears a burgundy-coloured cardigan and thick tights. I told her I liked her shoes which are also burgundy colour with laces. I asked her where she got them. Perhaps she didn't hear me, because she didn't answer so I told her where I'd bought mine. The next time I saw her she just sat there, saying nothing. I think she lives in the house where we meet, because sometimes I can smell cooking. Perhaps that's what she was thinking about, because after about twenty minutes, she glanced at the clock on her table, and asked me if there was anything I wanted to talk to her about. I don't know why but suddenly I heard myself start to talk about working at the agency and about Charlie. Then I started to think about Adele. I told her I'd had a friend who died and that it was horrible and that nobody had been caught for her murder. She didn't seem surprised to hear me talking about murder, so I suppose she already knew that from the police.

I wondered if I should tell her about Luk and my suspicions but, before I had a chance, I found myself weeping and she held out a box of tissues. I was embarrassed to tell the truth and wish I'd been able to keep better control of my emotions. But she didn't seem to mind and just said well done, and see you same time next week. I felt better afterwards.

I felt exhausted and had to go home and lie down. The room is warm and my eyes soon close. I'm dozing lightly when I hear my phone vibrate. I almost drop it as I reach to pick it up.

'Did you leave a message for me?'

'Who is this?'

'This is Luk,' he says. 'What is it you want?'

39

His voice is curt, his accent clipped. It reminds me of somebody else. It's what I have thought about all these months. Yet, now it is here, I don't know what to say.

'Well?' He asks.

My heart has started to beat so fast it could leap out of my chest onto the floor. I imagine it rolling its bloody way across the carpet, bouncing against the wardrobe and coming to rest under the bed next to Madame Bovary.

'I need to talk to you,' my voice is almost a whisper.

'What about?'

'I'd rather not say over the phone.'

He doesn't respond and I think he's going to end the call. My thoughts are racing. Why didn't I look more closely at the photo D.I. Naomi showed me. If I could recognise him as the man with Adele, I could go to the police with everything I know.

'What about meeting me tomorrow morning?' I search hurriedly for a public place and stumble over my words. 'The Blue Banana in the High St. Eleven o'clock? How will I know you?'

'I will know you.'

The line goes dead. I check, but know already he will have withheld his number.

I sit on the edge of the bed and go over the brief dialogue. I tell myself I don't have to go. But surely no harm will come to me in broad daylight in the high street. The main thing is I've managed to flush Luk out of his hole. I take a shower and gather my thoughts. The cool water clears my head. I will make a list of things I want to ask Luk.

I spend the rest of the day clearing up. The flat is a mess. I do my neglected washing and ironing and hang up my clothes in an orderly way. I haven't even separated out my summer and winter wardrobes. I start on the cupboards and while looking for a lost sandal, I come across the unopened bottle of weed killer in a box under the stairs. I look at its black label for a long time. I've blotted out the memory of why I bought it in the first place. Perhaps I should show it to P.O. Morgan and prove myself innocent of criminal damage. But on the other hand, perhaps it would be better to just dispose of it. But where? I can't quite think what to do, so I put it back in the box and close the cupboard door.

I'm surprised to look at the clock and find it's already turned nine o'clock. I turn on the TV and try to watch a sitcom, but the forced cheerfulness puts me off and I go to bed early. I sleep well, despite all that's on my mind, and wake to the sound of thin summer rain blowing against the bedroom window.

I have no problem finding some suitable clothes after all my efforts yesterday, but I can't decide between my black trousers or the beige. It's stopped raining and the sun's come out. Perhaps black trousers are a little formal, but I think they will set the right tone. I find a white t-shirt and top it off with my short grey jacket. I am ready to leave by ten o'clock. I drive to the High Street and park in a convenient space opposite the Blue Banana. I congratulate myself on getting there early. It will give me the advantage. I'll be able to watch him arrive. I'm starting to think like P.O. Morgan and D.I. Naomi.

I listen to the radio for a while and keep my eyes fixed on the street outside. It occurs to me how much time I've spent lately watching and waiting. I glance across to the bistro from time to time and it's then I see Sam. She's crossing the road and coming towards me. She's wearing cut-off shorts and a beret, perched on her head in a chic way. There's a brief spark of red ash as she flicks a cigarette end away into the gutter. I shrug down in my seat, not wanting to be seen. But it's too late.

She's knocking on the window. 'If you want to be invisible, you shouldn't have bought a red car.'

'Shouldn't you be in school?'

As expected, she ignores the question. 'Why are you hiding here?' she asks.

I keep glancing over her shoulder. It's after eleven now. I wonder if Luk's already inside the bistro.

'Just waiting for someone,' I say.

'Is it a man?'

'Not exactly… not in the way you think.'

I want her to go away. She's blocking my view and I have no idea if Luk has turned up or not. A group of teenagers comes into view and Sam shifts her attention as she hears their voices.

'My mates are here,' she says.

162

I should like to ask her about Simon. But wouldn't know what to ask and it's no longer any of my business. With a casual wave, she sways across the road to join her friends. Those shorts really are too short. One of the boys pushes open the door of the Blue Banana and they disappear inside.

I wait in the car for a bit longer. By mid-day it's obvious Luk's not coming. I've been a fool to think he would. It occurs that he might have been watching for me, driven past. Seen me sitting here. Had no intention ever of meeting me face to face. 'I'll know you,' he said. Despite the warm afternoon, the thought makes me shiver.

Sam and her mates have crowded themselves into the soft window seats of the Blue Banana. They're laughing, leaning into each other. It's a long time since I saw Sam laugh like that. A long time since I laughed like that, too.

40

I go home because I can't think of anywhere else to go. I meet Mrs Baxter on the stairs. My thoughts are still dwelling on the morning's events and I don't want to stop and talk but she says she wants to show me something. I follow her upstairs and we go into her bedroom. Hanging over the wardrobe under a garment bag is a smart apricot coloured dress.

'This is my outfit,' she says. 'I asked Julie to go with me to choose something but she didn't have time, so I went by myself. What do you think?'

'It's lovely Mrs Baxter,' I say.

'I've got pale grey sandals and a little Dorothy bag to go with it. I've not decided on a hat yet. What do you think?'

'It's lovely, Mrs Baxter,' I say again.

A pink spot has appeared on her cheeks as she holds up the dress. She looks happy.

'It's not long to go now, less than a week away. Jack mustn't see this yet,' she says, thrusting the dress back into its cover.

I'm surprised to hear the wedding day is so close.

'You've had your invitation, haven't you dear? I hope you can get the day off. It's only a small ceremony. Julie's going to be a witness and Jack's son is going to be best man. He's been working out in Saudi for the past couple of years – something to do with oil. He's coming home specially. I think he's pleased for his father, though you never really know, do you?'

While Mrs Baxter keeps talking my thoughts drift away. There was a time when I might have been telling her about my own future plans, but now they seem as distant as Saudi Arabia.

As though reading my thoughts, she breaks in. 'What's happened to that nice young man of yours? He used to be here a lot. I've not seen him for ages. Of course, it's difficult when there's a child from the previous…'

'Actually, Mrs Baxter, I have to go, I've got some notes to look out for work tomorrow. I'm looking forward to next Wednesday, and your dress is lovely…'

'Good bye then dear,' she says. 'Glad you like my dress.'

I'm searching through my chest of drawers, wondering what I'll wear to Mrs Baxter's wedding when I come across a white card. Printed in green letters, is the name Sarah Fielding, freelance journalist. I take it out and look at it for a while.

41

It's not out of my way to drive down Albert Terrace. I haven't felt able to drive down there for some time. I go slowly, not wanting to miss anything, though couldn't tell you what I was expecting to see. Outside one of the houses a couple of doors away from number three, Rob is in his front garden fiddling with a bicycle tyre. He stops what he's doing and straightens up. I hope he hasn't seen me, but he's recognised the car and it's too late. He's out on the pavement with his hand up, almost forcing me to brake. I wind down the window.

'Well, we meet again. What brings you down Albert Terrace after all this time?'

'Charlie sent me on an errand,' I lie. I am embarrassed and hope he doesn't think I've driven down his street hoping to see him.

'Is number three going back on the market then?'

If I let him talk on, he'll run out of things to say, then I can go.

'Actually, I've got something to ask you. Had been meaning to come to your office, but now you're here… well it wouldn't take a minute.'

'What is it?' I say.

'We could talk better if you come inside.'

He nods towards his front door. I don't want to go with him, but find myself switching off the engine and undoing my seat belt.

'I've only got a couple of minutes,' I say, looking at my watch.

The hallway is dark, in contrast to the bright sun lit street outside. He leads me into a small sitting room. It's cluttered with too much oversized furniture. Books and papers are piled on a carpet that has seen better days. He moves some stuff out of the way, so I can sit down.

'I've only got a minute,' I say again, perching on the edge of a chair. I try to remember if he shut the front door or whether it's still standing open.

'Would you like a cup of tea?' he asks. 'I've got green, or perhaps you'd prefer something cold?'

'I'm fine, thanks, Rob. What was it you wanted to tell me?'

I shift back in the chair, which is so deep I feel swallowed up in the upholstery. The cushions smell of dust, as though they're seldom moved. Not surprising I suppose, for a bloke living on his own.

'I've coke in the fridge, or a beer? I may even have some elderflower somewhere.'

'Anything, Rob. Whatever you're having.'

He disappears out to the kitchen and I hear him searching for glasses and the chink of ice.

'Biscuit?' He calls out.

'Can I use your bathroom?' I call out.

'Upstairs, end of passage.'

I pick up my bag and make for the stairs. On the landing I pass a small room with an open door. It's an office with computer and a muddle of paperwork and files. This must be where he does his writing. My eye is drawn to a sheet of A4 paper blu-tacked to the wall. It's a black and white computer print-out of a man and woman sitting on a garden bench. It's indistinct, a heavy dark ink masks detail but at a quick glance it looks a lot like a copy of the photo D.I. Naomi showed me. I take a few steps into the room, trying to get a better look. Why would Rob have that image on his wall? Hearing sounds from downstairs, I back away out of the room.

The bathroom is clean enough but impersonal. I didn't expect candles. The open window looks out over the back gardens of the neighbouring houses. I can make out number three with its wooden bench next to a small shrub. It's obvious to me the photo was taken from here.

I flush the loo and run the water as if washing my hands. I want to get another look at the picture, but when I open the door, Rob is standing on the landing.

'Did you get lost?'

'No, everything's fine, thank you.'

I see that he's closed the door to his study. He turns and starts back down the stairs and I follow him back to the sitting room.

'Biscuit?' he asks again.

There's a rustle as he opens a packet and cupboard doors bang as he searches for a plate. My eye catches something glinting on the mantelpiece where the light has caught it. It's a small tin figure.

'Oh, you're admiring my spaceman.' He sets a tray

down on the table and hands me a glass. 'I won him in a sci-fi competition last year.'

'Congratulations.' I say. Are you doing much writing these days?

'Well, the inspiration comes and goes. I don't do much entertaining. Let me know if the elderflower's too strong.

There's a small silence. I need to get another look at that photo. If it is the same as the one the police showed me, I want to know if he took it and when. I could ask him straight out, but something holds me back. I need to be certain. The thought of him photographing Adele through his bathroom window is sickening.

'Would you like some music?' he asks. I should have asked you what sort of music you like.'

It's quite dark in the room. The blinds are partly pulled down against the afternoon sun. I shake my head to the offer of some music.

'What was it you wanted to tell me?'

Rob looks surprised, as if he's forgotten why he asked me in. But perhaps I know why he's asked me in.

'It's about Book Club. We've missed you. We're doing Scott Fitzgerald. Do you like his stuff?'

'I haven't read a lot.'

'Gatsby,' he says. 'Do you know it?'

I shake my head. 'I saw the film.'

The sun must have gone behind the clouds because the room suddenly feels chill and the cold drink has had a numbing effect on my hands. Of course I know Gatsby. It's about a writer who spies on his neighbour. Does he know about the Watch? Or has he been watching me? Was he watching Adele? I stand up and put the glass back on the tray.

'I think I've left something in your bathroom.'

He looks surprised. 'Well, you know where it is.'

I'm conscious of his eyes on me as I climb the stairs. I go straight to the study and open the door. It's immediately evident the photo has gone. I look round the room to see where he might have put it. I start to fumble through the papers on his desk.

'Have you found what you're looking for?'

He's standing in the doorway.

'I saw a picture of Adele in here.'

'I don't know what you're talking about.'

'It was there, on that wall. I saw it.' I point.

He says nothing, but keeps looking at me.

'You took it, didn't you? From your bathroom window. Do the police know you've got it?

'Even if I had such a picture why would the police be interested?'

He's walked into the study, forcing me to take a few steps back. If he hasn't anything to hide why is he acting this way. He's standing very close and my heart's starting to thump. I realise I've been a fool to confront him.

'I must be mistaken then,' I say. 'I have to go now.'

He laughs. It's a silly, forced laugh.

'I thought you left something in the bathroom.'

'I was mistaken. Please let me pass.'

'Another mistake.' He reaches out and catches hold of my arm. 'Didn't your daddy ever tell you about the dangers of finding yourself alone like this with a man in an empty house?'

I glance around, looking to see if there is something I could defend myself with. There's a hefty book on his desk.

I wonder if I could reach it. He sees me looking and laughs again.

'So you think you could knock me out with the Scrabble dictionary?'

'Rob, this is silly. It's none of my business. I should go now.'

He's looking at a pile of papers on the floor. It's where he's probably hidden the photo. He's let go of my arm and I see my chance and push past him onto the landing. He's close behind, and I have this sudden fantasy that he's going to shove me down the stairs, but I stumble to the bottom and make for the door. I can't seem to open it. Then he's reaching past me to release the catch.

'Don't look so worried. Did you think I'd locked you in?'

'No, of course not.'

He opens the door and gives a mock bow. My glass of elderflower remains untouched in the sitting room, but he's not going to suggest finishing it. No more mention of Book Club. Rob's pretending to ignore what just took place upstairs. Had he really threatened me? Was it his idea of a joke? Or was he just taking advantage of the situation. I no longer feel able to trust my judgement. I stumble outside, grateful for the air on my face. I try not to run to the car, and don't look back.

42

When the phone rings later that evening, my heart starts to pound. I dread it will be Rob, and I'm half afraid it will be Luk, but am relieved to hear Simon's voice.

'I wasn't sure if you'd be in,' he says. Where did he think I'd be, or is this his clumsy attempt to find out.

'What do you want?' I say.

'Well, to see how you are.'

'I'm OK. Is that why you rang?'

'Sam said she saw you.'

'What of it?'

'Well, she slipped up. Said it was outside the Blue Banana.'

'And?'

'At eleven o'clock in the morning. She should have been in school.'

There we have it. The call has nothing to do with me. He just wants to talk about his daughter.

'Well, you'll have to take that up with her, won't you. Is there anything else?'

There is a long silence. Simon has instigated this, and I am not going to make it easy for him.

'Hanna…'

'What?'

'I've missed you.'

Once, I longed to hear him say it, but now I can't see the point, can't actually be bothered to think up a reply.

'Did you hear what I said? I'm trying to say, I still miss you, Hanna.'

'I think it's a bit late for that, don't you?'

'Can't we at least talk about it?'

But we never talked about it. That's the problem.

'What would Claire say about that?' I say.

He's quiet for a second or two. Then I get it. Sometimes I can be so slow. Sometimes I miss the point altogether.

'You've split up, have you?'

'Not exactly.'

'What does that mean?'

'Words. We had words. She was convinced she saw you outside her house.'

'Yes. I suppose she would find that irritating.'

'I asked her not to go to the police. But she wouldn't have it. Said she was scared. Found weed killer in her bin, thought you were trying to bump her off .' He attempts a laugh, to show how ludicrous he finds it.

'I had nothing to do with that!' I'm about to explain about the unopened weed killer under the stairs, then change my mind.

'I absolutely knew you'd do nothing like that.'

I try to picture Simon. He'll be lying on the bed, his long legs crossed, phone crooked by his ear. He'll be lying on the right hand side of the bed which habitually was his side. The bedside lamp will be casting a cosy glow. It's one of the pair we bought one weekend early on. When we felt like a couple. When it felt as if we were furnishing a home together. I'm on the verge of asking him what he's wearing, but remember that's his line.

'Couldn't we meet up, just for a drink or a meal, just for old times? Nothing heavy,' he asks.

He's picking his words carefully, anxious to say the right things. I wonder how long it took him to decide to pick up the phone. No doubt he's feeling lonely, now Claire has ditched him. Did she leave a half empty jar of body lotion in the bathroom? Or a forgotten item of underwear under the bed? I wonder how they get on during the working day. Do they still chat over the water-cooler?

As if in answer to my unasked question, he says, 'Claire's put in for promotion, to one of our regional offices.'

It takes a moment or two to take in the significance of this statement. 'So you have split up then?'

'Look, Hanna, can't we get together and talk face to face, like proper grown-ups?'

It would be so easy to say yes. So easy to say, come over, come now. 'I need to think,' I say.

He's silent for a few moments then, 'By the way,' he says 'did the police ever get back to you about the diary?'

'What are you talking about?'

Simon laughs. 'Don't pretend you don't know.' It's not a very attractive laugh. 'Lost in the oven, wasn't it?'

His tone has changed, and his blunt recall of my lie to D.I. Reynolds feels ominous, has come out of the blue.

'Don't worry, Hanna. Your secret's safe with me.' If he thinks this is the way to get me back, he's made a mistake. 'You can always talk to me you know.'

I think of the number of times I tried to talk to him in the past.

He laughs again. 'You haven't answered my question. Can we get together?'

'I'll have to think about it,' I say.

'Can I ring you in a day or so? Ask you again?'

'Hmm.' I mumble and put the phone down.

I can't think Simon would rat on me but neither do I like him thinking he's got something over me.

43

I'm still awake. It's two in the morning and I can't stop thinking about the picture pinned to Rob's study wall. Why did he prevaricate when he realised I'd seen it? I'm sure it was Adele, probably sitting with Luk. Who else could it have been?

Despite the lack of sleep, I wake early with all manner of thoughts buzzing in my head. I am spending too much time and energy getting nowhere and need to get back to work. I ring Charlie first thing and tell him to expect me in.

I'm leaving the flat just before ten o'clock and meet Mrs Baxter on the stairs. She's dressed in the apricot coloured dress with dove grey accessories. On her head is a light feathery creation that puts in mind a pigeon fluttering on its nest. As if she reads my thoughts, she puts up her hand and adjusts it.

'What do you think, dear?' she asks. 'It doesn't fit very well. Keeps wobbling off. You are coming, aren't you?' She looks doubtfully at my basic going to work outfit. I had completely forgotten about the wedding today.

'Julie's driving me,' she says. 'She's gone to get the car. Would you like to go with us?'

I calculate whether I have time to change. As if reading my mind, she says. 'Come just as you are dear, if you like.'

I wish I hadn't told Charlie I'd be in this morning. He said he's got some new work lined up for me. Seemed pleased I was coming back.

'Just give me a minute to let my boss know,' I say. 'And thank you. I'd love to come with you and Julie.'

The wedding takes place in a small room in the Town Hall. Someone has thoughtfully placed a vase of flowers on the table. I recognise Sweet William, summer flowers Dad used to grow in the garden at home. There are only a handful of us there. Julie drives us to the Town Hall in silence. She is wearing a short, tight brown skirt rather creased with a pink jacket clearly not bought especially for the occasion. Maybe it signals her thoughts about her mother's re-marriage. Maybe she's thinking about her inheritance. I overhear her advising her mother to remove her hat, which makes me sad. Mr Sellers is already there, beaming at everybody, kissing each arrival on the cheek.

'You look beautiful, lovely,' he says to Mrs Baxter.

The service is short and there is a sprinkling of applause when Mr Sellers places a ring on Mrs Baxter now Sellers left hand. Then Mr Sellers kissed everybody again. We are all invited to the pub next door for a glass of champagne. I don't see any sign of Mr Sellers' son, so obviously he hasn't made it back from Saudi Arabia. Mr Sellers is telling everyone how he met his new bride and how lucky he is. I hope he isn't going to tell everybody about how his ex-wife left him, but anybody here will already know that. Mrs Baxter, now Sellers, is smiling too and gives me a kiss.

'Sorry your young man couldn't make it,' she says.

She picks a bloom out of the vase and hands it to me. It drips water and is already shedding its tiny leaves. 'You'll be next,' she says. I wish them both good luck and make my excuses.

44

It's afternoon by the time I get to the office. I apologise again to Charlie for being late. He tells me not to worry and asks how I am. It feels as though I've been away longer than a few days. My desk with its blank computer screen is still where I left it. There's no sign of Jason. I'm about to ask about him but Charlie ushers me into his office.

'Have you been busy?' I ask, not knowing what else to say.

'The usual,' he replies, cryptically.

'You said there were some new clients.'

'Yes. I'll come to that. But there have been some developments at Riverside Apartments. Someone's interested. I'd like you to follow it up. Riverside has been hanging around for too long.'

An unfortunate word to use, I think, remembering the likely fate of the last occupant. I write something down on the note pad I've bought in with me.

'The Caswell place on the Golf Course,' he goes on, 'was completed a couple of weeks ago. Jason handled that.' Charlie looks down at his desk as he speaks, not wanting to meet my eye. It should have been my sale, of course.

'What about the doctors place?' I ask, 'Up at... '

'Yes. That's the one I'd like you to follow up asap. No reason why that shouldn't have sold.' If there is an implied criticism in the statement, I'm not sure, but I think Charlie's trying to be kind. 'Anyway, as I say, look at the old stuff first then have a look at the couple of new properties that have come in.'

'Where is Jason?' I ask.

'He won't be in for a couple of days. Personal issues.'

He stands up at this point, and I take it as my clue we're through. I open up my computer and search for Riverside Apartments. Charlie has linked the property to James Batley. I dimly recall meeting him last year. He's obviously lowered his budget. I call his number and leave a message.

I go to my list of prospective buyers. There are not many looking for houses in the price range of Dr Elliott's property. I ignore anyone who still has a house to sell, and finding two in a position to make an offer, I pick up the phone again. There's no reply to my first call. The second someone picks up.

'Yes, it's a lovely house,' I hear myself say. 'No. Not long on the market.'

I remember the day I visited, the chill of the detached atmosphere, the emotional distance between the two doctors.

'A lovely family house,' I repeat. 'Would you like me to send details?'

I feel exhausted, yet I've only been in the office a couple of hours. Charlie has popped out. I glance over at Jason's desk that used to be Adele's desk and wonder what his personal issues are. Could be anything from a death in the family to something wrong with his car. I make a cup of coffee and am thinking what to do next when the phone rings.

'James Batley here. I want to have a look at Riverside Apartments. Friday suits me.'

'No problem,' I reply. It's a relief to think I've managed one small achievement, but I can't seem to stop other worries intruding.

What I'd really like to do would be to go home, draw the curtains, lie down, read a book, watch TV. Anything to take my mind off the dark thoughts that have settled in my head like storm clouds. Some drift in like snow, mist-like and opaque, others dense and threatening. There is the question of Rob. I want nothing more to do with him now. And Luk. How stupid I'd been to think he was going to turn up at the Blue Banana. He must have something to hide.

It's time I voiced these concerns to the police. Tell them Rob's got a copy of the photo they showed me and that it was taken from his bathroom window. I pick up the phone, dial the station and ask to be put through to P.O. Morgan.

'Name, please,' said the woman. 'What is it in connection with?'

'Hanna Summers. He'll know,' I answer, my voice sounding faint.

'One moment.'

I'm surprised when after a few seconds I hear P.O. Morgan. His voice is a comfort, like that of an old friend or an elderly uncle, though he is probably not much older than me.

'What is it, Hanna?' he says.

'Um, well, it's about that bottle of weed-killer found in the bin… at Percival Street…' I struggle to say the words.

P.O. Morgan says nothing. He waits for me to go on.

'The one you came to see me about,' I add.

'Go on,' is all he says.

'It wasn't mine.' I can't hide a hint of triumph in my voice. 'I know it wasn't mine, because I found my Go-Weeds under the stairs. Unopened.'

'Is this what you've called to tell me, Hanna?'

'Well, yes. I thought you should know. If you like, you can come over, if you've got a spare moment, of course, and I'll show it to you.'

'Showing me a container of weed-killer proves nothing, Hanna. You could have bought it yesterday.'

I hadn't thought of that. I wonder if I could find the receipt to prove when I bought it. But I think it unlikely. No, impossible.

'Is there anything else you want to tell me, Hanna?'

Here's my chance. It's why I've called. To tell him about Luk, to tell him about Rob and the creepy photo. But I need to be sure.

'No, I say. Not really.' I would like to say more, but the words stick in my throat. Anyway, P.O. Morgan only seems interested in solving the stalking complaint.

'Well,' he says, 'if that's everything? I'll make a note of your call. Let me know if there's anything else you want to talk to me about.'

Later that night, Dad rings. 'We've had an offer,' he says, 'on Auntie Jean's flat.'

'Do you want me to come up?' I ask.

'No need. Agent's handling it.'

I hope they don't find a body in there I think, but of course I don't say.

'I miss you, Dad.'

Dad doesn't reply. He never was very good at talking about that sort of thing.

'How are you?' I say.

'Well, you know…'

'Yes, I know,' I echo. But in many ways, I don't. I think back to the icy chill of his hand as he squeezed mine at his sister's funeral. It's about as close as he got to expressing his feelings.

'Well, let's trust the agent to get the best price,' I say.

'Well, you'd know all about that. I'll let you know of any developments.'

'Take care of yourself, Dad.'

'You too, love.'

There's been a strange man on the stairs. I've seen him once or twice coming and going from work. He was outside the flat tonight, leaning against the wall smoking. He always glances in my direction and I think he might be trying to pick me up. This morning, he tried to speak to me when I was getting into the car, but I slammed the door before he was in earshot and drove off. He's quite handsome – broad-shouldered, his skin tanned, so what would he want with me? I have this sudden wild thought that it's Luk. He's come to check me out, come to find out what I know, come to look for the photo, look for the weed killer, come to put a knife in me…

He was there again tonight, loitering outside. He's seen me and he's coming up the stairs behind me. I try to walk faster but my heart is racing. I want to run, but I'm trapped on the stairs. I turn to face him. I'll ask him what he wants, though I dread to hear the answer.

'You must be Hanna,' he says, holding out his hand.

It's too late. I should scream. I open my mouth, but no sound comes.

'I'm Paul Sellers.'

Of course, the son who works in Saudi Arabia. The one who couldn't get back for the wedding.

He's taken hold of my hand. The skin feels rough, yet smooth. How can that be? I think how long it is since I felt the touch of a man's hand. Wonder how those hands would feel on my body. I turn away, afraid he'll read my thoughts. He's said something, but I don't quite catch it.

'It's a shame you missed the wedding,' I say.

'I've seen the photos,' he replies.

'How long are you here for?' I ask.

'Just a few more days.' Neither of us knows what else to say, but we seem to be sharing a moment. As though we both want to linger a while. It might be a moment for him to suggest having a drink before he goes back to Saudi. Or a walk in the park. Maybe I could invite him, his father and the new Mrs Sellers to my flat one evening before he leaves.

'Pleased to meet you,' I say, pulling away.

His eyes are very blue. 'You too.' He replies, before making his way upstairs to the former Mrs Baxter's flat. Going back to Saudi. In only a few days, he'd said.

45

Charlie's looking at paint charts. 'Riverside's been on the market too long,' he says. 'I've advised the owner it needs a paint job.'

'What's wrong with magnolia?' I say.

'See when Vivien can fit us in,' he replies.

I think back to the number of times I showed Riverside to Angela Marriott. Wonder what happened to her. Nothing ever came of my opening day either. Perhaps there is some kind of negative energy lingering in the walls. A kind of ghostly presence that people pick up on. I tell myself not to be ridiculous. More likely it's local gossip that puts enquiries off.

As it happened, Vivien couldn't fit us in, so Jason piped up with a 'reliable guy' he knows who could start immediately. We're driving over now in his Focus to inspect the finish. The car's a bit noisy but it's a nice feeling to be doing something that appears to be useful but makes few demands. I sit back and let Jason negotiate the traffic.

'So how long has it been on the market?' he asks as we climb up to the third floor.

'Quite long,' I reply. I sense an implied criticism in the remark. He must have looked at the notes.

'Did anything ever come of your Open Day?' There, I knew it. He had read the notes.

'Some interest at the time.'

'Shame there's no lift. So there were no offers?'

He's puffing a bit so I don't bother to answer. The key is ready in my hand and I open up.

'Phew. Bit whiffy in here isn't it? Problem with the drains?'

It's true. There is a slight effluence here that I'd never noticed before. But it's been months since I brought anybody here.

'Probably from the river,' I say. 'Nice smell of fresh paint though.'

'Yeah, he's a reliable guy.'

There he goes again. I'm not usually touchy but I sense a put down in everything he says. Perhaps I should have thought of the re-paint myself. I should have known Vivien would be booked up and could easily have found another decorator. I pick up the free newspapers and junk mail and open the window.

'Have there been any offers on it at all, then?'

I don't want to admit that I can't remember. 'There was a nasty incident here that may affect a sale,' I say, my tone prim.

'Fortune Estates seem a bit unlucky there, don't they? Suicide, wasn't it?'

So he knows everything about the place. Charlie must have told him. Perhaps Charlie wants Jason to take it over, though he hasn't said anything to me.

'How you'll ever get rid of Albert Terrace, God knows. Murder wasn't it?'

I walk out onto the narrow balcony and look down at the river. There's a definite smell coming up from the green algae below. Probably a dead animal.

'How did they get into the house, anyway?'

'Who?'

'Albert Terrace. Did somebody give them a key?'

Jason has joined me on the narrow balcony, his back turned to the river, his arms resting on the iron struts, looking at me. The sun has gone behind the clouds and I feel a sudden chill. A ripple on the hairs of my arm.

'Why do you think that?'

'Well, obvious isn't it? Empty property, someone gets hold of a key. Maybe a neighbour, they find it under the plant pot, or perhaps somebody gives them one. Could even be the estate agent.'

There's a ringing in my ears. I pretend I haven't heard, and almost believe it. I fix my gaze past the river onto the fields on the other side, then turn back into the room.

'I think we've finished here, don't you?' I hold open the French doors signalling him to come inside

'Well, it wouldn't be the first time, would it?'

'I really wouldn't know.'

'Happens all the time. So many empty properties, couples looking for somewhere to go. Bet your Vivien could tell a tale or two.'

'You seem to know a lot about it.'

Jason is walking round the room. Puts his head round the bathroom door, now opening a cupboard door.

'I think the mice have been in here,' is his reply. 'Better bring a trap next time.'

His sudden shift reminds me of my viewing with

James Batley on Friday. I'll plan to get here early, bring air freshener.

'I think we're finished here, don't you?' I say. 'Let's go.'

*

Simon never got back to me though he made it clear he was missing me. But, after the initial break-up, do I really miss him? And all the hassles that went with our on-off relationship. I'm thinking it over, when there's a ring at the doorbell. Paul Sellers is standing there.

'I've come to borrow a cup of sugar,' he says. I'm halfway to the kitchen when I realise it's a joke. He's followed me into the hall, and pushed the door shut behind him.

'I thought you'd gone back to Saudi,' I say.

'Few more days to go.'

He's wearing a faded denim shirt. His eyes the colour of the Aegean and they're looking straight into mine. I wish I'd known he was coming and made a bit of effort.

'Come in,' I say.

'Nice place,' he says, looking around.

He follows me into the sitting room. I can hear Mr Sellers' dog, Bobby, barking upstairs but we both pretend not to hear.

'Nice.' He says again.

We stand looking at each other. I ought to look away, but can't seem to manage it. I should offer him something, ask about his work, what he thinks about his father's marriage, about his father's dog, anything to detain him. But he seems in no hurry to move. We're standing so close I can catch the faint smell of sweat and tobacco. As if he knows, he takes a crumpled packet of an unfamiliar brand from his top pocket and drops it on the coffee table.

'Trying to give them up, but I have no will-power.'

'You're not really here to borrow sugar, are you?'

'What do you think?'

I reach out and touch his shoulder. The denim feels soft under my hand. He catches hold of my arm, manoeuvres his leg between mine then pushes me gently back against the wall.

'Then what are you here for?' I breathe into his ear, reaching for his belt.

No further words are needed. We both know exactly what we're here for.

46

It's Saturday morning. Charlie has asked me to cover the office for a couple of hours while he's out doing an estimate. I find myself humming a tune, warming myself in the sunlight that's flooding the office with light. I wonder if I'll see Paul again tonight. I feel sure I will. I wonder how much longer he will be around before he has to go back out to Saudi. A few days, he said. But he has holidays, maybe I'll be able to visit him. I'll have to ask him when is the best time of year to go. I water the plants, dust the ledges, read my emails.

'Busy?' says a voice.

Without having to look round, I know who it is.

'Have you had your phone turned off?' asks Simon. 'I've been trying to reach you.'

I turn to face him and wonder if he sees guilt in my face. 'Yes, I just wanted a couple of early nights, that's all.'

'You're not poorly are you?'

'No.'

'Actually, you're looking rather good.'

I can't remember when Simon made any comment like that. 'Did you want me for any special reason?' I ask.

'Well, we were going to talk things over,' he replies.

Ah yes. The talking things over moment. I wonder how long it will be before he mentions Sam.

'Sam's away for a few days. School trip to Bruges. Thought it might be a good opportunity.'

'Really.'

'I wonder if I could come over to yours.'

We haven't seen each other for months, not in that sort of way. 'I take it Claire got her promotion,' I say, nastily.

He has the good grace to look away. 'I hoped we might put all that behind us,' he says.

I bet he does. I cast my eyes round the empty office and my tidy desk, the nothing much happening look of the place. 'Actually, Simon, I've got quite a lot on at the moment.'

'Oh?'

'Viewings lined up, that sort of thing.'

'What, in the evenings?'

I can't bother to try to lie any more. 'And I can't see the point,' I say.

He's obviously disappointed. Must have a very short memory. 'Is there somebody else?' He asks.

I'm surprised he would even consider it a possibility. 'It's not that,' I say.

'It's not that sci-fi writer chap, is it?'

I smile to myself at the thought. 'Why ever would you think that?' I ask.

'It's just that I've seen him a few times, you know, near your place.'

'You've seen him near my place? You mean my flat?'

'Only a couple of times.'

'Did you speak to him? How did you recognise him?'

'Well, I did meet him once – you introduced me, at that restaurant.'

It was a long time ago, and I'm surprised he remembers. 'But that was ages ago.'

'So, is it him?'

'No. Simon, you've got it all wrong.'

But the thought of Rob hanging around outside the flat is disturbing. I remember how he turned up at the mall that time. The picture of Adele sitting next to a man on a bench in the garden of Albert Terrace shoots into my thoughts. The photo taken from his bathroom window. It's only later I wish I'd asked Simon why he'd been in the vicinity of my flat enough times to notice Rob, yet never rung my doorbell. What had he been doing there? At least there was no more mention of the diary.

'I'd better get on,' I say, opening up my inbox. 'Charlie will be in soon and…'

'OK I get it.'

What he gets is unclear. The door clicks open and a couple I've already observed looking at the display photos in the window enter.

'Can I help you?' I say as I rise to greet them.

Simon makes his way back out on to the street.

*

The evening air is still warm, even humid. I stand at the bottom of the stairs for a few seconds but hear no sound. And that's another thing. Part of me expected Paul might be listening out for my return, would be waiting for me outside on the street, or would hear the outside door, come down to meet me, but all remains silent. Other than knocking on the door of the flat upstairs, I have no means of contacting him, no mobile number. I've got Mrs Baxter-Sellers number but would hold back from using it.

I take a long shower, wash my hair and change into a linen sun frock that is probably not quite right for early September, but its bright colours are cheering. Make me feel sexy. It's a good feeling.

The phone rings at just after eight. I wish I'd bought in some food, anything to throw together for a quick meal. I let it ring four times before picking up.

"Hi,' I say. 'I was hoping to hear from you.'

'Oh and why is that, Hanna?'

'Oh, P.O. Morgan.'

'Sorry to disappoint you. Were you expecting someone else?'

It's none of his business actually. Does the man never stop asking questions? I suppose that's what he learned at Policeman's school. Well, two can play that game.

'What did you want me for?'

'We've had a breakthrough.'

'Oh?'

I try to think what he might be talking about. Has Rob seen the only way forward for him is to confess all he knows?

'What sort of breakthrough?'

'We've arrested a man in connection with the murder of the woman at three Albert Terrace.'

'Oh, so he's come forward.'

'It sounds as though you already know what I'm going to say.'

'Oh no. Please tell me.'

'We took him in for questioning a few days ago. We've had him under observation for a while.'

It must be Luk, I think to myself. They've managed to track him down, find him, while my attempts failed utterly. 'You've found Luk, then,' I say.

'Who?' he replies. Again, that irritating use of a question to answer a question.

'Sorry,' I say. 'I'm a bit confused.'

'He's a gardener, Marek Kowski.'

I'm fidgeting with a pencil, shuffling names through my head. Marek. Of course. The gardener I spoke to at Zoe Caswell's house back in the spring.

'Oh, no, I start to say, 'it's not…'

But P.O. Morgan hasn't finished. 'He came forward and we brought him in for questioning. I thought you'd want to know.'

I can't quite get my thoughts round it. Marek. The man who walked Zoe Caswell's dog. The good-looking gardener willing to offer his varied services to a lonely widow.

'I don't think…'

'What don't you think, Hanna?'

'No. I mean to say are you sure?' I ask.

He doesn't answer. 'I'm not following you, Hanna.'

'How do you know it was him?'

'There is enough evidence to question him. That's all I can tell you at this stage.' He sounds a little snappy. Doesn't like me querying his judgement. 'Anyway, I thought you'd want to hear. I already told Charlie, but I thought you'd probably like to hear it from me direct.'

'Yes,' I say. 'Of course. It was good of you to let me know.'

'No problem. Goodnight.' He says and rings off.

I try very hard, but cannot get my thoughts around the likelihood of Marek the gardener being Marek the murderer. P.O. Morgan's got it all wrong. I should have had the guts to tell him he's made a mistake. And it's clear he knows nothing about Luk. And where does Rob fit into all this? I feel suddenly weary. I make a cup of coffee and try to settle my thoughts. My mind goes blank. I close my eyes for a few minutes and when I come to, I realise it's already turned nine o'clock. I've heard nothing from Paul. No sound at all from upstairs. Not even the yapping of a dog.

47

Next morning, Charlie is full of talk of Marek's arrest. 'To think he was there, under our noses,' he says. 'It's going to lead us to Adele's murder, there has to be a connection.'

Jason is sitting at his desk, his head down, trying to give the impression he's working.

'Do you remember meeting this Marek?' Charlie asks me.

At this, Jason looks up. 'He's the chap who was supposed to do the work at Zoe Caswell's.'

Thank you for reminding us Jason, I think. We all know who arranged for the garden to be tidied, and who completed on the sale.

'Yes, I was ill,' I say.

'But before that,' says Charlie, turning to me. 'Did you see him on those earlier viewings?'

As I recall, there were very few viewings, that was the problem, but I can't say that. 'I do remember meeting him,' I say. 'I thought he was a nice young man. Spoke good English, looked after Zoe's dog.'

Charlie and Jason both look at me, expecting more.

'Well, it takes a clever judge of character to suss out someone as psychopathic as that,' says Jason.

'Is this a comment on my judgement?' I ask.

Charlie, sensing the tension, steps in. 'Well, it's in police hands now. We've got our own work to do. Let's get on.'

It's a relief to turn to my computer.

I've received an email from a client with a house to sell at Hill Vale, asking me to do a valuation. We don't get many houses offered to us up there. I'm a bit surprised it's come to me direct, though it does sometimes happen. Someone obviously passed on my name by word of mouth. If I pass it over to Charlie, he'll probably give it to Jason. I email back and suggest an appointment tomorrow afternoon. Strictly speaking, this is something that Charlie doesn't approve of. He likes to vet the enquiries himself and the rule is that someone in the office is always aware when an agent goes out somewhere new. I tell myself it will be OK this once and Charlie will be delighted if we get sole agency of a house in Hill Vale.

The weather's cooling off, a hint of autumn in the air. There's a knock on my door as soon as I get home. I'm somehow expecting P.O. Morgan to come to tell me it's all a big mistake. Marek's in the clear and who is this Luk you mentioned? This time I'll definitely tell him my suspicions about Rob.

'I've been listening out for you,' says Paul. He walks into the hallway and puts his arms round me. Touches my hair. Leans down to kiss me on the mouth.

'I wasn't expecting you,' I say, extricating myself. I wonder what he does all day while I'm at work. If he has friends he sees. He surely can't spend all day upstairs with his father and Mrs Baxter, who's no longer Mrs Baxter. And is his father aware of this new development with the estate agent who lives downstairs? I think probably not.

'Are your feelings for me cooling already?' he asks, stepping away.

It occurs to me that we've started this affair, if that's what it is, the wrong way round. It's the same way it was with Simon. Slept together the first day we met, before we'd even had a half decent conversation. Perhaps I give off some sort clue, a kind of scent, like an animal. The thought disgusts me and I try to push it away.

'Would you like a coffee?' I ask.

'I'd prefer a beer.'

'Don't think I've got any.' I know I haven't. Those years with Simon mean I rarely keep alcohol in the house.

'Shall we talk?' He asks.

I sit on the couch, somewhere in the middle, spreading myself, leaving no space for him to join me. It's not that I don't fancy him. I fancy him too much. He's wearing the same faded blue shirt he wore before. I wonder if it's the same one or if he's got a suitcase full of them. Perhaps this one's his lucky shirt.

'How long are you here for?' I ask.

'A few more days.'

'Can't you be more precise?' I don't like myself for asking this. I have no right to ask anyway. It's the sort of remark a jealous wife might make.

'I'm here for an interview with head office,' he says after a short silence.

'I thought it was for your father's wedding,' I say.

'Well, that too, though I didn't get back in time.'

'What is it you do?'

'Engineering.'

A word that covers a thousand possibilities. A word

that says nothing. Another silence hangs in the room. Maybe we're both wondering where this is going.

'I've been looking for a transfer,' he volunteers.

'Where to?'

'Not sure yet.'

He's not going to say any more. There are a hundred things I'd like to know, but don't want to keep asking questions. I would like it if he would ask me some questions. He doesn't wear a ring, but that doesn't mean anything. He doesn't strike me as the sort of man who'd wear jewellery.

'Are you married?' I ask.

'Divorced,' he says briefly. 'She couldn't handle me being half way across the world all the time. Not many women could. No kids though,' he adds as an afterthought.

'And are you seeing somebody, out there in Saudi Arabia?'

He laughs. His teeth are very white. He must have good dental care. 'Riyadh isn't the sort of place you "see someone". I'm there for the work and the money. Actually, I will have that coffee, if it's still on offer.'

He surprises me by getting up and going into the kitchen. 'I see you've got one of these fancy machines.' He methodically puts out two mugs, spoons and looks in the fridge for some milk. 'Black or white?' he calls out. 'Sugar?'

This is all the wrong way round, I think. We've had sex, but he doesn't even know how I drink my coffee. 'White,' I say. 'If you can find any milk.'

'So what about you?' he asks, handing me a mug. 'You must have many admirers.'

This is probably where I should mention my break-up with Simon. 'Well, if I have, they don't let on,' I say.

He wanders over to the CD player and picks out some Miles Davis. 'Do you like him?' he asks, putting it on anyway.

The cool blues alters the mood in the room. I move along the couch and he sits down beside me. We finish our coffees. He puts his arm round me. Neither of us speaks much after that.

48

There's a small news item on page one of the local paper to say a man of Romanian origin has been arrested in connection with a woman's murder. It's mentioned briefly on local radio and TV but no further details. I'm surprised more hasn't been made of it. I picture Marek in a cell, waiting to go on trial for a murder he didn't commit. I hope he's got good legal advice. But perhaps I've been disingenuous. Maybe my judgement is poor, like Jason suggested. Maybe Zoe Caswell had a lucky escape.

Later in the day, I drive out to Hill Vale. It's a lovely drive on an autumn afternoon, out past the golf course, then onto quieter roads, opening up vistas of rolling countryside. The houses on Hill Vale are detached, red-brick, early twentieth century. After a mile or two the road narrows and they become more spread out. I'm looking for number eight, but high hedgerows obscure the numbers. I pass an elderly man walking a dog. I slow down and wait for him to catch up, wind down the window.

'Number eight?' I say.

'You've passed it,' he says.

I think he's mistaken, but don't contradict him.

'There's nobody living there,' he says.

I'm not surprised to hear there's no one living there. It's likely the owner has already died or moved out, and whoever is handling the estate wants it valued before it goes on the market. I check my rear mirror and glance over my shoulder.

'You can't turn here,' says the man.

I have to drive a mile before finding a place wide enough to turn. I go back slowly looking out for number eight, or any sign of an empty house. A strong breeze has got up, blowing leaves down in gusts and across the road. Peering through the windscreen, I think I see a number on a post box and I'm relieved to see it's number eight. As the entrance to the drive is overgrown, I park on the verge and walk to the door.

The house certainly appears empty. The blinds are drawn down at the windows and there is a neglected look to the garden and the house. Such a promising house, with such a good address, it will be great to have it on our books. I've rung the bell twice now, but no one answers. I stare up at the windows, hoping for a sign of life. I'm sure I've got the time and date right. I'm looking in my diary when I hear a voice. I turn and it's the man I saw earlier, calling his dog who's running around loose in the driveway.

'Told you. It's been empty for months.'

'Do you know anything about it?' I say, 'Who owns it.'

The man shakes his head. 'No. They keep to themselves up here. Rudi come here!' He calls to his dog who's been sniffing at the bushes with interest.

I can only think I've misread the email, or the owner has changed their mind. It's annoying. It's a wasted afternoon.

'Rudi!' Shouts the man again. Hearing his owner's voice, the dog ambles back to the road.

'Thank you anyway,' I say.

'Empty for months,' is the man's response as he stoops to attach the dog's lead.

49

Later, I see Sam on the pavement, walking in the direction of the flat. She sees me and waves. Behind her lopes a lanky long-legged youth, trousers too low-slung, over-smoking a cigarette. I don't think Sam is smoking which is a good sign. I slow down and pull up, ignoring the aggressive driver who sounds his horn behind me.

'Hi Sam,' I say, leaning out of the window. 'What are you doing over here? Were you coming to see me?'

'Sort of,' she replies.

What kind of reply is that I ask myself. 'I can't park here. Is it a yes, or a no?'

'I have a message from Dad,' she says.

My heart fails to leap, like once it would have. In fact, I feel a slight stab between my ribs. Simon's been completely out of my thoughts.

'What's the message?' I ask.

'He thinks he left some of his stuff at your flat. Wants to pick it up.'

What a nerve, I think. Then I rack my brains to think what he could have left behind. Or is he going to try to corner me about the diary again. Is this his weird way of trying to start up again? Should I have told him about Paul?

But what would I have said? What is the situation anyway? A bus roars past too close. I think I've have stopped in a bus lane as the driver makes a gesture.

'I've got to move on,' I say. 'Why don't you come up to the flat?'

She shakes her head. She's turned away and is talking to the boy. She should be at home this time of day, not hanging about the streets. Romeo throws his cigarette to the ground, pulls ineffectively at his trousers and hangs a possessive arm round Sam's shoulders. I'd like to tell him about litter and the inconsequential gestures men make to show control, but another blaring horn interrupts.

'Got to go,' I say. I wind up my window, switch on my turn signal and pull out with a foot or two to spare.

I pass the office on the way home and notice the light still on. I'm surprised to see Charlie still at his desk. 'Hi Charlie,' I say.

He swivels round to face me. 'Where have you been all afternoon?'

I can see something's upset him. 'Has James Batley pulled out of Riverside?'

'I asked where you'd been all afternoon.'

'Well, I had one or two things to follow up…'

'Hanna, I asked you specifically, where you'd been all afternoon.'

He's only asking because knows where I've been. Knows all about Hill Vale. I can't imagine how he found out, but he knows.

'You've been on a viewing, haven't you? On your own. Without telling anybody where you were going.' He's almost shouting It's not really like Charlie to get angry. 'After all the problems we've had this year, you think it's OK to go swanning around empty properties without any thought of your own security.'

Oh, if that's all that's upset him, when I tell him about Hill Vale, it will bring a smile back to his face. 'Well, Charlie, wait until you hear where I've been…'

'I know exactly where you've been.'

I don't know how to answer that. 'How…'

'It doesn't matter how I know. The fact is you've put yourself into possible danger for nothing.'

'Well, it might come to something. '

'Jason's already looked into it. It's a hoax.'

I feel bewildered. Whatever has Jason got to do with it? 'Whatever has Jason…' I start.

'It hardly matters. You know you just don't go haring off to a property on the strength of an email. Especially not without telling somebody in the office where you're going.'

He's right, of course. And his concern for my safety is touching. But I don't know where Jason fits in. Charlie is running his hands through his hair. I wonder why Ed doesn't advise him to get a haircut. Charlie never talks about Ed anymore and I wonder if things aren't going so well. I feel bad adding to his worries. But something else is bothering me.

'Has Jason been reading my emails?'

Charlie doesn't answer. It's answer enough. I can't believe it. I'm shocked at his betrayal. 'Don't you trust me anymore, Charlie?'

'Jason got the same email and brought it straight to me.'

'Oh.' There's nothing more I can say to this.

'You've not been yourself for a long time, Hanna. You don't act as if you're in a team.'

I feel like laughing. 'Do you think Jason believes we're in a team?'

'Jason acted in your best interests. He was worried for your safety.'

'So what was he going to do about it?'

'He checked out the house in Hill Vale. Made a note of your appointment.'

'Met Rudi the dog too, I suppose.'

'What? '

So there is something Charlie doesn't know about. I feel suddenly defeated. 'I'm sorry, I should have said something.'

'Too right. I've got to feel I can trust you, Hanna.'

So does he think Jason the worm who looks at his colleague's emails and tells tales on her is trustworthy?

'Anyway, what did Jason make of the Hill Vale house?'

'Well, like I said. Probably a hoax. Empty property. End of story.' Glancing at his watch, 'It's time we went home.'

I'd like to say more, question what's going on here, but Charlie's getting ready to leave.

'Go home, get some rest. See you in the morning,' he says.

'OK,' I say.

50

When I get home, the light's flashing on my landline. When I pick up, it's Mrs Baxter-Sellers. I'll never get used to calling her Mrs Sellers.

'Can you come up, dear? Just for a quick drink after work – six-thirty? Paul is leaving. We want to give him a send-off.'

My heart does a flip. Paul leaving. So soon. I wonder if she has any idea of how the relationship between me and her new step-son has taken off. I tell myself probably not, otherwise she would realise that he will want to say goodbye to me in his own way.

It's only five thirty, but I want to look my best and take my time getting ready. Pick out a knee-length wrap-around dress to wear with my highest heels.

When I get there later, Paul is in the kitchen doing something with a cloth and the glasses and he gives me a friendly peck on the cheek in greeting. 'Hello, gorgeous,' he says.

I feel an exquisite pain deep inside my gut. It might be love. I would like to reach up, would like him to kiss me on the mouth, want him to put his hand on my thigh, push me back and ravish me against the sink, but he's turned away, talking to his new step-mother, Mrs Baxter-Sellers.

'So you two have already met, have you?' She says.

'That's right, Elaine. Let me refresh your glass?'

'Just a splash for me, please, Paul.'

She walks away into the sitting room where Mr Sellers is holding forth. I wonder who else they have invited. I'm about to follow her when Paul catches hold of my arm.

'Wait a minute,' he says.

'You didn't tell me you were leaving,' I reply.

'Something came up. I had no choice.'

'I thought you were looking for a new job?'

'That too, but I have things to sort out first.'

He is being infuriatingly cryptic. I want to know more, but don't want to ask. Probably don't want to hear the answer. 'When are you coming back?'

'It depends.'

'On what?'

At this point, Mr Sellers comes into the kitchen. 'Have you given this young lady something to drink, Paul? If it wasn't for her, Elaine and I might never have met, you know.'

Mr Sellers looks happy. He no longer launches into bitter details of previous marital disappointments. I gather Paul is his only son from the first marriage. Nothing to do with wife number two who upped and left. I wonder if Mrs Baxter-Sellers realises what a lothario she has married. I hope it's not a family trait. I look at Paul. He looks back at me. I know I'm in love.

We drift into the sitting room. There's nobody else in there, so I'm a bit confused. I'm sure I heard people talking. Perhaps Mr Sellers was on the telephone, perhaps I imagined it. It doesn't matter anyway. Paul has come into the room holding a bottle.

'Any more for a top up?' he asks. He holds out a bowl of crisps.

'We've got so used to having Paul with us; we're going to miss him.'

Elaine, as I'm getting used to calling her, is fussing with her cushions. Bobby the dog is asleep under one of them and gives a sharp bark, doesn't want to be disturbed. That's who he was talking to, of course.

'Perhaps Paul will be coming back again soon?' I say.

We all look hopefully in Paul's direction, but he's disappeared back into the kitchen.

'Haven't we got some music to put on?' He calls out. 'This is a party, isn't it?'

Mr Sellers looks at Elaine.

'We could put the radio on, quietly,' she says.

'Bobby doesn't like too much noise,' Mr Sellers says to me. So we sit looking at each other until Paul comes back. I watch him move across the room, gracefully refilling glasses, offering snacks, pretending interest in a conversation about how long it takes to get an appointment with the doctor. At one point I catch him looking at me and I wonder if he's thinking the same as me. How soon will we be able to quietly disappear downstairs and say goodbye properly.

At about eight o'clock I've had enough. My dress feels tight, and my feet hurt. I stand up and pretend to stifle a yawn. 'Work tomorrow,' I say. 'Lovely party. Thank you so much for inviting me.'

Paul comes over and gives me another friendly kiss on the cheek. The sort of thing everyone does now, that means nothing.

'Good luck with your travels, Paul.' I say. I'm sure he'll be joining me downstairs as soon as he can decently get away. I wonder what excuse he'll give.

I let myself into my flat, kick off my heels and change into my dressing gown. I stay awake until eleven, but there's no sign of Paul.

51

There's so much I want to ask Paul, but it will have to wait. I've planned to get to the office early. I want to speak to Jason. He needs to answer a few questions. I am very concerned to find out he's been tracking my movements, looking at my emails, talking about me to Charlie behind my back. I know I should have said something before going out to Hill Vale yesterday, but that's not a good enough excuse for him to snoop. He's not in the office and when I ask Charlie when he'll be in, he just shrugs.

Half way through the morning the phone rings. I'm surprised to hear P.O. Morgan's voice. He comes straight to the point. 'Marek Kowski was released from custody this morning. I've spoken to Mr Porter, but I thought you'd want to know.'

'Well, of course he's been released,' I reply. 'He didn't do it, did he?'

If P.O. Morgan is surprised at my response, it's not obvious. 'We ran further DNA tests,' he goes on. 'They're inconclusive.'

I could have told him that ages ago. In fact, I'm wondering what held me back. 'So what happens next?'

'We are still pursuing a number of active lines of enquiry,' he says.

'What does that mean?'

'I am not at liberty to say. But if there is anything you want to...'

My thoughts shift and shuffle around in my head like a deck of cards. The murdered woman shows herself as a two-faced Queen. Luk, the Ace of spades. And what about Rob the Joker, and the photos... I'm trying to make sense of it all when Jason walks through the door.

'I need to go,' I say. There's a soft click as P.O. Morgan hangs up.

Jason has gone into Charlie's office and shut the door. In Adele's day, Charlie's door was never shut. I am completely closed out of whatever is going on in there.

After twenty minutes, Jason comes out. 'Can't stop, I'm afraid.'

He must know I want to have it out with him about the emails. 'Jason,' I say, 'can I buy you a coffee at lunch time?'

'Any time, Hanna, but not today. I've an errand to do for Charlie.'

He doesn't say what the errand is. Charlie hasn't said anything about any errand to me. Jason picks up the man-bag he takes everywhere and makes for the door. 'Catch you later,' he says.

I sit at my desk for what seems a long time. Then Charlie comes out and says he's got something he wants me to take a look at.

'It's about Albert Terrace,' he says. 'Number three. The police finished with it months ago.' He doesn't quite look at

213

me as he says, 'The owner wants it back on the market. I'll understand if you say no.'

There is a silence as we both avoid looking at each other and gaze out of the window. The skies are heavy, it looks like rain.

'You want me to take it on?' I ask.

'Only if you're OK about it,' he replies. 'It's been freshened up, re-painted, new carpets. New locks, obviously.'

I express surprise that the owner wants to instruct us again.

'He's gone back to Spain. And who else would want it? Jason and I had a look. You'd never know anything happened there.'

So that's what all the secrecy was about. They didn't want to upset me. I expect Charlie has already asked Jason to handle the property and he's turned it down.

'I haven't got a problem with it,' I say.

'Thought you'd say that. We'll do new brochures. Market it like a new property.' Charlie hands me the keys. 'I was going to offer it to Jason, but I thought I'd ask you first.'

I am grateful to Charlie. Perhaps he still has some faith in me. I go back to my computer and dig out any information I can about Albert Terrace. There's not a lot. The police took away anything they thought significant over a year ago. I print off a couple of pages, put them into a folder and make a plan.

Half an hour later, I'm driving down Albert Terrace. I park the car, locate the keys, take a deep breath and prepare myself to enter number three's blue door for the first time. Someone, must be Jason, has left a small pile of junk-mail on the side. A cheap beige carpet spreads from the hall to the small sitting room and up the stairs. There's a chemical smell of new paint and rubber underlay and an echo from the empty rooms. I walk into the kitchen and try to imagine a family living here. It's difficult. I open one cupboard after another and look under the sink. I turn the key in the back door and look outside. The small hedge has been sharply trimmed back. Though it's stopped raining, droplets cling to the leaves. The garden bench is no longer there. I go back inside, lock the back door and steel myself to go to the foot of the stairs. It was in one of the bedrooms the woman's body was found.

I realise I've been a fool to agree to take on the marketing of this house. The horror is too fresh. It will live on in the collective memory of the neighbourhood for decades. The first thing any new owner finds out about their new home.

I'll take a quick look upstairs, then go back to Charlie and tell him I've changed my mind. Let him give it to Jason. I mount the stairs and peer into the bathroom. Pity the owner didn't make some changes in here. The tiles are a dated dull brown, decorated with sheaves of wheat. I go into the larger of the two bedrooms. This must be where it happened. I try to picture where the body was found, but the walls give nothing away. No stains, no smells. Its hideousness now covered in tufted beige. I think about Marek, now released from custody. I remember Adele's words. She and Luk seldom came here, but his friends used it for sleepovers. A euphemism for sex, I suppose. It was used as some kind of brothel. I feel a flash of anger towards Adele but try to suppress it.

My thoughts are interrupted by a noise. Someone is at the door. I glance into the other bedroom, an empty box-room and make my way downstairs. A flyer advertising a new pizza restaurant lies on the mat. I toss it onto the junk pile and open the door, but there's nobody there. I need to get out of here. I grab my bag and make for the car. It's a relief to breathe in fresh clean air. I nod to a passer-by who glances at me with interest then looks away. I feel angry with Charlie. Angry with Jason and angry with myself for agreeing so stupidly to come here today.

When I get back to the office, I realise I've left my folder behind. I fiddle around for an hour or so, answering the phone, checking texts and emails. Nobody walks through the door and the phones are quiet. I decide to leave work early, go back to Albert Terrace and pick up the folder on the way home. I don't want to say anything to Charlie until I've retrieved it. Jason would find it and be sure to tell Charlie. They'd both shake their heads and say it's more proof of my incompetence. It's almost dark when I park outside number three. I plan to dash in and out. I don't even think the electricity is on. I nearly leave my car engine running, but decide against it. I find the folder in the kitchen where I left it. I'm startled by a ring at the bell and somebody shouting out "hello!" I'm not exactly nervous, but it's inevitable this place spooks me. I check the back door is locked, tell myself not to be stupid and walk back into the hall.

'I thought I recognised your car.'

'What can I do for you, Rob?'

'Nothing. Just thought I'd come and say hello. You left the front door open.'

'I'm just leaving.'

'So it's back on the market, then?'

I don't want to get into this conversation. I make as though to switch off the lights, although as I'd thought, the electricity is turned off.

'Did you leave something behind?' He says. He's spotted the folder.

'Nothing important,' I say.

'I saw your car here earlier.'

'You're a one-man neighbourhood watch,' I say.

He's got something in his hand, holding something out to me. 'I thought you'd like a copy of this,' he says. He holds out a sheet of A4.

Adele's face smiles up at me in smudgy black and white. It's the photo he claimed to know nothing about.

'I thought you said you didn't have it.'

'I felt embarrassed. You'd caught me out. I saw them from my bathroom window. It was stupid of me to take a photo.'

So he had been watching Adele, spying on her. 'Why did you lie about it?'

'I admit I found her attractive. I'd seen her in the street a few times. We smiled. I used to look out for her car. It was a dark green Mini. Then one day I saw her with the man.'

He indicates the man sitting beside her, on the garden bench, in the sunlight. 'I took a few photos, some on different days, but this was the best of Adele.'

It's the first time I've looked at it properly. Undoubtedly it is Adele, but what of the man next to her? It must be Luk. I peer more closely. Try to get a good look at last. The image is dark and smudgy.

'The police have a copy of this. Do they know you took it?'

'No. I didn't want to get involved. But I thought you should have it. She was your friend.'

The front door still stands ajar. It feels as cold and dark here in the narrow hallway as it is outside. My thoughts are awash with new information I don't know how to process. I keep looking at the face I now recognise as James Batley.

'You can keep it, if you like,' he says, indicating the photograph.

How does James Batley fit into all this? Batley, who's just bought Riverside apartments. There must be some mistake.

'I must be going,' I say. I don't want to say any more. My voice is too shaky. I put the photo in the folder as though it's just another insignificant piece of paper connected to the house sale.

'I expect I'll be seeing quite a bit of you then.' I must look surprised because he goes on, 'When you show the property, I mean.' He's looking past me. 'I saw the carpet fitters van... you'd never know anything...'

I don't hear the rest. I no longer fear him, he's just stupid and small. I'm practically pushing him out into the street.

'I have to go. Thank you for the...' I indicate the folder.

'Let me know if I can help in any way – with the viewings, I mean.'

I start the car and drive round the corner and stop. I turn on the overhead light, open the folder and stare at the photo Rob has just given me. There's no mistaking it. James Batley is the man sitting beside Adele on the bench in the garden of number three. No mistaking him at all.

52

I am so lost in my thoughts I have little recollection of the journey home. It comes as a surprise to find I've reached my flat. I let myself in and throw my bag down on the table. The doorbell rings almost immediately.

'I've been waiting for you,' says Paul. He puts his arms round me and leans over to kiss me.

'I wondered if you'd like to go out somewhere tonight. Dinner, a drink, or a walk somewhere? I'm sorry about last night,' he says. He means the party. It already seems a million years away.

'It came as a surprise to hear you were leaving so soon.'

'I'd like to talk about it. Or do you have other plans tonight.'

'No. No other plans.'

'What do you say, then, it's a fine evening.'

'I'll change my shoes.'

I suggest a lake, a quiet beauty spot a little way out of town and he drives us there in his rental car. It has been a warm day and the evening is thick with midges rising out of the water. We lie down on the grass looking up at the leaves rustling overhead. He asks about my family and I tell him about Dad. I tell him about my job, about everything that's happened over the past few months. Though I don't tell him everything. Eventually, I tell him about Simon. When I hear myself talking about Simon, it's clearer to me than ever he is a chapter in my life that's finally closed. We get back in the car and drive to a popular lakeside pub, manage to get a table and sit for an hour or so as dusk starts to fall, nibbling tapas, sipping prosecco, and telling each other the story of our lives.

'When are you leaving?' I ask, eventually.

'In the morning.'

My heart jolts. 'So soon? Are you going back to Saudi?'

'That's the plan.'

'What happened to the new job?'

'I'm working on it. Nothing's settled but I've got to go back to Riyadh.'

'When will you be coming back?'

I don't think he's going to answer and there's a silence between us as we walk to the car.

'I only know I want to see you again, Hanna. You're special.'

He takes hold of my hand and kisses it, puts his arms round me and we stay like that until he lets me go. On the way back we hear a song on the radio we both recognise. We sing along, laughing, because neither of us know the words. But it doesn't matter, because we both know something more important is taking place.

Paul stays until the early hours, but I tell him I need to be at the office early. I expect to see him before he leaves. I try not to think about it too much.

I can't stop looking at the photo of Adele and James Batley. Is it possible Rob's photo is simply a record of an innocent moment she spent with him on a sunny morning while they discussed rights of way and double glazing? There's only one way to find out.

I try all morning to contact Batley but only get his voicemail. I leave a couple of messages asking him to contact me but don't get any reply. The only thing is to go to Riverside. I'm thinking of doing just that when Charlie puts his head round the door and asks me if I've read the email he's sent regarding a new property we've been asked to value.

'Get onto this asap,' he says.

I scan the details and nod brightly. 'Will do,' I say.

I plan to drive there first but, somehow, I find myself on the road leading to Riverside.

From outside the apartments look exactly the same. Blinds pulled down, bistro chairs sit empty on the veranda. Nobody around. I walk up to the fourth floor and ring the bell. I don't expect anybody to answer it. James Batley still hasn't responded to any of my phone messages and I'm about to turn away when the door opens. He looks disappointed to see me. Perhaps he's expecting somebody else.

'Good morning, James,' I say, smiling, showing him my teeth, running my tongue along my lips.

'What is it?' he says.

He is dressed in shabby track suit bottoms and his T-shirt is stained with last night's dinner. He looks changed. Not the same in control of life man I showed the apartment to. I try to peer past him but he pulls the door slightly, positioning himself so I can't see inside.

'Well?'

Now that I'm here, I don't know what to say. How to justify my visit, how to broach the subject of his weird appearance in the garden of three Albert Terrace sitting next to Adele, my friend, my dead friend.

'Just thought I'd drop by and see how you're settling in,' I say, still smiling falsely.

'Fine,' he says, 'everything's fine,' and goes to close the door.

'All part of the service.' I've pushed my way through the door and I've got my foot on the mat. We're standing uncomfortably close.

'No need for that, everything's fine,' he says again looking at his watch. 'I'm about to…'

I don't give him a chance to say what he's about to. 'I tried phoning, but never seemed to get you. I was in the area and…'

I squeeze past him and walk inside. He's not bought much furniture. No pictures on the wall. Two big chairs, one facing a large TV screen, sound off, picture on, showing a cartoon. I glance into the kitchen. Several empty beer cans, a couple of wine bottles and dirty dishes fill the sink.

'You've made it look very nice,' I say, indicating the new chairs and manoeuvring myself towards the window. 'It can take time, I know.'

He doesn't answer. He's closed the front door and followed me into the sitting room. I don't think he's going to offer coffee. I look out of the window and down at the river. The green algae is still evident, but the windows are closed so there's no smell today. I feel faintly sick at the memory, but tell myself I've got to go on.

'A lovely light room,' I say.

'You've already sold it to me once,' he replies. 'You don't have to do it again. What's all this about?'

'Fortune Estates are having a sales promotion,' I say. I'm rather surprised at the ease and speed with which I've come up with this lie. 'We'd love to have some photos and a few quotes from satisfied clients. We hoped you'd be willing to participate.'

'Maybe some other time.'

'It won't take long,' I say, sitting down and taking my pen and notebook out of my bag.

'I'm busy.'

He doesn't look busy. He knows I know he's not busy. Perhaps he's lost his job. Is that why he's home at this time of day, hanging around in odd socks.

The cartoon characters flicker and chase each other wildly across the screen. They inevitably draw our eyes but he makes no effort to turn them off.

'It won't take long. Just one or two questions.' I feel like P.O. Morgan or D.I. Naomi preparing to winkle out the truth from a reluctant witness.

'Did you look at many properties before deciding on this one?'

'I'm sorry, but this is an intrusion.'

'Perhaps you met a colleague of mine…'

He's not going to sit down. Feels uncomfortable, doesn't want to prolong this exchange. But I mustn't draw any conclusions from that.

'You're still having your house-warming parties then.'

He looks startled. I nod towards the kitchen and the empty bottles. A voice inside me is screaming *You can't do this, it's not professional, Charlie will kill you!* but I've conjured up the image of Adele sitting beside him on a garden bench at Albert Terrace before she was murdered.

'You must have it on record how many properties I looked at.'

My phone is ringing. I want to ignore it, but it persists.

'Aren't you going to answer?' he asks.

I take it out of my bag. It's Charlie. 'Nothing that can't wait,' I say.

At last he sits down on the other chair. 'What is it you want to know, then? Let's get on with it.'

Whether he believes my lie about a sales promotion is neither here or there. I take the photo out of my bag to show him. He is clearly startled.

'Where did you get this?'

'It is you, isn't it?'

'Who took it?'

'Do you remember going there?'

'How did you get hold of it?'

'So you did go there?'

'I looked at other places before this, but what of it?'

'Can you tell me what you remember about Albert Terrace?'

'Who took this picture?'

'No idea. Thought it might ring a bell with you.'

He's unsettled. Stands up. 'This is a waste of my time. I think you should leave.'

'So was it a property you visited with one of our agents?' He must hear the urgency in my voice.

'Why do you keep going on about it? How many times do I have to say it?' He's raised his voice. Waves his hand over the print and it falls to the floor.

I think he'd like to stamp on it.

'I hate those properties. That's why I bought here.'

'Just part of our survey, James, that's all.'

He sounds so convincing I begin to doubt myself. Perhaps he really doesn't remember going to Albert Terrace. I decide to change the subject and ask him how work is going, how the commute is working out.

'I've been off work.'

'Oh?'

'Medical reasons.'

When I hear this, I feel bad about bothering him. My theories have already started to unravel. When his phone rings I guess it's work-connected, so grab my bag, give a little wave, mouth a thank you and let myself out. I deliberately leave the photo behind. Let him look at it a bit. It might bring back some memories. It would give me a good excuse to go back later if necessary. Of course, I've made a copy.

There was still time for me to get over to Gilbert Avenue to meet the new clients. I phoned, apologised for the delay and said I was on my way. Mr and Mrs Carter are both standing in the garden, and Mr Carter looks pointedly at his watch, then up at the sky before shaking my hand.

'One of you works hard in the garden,' I say brightly. Mrs Carter looks up, but neither reply.

The house smells strongly of chemical cleaning products and any sign of normal daily habitation has been tidied away out of sight. They briskly walk me through the rooms, explaining they want to move to the south coast where their daughter is settled with her partner. 'She's got the little ones now. We can help her out.'

I can't understand why Charlie thinks this property is such a catch, but perhaps he has already got some clients in mind for it. I take some measurements, hand them the brochure with our terms, give a verbal estimate of the kind of price a house like theirs is selling for in this part of town and tell them I'll be in touch. I don't think they are impressed with the estimate and feel sure they will be consulting other agents before committing themselves. I feel exhausted and, looking at my watch, see it's nearly six o'clock, so turn the car in the direction of home.

53

The nearer I get to home, the more my thoughts turn to Paul. I expect to see him outside the flat, but I climb the stairs to see Sam sitting outside on the concrete, leaning back against the door. She's got a grubby roll up between her fingers. I sniff the air. At least it's not dope.

This is a no-smoking building, I should say, but instead put out my hand and haul her to her feet and give her a half-hug. She's on the verge of tears.

'Come in,' I say, 'but put out that cigarette first. Coffee?' I ask. She just nods.

'What's up, Sam?' I ask.

She sits down on the sofa and clutches a cushion to her stomach. 'I think I'm pregnant.'

My heart sinks. It can't be with that weasly, ratty-looking boy-man I saw her with.

'Are you sure?'

She nods, her tears, mingling with snot. I pass her a box of tissues.

'I did a test. It turned blue.'

'Does your father know?'

'What do you think?'

'Do you want to keep it?'

Sam doesn't answer. She keeps the cushion hugged tightly to her stomach as if to announce the baby's here already. Which in a way, it is.

'Perhaps we'd better have a hot chocolate instead,' I say, putting on the kettle. 'Have you told your mother?'

Outside, the leafy trees wave their branches; the sky behind them is dotted with cloud. I would like to turn the clock back a few hours or, better still, a few weeks.

'I can't tell them,' she says at last.

'Well, they'll have to know some time.'

I'm filled with anger with the weasly man-boy. Angry with her parents for allowing their break-up to screw up her teenage years. Guilty with myself for ending it with Simon. Angry with Simon and the woman with the hair extensions. But mostly I feel sad for Sam. Two mugs of chocolate sit on the table between us. It's steamy sugar redolent of lakeside cafes and mountain slopes. Life-enhancing images, how her first pregnancy should be; smiling grandparents, baby clothes. After her big announcement, however, Sam seems to have little else to say.

I try again. 'Does the father know?'

'No. I'm not telling him either.'

'Does he realise this is illegal, that you're underage? And he could go on the sex-offenders register for life?'

She rolls her eyes and looks at me as though I'm mad, but I'm glad to see a hint of defiance return. I wonder why she's chosen to make this big announcement to me.

'Have you seen a doctor?'

'What for?'

'For the baby, of course, not just for you. And you shouldn't be smoking.'

A look of discomfort flickers across her face. She wants to appear grown up.

'I'll go with you if you like.'

The cushion has fallen to the floor. 'This is frigging hot,' she says, picking up the chocolate and putting it down again.

There is a knock at the door and at the same time I hear my phone vibrate.

I glance quickly. It's Paul.

'Shouldn't you get that?' asks Sam.

'It's nothing important.'

The door-bell goes again.

'Somebody wants you bad.'

'Yes,' I say, getting up and going to the door.

Paul stands there. 'Aren't you going to ask me in?' He says. He's reaching for my hands, putting his arms out to touch me. I nod my head in the direction of the sitting room, trying to indicate I've got a visitor.

'If it's my father or his new bride, tell them to go home.'

Hearing voices, Sam comes to the door. She takes in the situation and pushes past us. 'I can see you're busy,' she spits out.

'No, wait Sam,' I say.

I try to catch her arm but she pulls away. Paul looks at us, trying to figure out what's going on but Sam is tripping down the stairs without a backward glance.

'Who's that,' asks Paul. 'Not your secret love-child, is she?'

I suddenly feel weary. Weary of Sam, weary of life. I seem to spend my time lately not sure what to tell people, uncomfortable with the truth about everything.

'It's a young girl I know,' I say. 'She came for some advice.'

'I'm sure she came to the right place.'

I think of how I've waited for him, longed to hear his voice, or his footstep on the stair, just wanting his presence but now I just feel confused.

'Just came down to tell you my taxi's due in ten minutes.'

'So soon?'

'Afraid so. Wanted to tell you I really enjoyed last night.'

'Me too.'

'So, do I get a goodbye kiss?' he asks. He takes my hand and pulls me towards him.

'I'm going to miss you,' he says.

'Me too.' His rough stubble brushes my cheek. It's a vivid memory of our first encounter, here, in this hallway. I'd give anything to get that moment back but we pull apart and he turns away, closing the door behind him. The second person to walk out on me in less than five minutes. I walk through the sitting room, pick up two mugs of cold chocolate and empty them down the sink. With Paul gone, I don't know how I'll fill my nights.

54

I am unable to sleep. I turn the pillow this way and that.
Get up and make myself some camomile tea, look for a
book to read. I come across Madame Bovary, dusty and
long-forgotten. I never did get a copy of Gatsby. But why
would I anyway, I would never go back to the book club
where I was likely to meet Rob. But is Rob really so bad?
After all, he did voluntarily give me a copy of that photo
print of Adele and James Batley. I thought back to my
afternoon visit to Riverside Apartments. Surely Batley
holds some sort of clue. But perhaps he genuinely didn't
recognise Adele in the photo. Perhaps he had made an
innocent visit to view Albert Terrace and had forgotten. It
happens. And what about Luk? I hadn't been able to find
out anything about him. Who he was, where he was. Back
in Romania probably. Or wherever it was he came from.
I ask myself why I'm letting these thoughts rob me of my
sleep. I wish I had someone to talk it over with. If Paul was
here... somehow my thoughts reach back to Simon. Simon
has issues of his own to deal with now. About to become
a grandfather. The thought makes me smile. I must fall
asleep eventually, because when I come to, it's morning.

There's a missed call on my phone. Paul has texted to say missing you already.

Charlie asks how I got on with the Carters and what did I think of their property.

'Let's wait and see,' I say. 'They haven't decided to go with us yet.'

'How did things go at Albert Terrace?'

'Oh, you know.'

'What do you think of the clean up?'

Now is the time to tell Charlie I've changed my mind. Let Jason take it over. 'Clean-up is a strange way to describe it, but I'm sure someone will love it,' I say.

'Yes, that's what Jason said. We'll do a new brochure and email details out. You might have some thoughts yourself.'

I really want nothing more to do with Albert Terrace, but somehow I'm not saying it.

'Charlie?'

'Hmm?'

'Remember what we talked about at New Year. At your party?'

'What about it?'

'Adele having a boyfriend... you thought she'd had a bust up.'

'So?'

'Do you think it could have been a client? Someone she met in the course of her work?'

'What makes you think that?'

'She would have found it difficult to say, wouldn't she? Would have wanted to keep quiet about it, you know, ethics and that...'

'Do you know something you're not telling me?'

I could tell him about the photo. He can't have any awareness of its existence. I could say something about James Batley. But what could I say that made any sense. I think it best to sit on it for a few days. Wait until I've got more evidence.

'No, I'm just speculating I guess.'

Next morning is quiet in the office. I keep going over old ground, old thoughts that seem to lead nowhere. I suddenly have the urge to go back to Riverside and have another go at James Batley. I have the excuse of the photo I left behind. That should be enough. But I'm surprised to see him walk through the door just before midday.

'I've been thinking it over,' he says. 'I can't take part in your promotion.'

I blink, momentarily forgetting what he was talking about.

'Because I don't believe that you're having one,' he continues, looking me straight in the eye. 'In fact, I think your visit to me yesterday was just a ruse. Actually a lie.'

Well, at least he's got straight to the point. 'I'm sorry, Mr Batley, but…'

'If you persist in harassing me at my home, I shall have no alternative but to take action.'

It's obvious he hasn't spoken to Charlie. Charlie would have called me out of bed at midnight with a complaint like that. I feel like laughing out loud. Once I would have felt a cold shiver at his words, but now, even the thought of him talking to P.O. Morgan and D.I. Naomi is quite a comfort. I know they'd be on my side. They would know that I was doing it to help their enquiries into two gruesome murders. I would like to tell Batley this, put him in the frame.

'And here's your photo.'

He slings the now grubby-looking A 4 sheet down onto my desk. 'I suppose you deliberately left it behind, so you could bother me again when you came back to collect it.'

He's sharper than I thought. 'I can assure you, Mr Batley, I had no such thoughts.' I feel a bubbling up of mirth, but try to suppress it.

'I don't know what your game is but...'

Suddenly all thoughts of mirth leave me. I have had a lapse of judgment, been unprofessional. If he complained to Charlie, it would lead me into deep trouble. 'I'm sorry, Mr Batley. It was wrong of me...'

'I'm not interested in your apologies. Don't bother to tell me. I don't want to know. Just keep away.'

With that, he turns and walks to the door and doesn't bother closing it as he leaves. Which is handy for Jason who is just walking through it.

'Who's that?' he asks. 'He looks familiar.'

'He's the man who bought Riverside.'

'Problems already?'

'Came to complain that he'd been told a person had taken his life there and we should have told him before he bought it.'

'Some people want it with jam on it, don't they?'

55

Dad called me later that evening. It had been my turn to call and I feel bad when I remember how little we've spoken recently.

He asks, 'how are you?'

I say, 'Fine, Dad, I was just about to phone you. How are you?'

'Oh, fine. Auntie Jean's flat seems to have been sold – anyway, it's all going through.'

'The Animal Sanctuary will be happy. One less thing for you to worry about.'

'Oh, I wasn't worried.'

It occurs to me that he might have enjoyed the active involvement of sorting out probate. Gave him something to think about, something to do.

'How are you really, Dad?'

'OK.'

I know he'd like me to say I was coming up to see him. This weekend. Soon. But he is too proud to ask. 'I'll try to come up to see you soon, Dad,' I say.

'Oh, I know you're busy. Come whenever you can, it will be nice to see you.'

I try to think what it is that's keeping me from saying I'll visit him at the weekend. Paul is away. Charlie wouldn't mind, though I don't want to be away from the office too long with Jason getting his feet so comfortably under the table.

'I'll look at my diary,' I say. 'There's quite a lot going on at the office at the moment, but I'll come up as soon as I can.'

'I'll look forward to it,' he says.

I blow a kiss down the phone and he rings off.

I sit there for quite a while. I think about how long it is since I had a break of any sort. Adele and I sometimes talked about taking a holiday together, but we never did. Who would I go with? Paul seems to work all the time and he's gone anyway. He gave me no clue as to when he was coming back. Simon and I took a couple of long breaks in the country when we were first together, but traipsing through a muddy field never appealed to me. And now he's got Sam to think about. I wonder when that bombshell's going to drop. What's the betting he'll be on the phone to me as soon as he hears about the pregnancy? I send a text to Sam, get in touch if you want, but there's no reply.

As I can't think of anything better to do, I go back to Albert Terrace and take another tour of number three. I never told Charlie that I didn't want to take it on. Maybe it will be easier this time. In fact, I tour the premises methodically and take a number of photos for the new brochure. The kitchen, the sitting room and the bedrooms. I try to avert the lens from the spot where I think the body was found. I go into the back garden and this time have a wander round. It's a rather uninteresting space; a path runs down the centre cutting it in two, boasting one or two dry and untended bushes and a brick wall at the bottom. I take another couple of photos looking back up at the house and it's then I glance up and see Rob watching me from what I now know to be his bathroom window. I wonder if he's taking my photo. Nothing would surprise me. I glance away, but not before I see him wave. I don't wave back but make my way back into the house. I hear the doorbell and see his shape through the glass in the front door. Will it be the same every time I visit this place? Perhaps I should have listened to my instincts to have nothing to do with it.

'You again, Rob. Can't keep away, can you?'

'I thought I saw your car,' he says.

'And…? So every time you see a red Clio in the street, you're going to come and harass me?'

I don't know why I use that word. It was the word James Batley said to me earlier.

'Rob, I'd like to ask you something.'

'What?'

'That photo you gave me the other day. I should have asked you at the time, but did you know who it was – the man in the photo?'

'What do you mean?'

'I think you know what I mean. Did you or didn't you?'

Rob stands there on the doorstep, looking down at his feet, over towards the front gate, then up at the sky. I think he'll stick his thumbs into his belt hooks soon and start whistling.

'Well, did you?'

'I was wondering when you'd ask me that,' he says at last.

I was right. There is more he can tell me. 'Well?' I say again, trying a different tone.

'Well,' he counters. 'We can't talk here on the doorstep. Come down to mine. I'll make you a cup of tea. I'll share my thoughts.'

I admit to a twinge of doubt, but I'm no longer anxious about being alone with him 'OK' I say. 'I'll be with you in a minute.'

He leaves and I'm checking I've locked up and collected my things when the doorbell goes again. Now what does he want, I think. I'm already regretting having agreed to go back to his house. But it's a woman standing on the doorstep.

'Forgive me for intruding,' she says. 'But I had to come over – seeing your car outside.'

That blasted car again. It's like a red flag. Next time I'm going to have one of those anonymous-looking silver jobs. 'How can I help you?' I say brightly.

She's a middle-aged sort of woman, with complicated hair, wearing a purple smock over the ubiquitous leggings. I try to think positive. Maybe she has a house to sell.

'I'm glad this place isn't going to be left empty indefinitely,' she says. 'Gives me the creeps. That poor girl. My name's Cynthia. Cynthia Mason.'

At first, I think the 'poor girl' is Adele, but then realise she's talking about the woman who was murdered here. I wonder if she knows anything about it, but the police must have spoken to her on one of their door-to-door enquiries.

'I live just over the way,' she says, 'Number ten. We've lived there for twenty years.' She's pointing vaguely down the street in the opposite direction to Rob's house. 'I expect you know Rob Green. He keeps an eye on everything. I'm surprised he didn't see anything happen here.'

I nod encouragingly.

'It's good to have a neighbour like that. Makes you feel safer in your bed at night.' I'm not sure I'd feel safer having Rob for a neighbour. 'Is there anything I can help you with today?' I ask, searching in my bag for a card to leave her with.

'I've seen the owner here a few times recently'

'Oh?'

'Yes, well he lives abroad, doesn't he? I suppose he thought he'd left his house in good hands.'

She means us. Fortune Estates. I don't like the way the conversation is going. 'Well, must get on, Mrs… err… Mrs…' I hold out the card for her but she doesn't take it.

'I never liked him.'

Are we still talking about Rob? 'Do you mean Mr Green,' I say?

'No. No. As I said, he keeps a eye on things. No I meant the owner, Fuller's his name.'

I'm surprised to hear the name. In all our dealings with number three I don't think I ever heard his name mentioned. 'Oh, you know him then?'

'Well, I couldn't say I know him. He did live here a couple of years back and I used to see him come and go. He wasn't a friendly type.'

'No?'

'Not at all friendly. I saw him over here a couple of months back, earlier in the year, while it was being done up. I came over to say hello, but he was very off-hand. Didn't really want to know. Suppose he's gone back to Spain.'

I give her a sympathetic nod. 'Well, that's a shame, in a friendly neighbourhood like this,' I say. 'It's been nice talking to you, Mrs… Mason, is it? I hope we get a nice new neighbour in here for you soon.'

Mrs Mason looks doubtful. 'Well, it won't be the easiest house to sell, will it?'

I give her a look, which she misinterprets.

'With all the horror that went on here, I mean. We saw it, Geoffrey and I. Men coming and going at all hours. Those girls too, so young, we'd see them smoking on the doorstep sometimes. I felt sorry for them really. I tried to speak to one of them once, but she couldn't understand a word I said. We reported it to the police, but nothing happened. They never even sent anybody to take a statement. Then it ends in murder and you couldn't move for police cars.'

'How long did all this go on for, Mrs Mason?'

'Can't be sure, but as I told the police it was probably the best part of three months.'

I'm shocked to hear this. Adele said she'd only let Luk have the key for a few days. Why would she lie about that? It didn't make sense. Surely if the police had been notified there was a brothel operating in this quiet street, it would have been investigated and closed down straight away?

'Are you quite sure it was as long as that, Mrs Mason?'

Mrs Mason looks offended. 'If you lived down here, dear, you'd have known all about it. '

'Well, we'll be keeping a close eye on the place now it's back on the market. If you've got any concerns…' I hand her my card, which she glances at but, having no pockets in her leggings, is uncertain what to do with it. She'll probably throw it away as soon as she gets home.

I look at my watch and see it's late afternoon already. It's only when I get back to the office and I'm putting the kettle on when I remember I didn't go to Rob's for the cup of tea and the "thoughts" he promised.

56

Jason is around in the office for once, so we exchange a few words on how busy we are, though there's no sign of it. I don't say anything to him about the Hill Vale incident. Perhaps it would be best to let it drop. I leave early and tell him I've got work to catch up on at home.

I find a letter from Beryl. She asks why I didn't keep my last appointment, and offers me another. I think I'm going to tell her I don't need any more therapy. At about six-thirty Simon rings. I've been expecting him to call.

'Sam says she's told you.'

'Yes, she's told me.' It's obvious he means the pregnancy but he'll find it hard to say the words.

'I don't know what to say,' says Simon. 'I mean I don't know what to say to Sam.'

'Perhaps it's best to leave the talking to Annie,' I say. 'Perhaps Sam would rather talk to her mother about it.'

'She wants to keep it,' he says at last. 'But that's impossible.'

'Well…' I counter.

'She's not even fourteen,' he explodes, showing his feelings for the first time.

'These things happen,' I say. How trite I sound.

'But how could it have happened?'

I smile in spite of myself. I remember him telling me proudly, yet anxiously, what seems to be a long time ago, that she was a woman now.

'In the usual way,' I say. 'We were all young once…'

Simon, rightly, ignores this. I try to bring my thoughts into focus.

'Is there somebody outside the family who can offer her some counselling? The pregnancy isn't too advanced yet, so there's time for her…'

'Well, Annie and I both thought you might talk to her. She won't discuss it with either of us.'

'I don't think I'm the best person.'

'But she came to you in the first place.'

This is undisputed. I try to imagine a conversation with her parents. The shock, the tears, the shouts. I can't imagine any hugs or talk of carry-cots and Pampers. As soon as she sees a doctor and the pregnancy is confirmed, social services will be involved.

'I'm sure there are professionals who are better at this sort of thing,' I say.

'She's refusing to do anything. She's stopped going to school. There'll be questions asked about that soon. She spends all day in her room listening to music on her headphones, lying on her bed trying to think up baby names. Simon's voice is full of despair. I hear it clearly. I hear it in a way that reminds me of the absence of passion in our own relationship. Once again, I am forced to accept, as I'd accepted it nearly a year ago, there can never be anything more between us. It even occurs to me that having this huge new complication in their daughter's life could bring him and Annie back together.

'I think the first thing is for Sam to see a doctor. Get this baby confirmed, then she will get plenty of advice about her health and well-being. She will be in a better position to look at her choices.'

This is not news to Simon. He and Annie know all this. I'm thinking and talking like Beryl. Maybe it would be a new career for me when Charlie throws me out. I wonder what training you need. I'll look into it when I've got a minute. My thoughts return to Sam. Part of me hopes she'll decide not to keep it. Not to throw away her youth so carelessly. I try to think myself into her situation, but fail.

'Sam knows she can call me whenever she wants to. I'll back her up whatever she decides.'

Simon mutters a brief thank you and cuts off.

Next day, I get a text from Sam wanting me to go with her to the doctor.

57

Sam's appointment is for ten o'clock. She asks me to pick her up at her father's house, but there's no sign of Simon. We check into the new surgery, its huge glass windows shedding a bright light over warnings about flu jabs. On a screen above our heads, pictures of grated carrots and slices of apple play on a continuous loop. I glance through a four-year-old copy of *Yachting Life*, and wish I'd bought along some back issues of *Marie Claire* as a contribution to the meagre reading distractions on offer. Sam fiddles with her phone. I wonder if she feels nervous. She looks pale and apart from saying she hasn't started feeling sick yet, has said very little. For the first time, I wonder if it isn't all a mistake. That she misunderstood the test result, whether she is imagining it all. We sit for half an hour behind an elderly couple. The woman's hand has a tremor; the man holds a stick. A mother tries to pacify an unhappy baby. I glance at Sam but she is too absorbed in her phone to notice anything. A smart young woman consults her watch. How skilled is a GP, I think, to manage the mysterious and varied problems brought daily to their attention.

Sam's name comes up on the screen, and we walk the few yards into the consulting room. Even though it's been over a year, I recognise Dr Elliott straight away.

'What can I do for you today?' she asks.

I'm feeling confused. It had never occurred to me that Sam's appointment was with the woman whose house I valued last year. I look at Sam. We've already agreed that she will do the talking, and I'm only there to offer support. She stares past the doctor, and in a muffled voice says, 'I think I'm pregnant.'

Dr Elliott shows no surprise. She probably deals with this sort of thing every day. 'And why do you think that?' She asks. 'Have you had sex with your boyfriend?'

'He's not my boyfriend anymore,' she says swiftly, eyes fixed on her mobile. 'I did a test, it turned blue.'

'I see from your notes you're thirteen,' says Dr Elliott.

As this is an indisputable fact, neither Sam nor I bother to reply.

'I'll be fourteen once the baby's born, though,' says Sam somewhat triumphantly. 'I want to keep it.'

'And do your parents know?'

Sam nods.

I feel it necessary to chip in with, 'I'm a friend of the family, I'm here to support Sam.'

'She was my Dad's girlfriend, but they split up,' Sam contributes unhelpfully.

'Well, do you think you could do a urine sample for me?' asks Dr Elliott, handing her a cardboard dish, 'in there.' She nods towards the door of a toilet. 'And when you come back, I'll take some details and do your blood tests. You'll need a referral to the hospital so they can keep an eye on you and the baby.'

Sam picks up the dish and leaves the room.

'I take it the parents are supportive?' Dr Elliott asks me.

'Well, they're shocked, of course, but…'

'I'll talk to Sam, but I can refer the family to Social Services. They will help her plan her future.'

I am grateful that help will be available. I picture a friendly social worker, a bright young woman with short spiky hair and ethnic earrings, someone a bit like me, but more useful. Somebody to help her with her choices.

'Of course,' I say.

I'm not sure whether Dr Janice recognises me or not. She shows no sign, but perhaps that's her style. Professional. Impersonal. I remember the day I did the valuation of her house. The kitchen granite chill. The enigmatic husband, also a doctor.

Wasn't Marek your gardener too? I almost blurt out, but remember not to in time. I try to catch my thoughts but they seem to be running away from me too fast.

Sam comes back into the room. 'I couldn't manage much,' she says.

'It'll be enough,' says Dr Elliott. She's got a firm manner, but is not unfriendly. 'I want you to make another appointment for a week's time. Try asking one of your parents to accompany you.'

She looks at me and says, 'By all means come too, if Sam asks you.' Sam and I rise together and thank the doctor, who's turned back to her computer screen, already updating her records.

58

I should go back to Albert Terrace and see Rob again. Find out what it was he wanted to tell me, though I expect it was probably just another excuse and he will make up something about book club. I drop Sam back at Simon's place, but don't go in with her. She doesn't have much to say on the way, but I think she must feel better about her situation now she's seen a medical professional. I go on into the office and am preparing myself for the trip to Albert Terrace when Charlie hears me and puts his head round the door.

"I've got something for you, Hanna."

'Yes?'

'Remember that hoax email we got about the house up at Hill Vale?'

Charlie has generously used the collective term "we". I remember it all too well. Jason ratting on me. Reading my emails. I never did manage to have it out with him.

'Yes.'

'Turns out it wasn't a hoax after all. Well, I don't know who sent it. It could even have been a neighbour fed up with seeing it so neglected, but I've had a visit from a Miss

Sanders. She's been working abroad. Her father died some time back. She's got probate sorted and she wants to put it on the market. We'll need to get the legal side checked, but it's good news for us.'

I think back to the visit I made months back. The empty property, the man with the dog.

'It's been empty for ages,' he'd said.

'So what was it all about then – the strange email?' I think it's quite brave of me to bring up my own foolish involvement, rushing off, telling nobody, on the strength of it. I know Charlie won't have forgotten. He never forgets that sort of misdemeanour. I'm surprised he hasn't given Hill Vale to Jason.

'Don't you want to give it to Jason?'

'Jason's got enough on his plate,' he replies.

I think back to Jason sitting at his empty desk yesterday, doing nothing.

'Well, if you're sure, of course,' I say. 'Yes, of course I'll take it.'

'I've got the keys. She wants a valuation, ASAP.'

Everything with Charlie is always ASAP.

'What's the rush, when it's been empty for so long?' I don't know why I say that. Charlie looks at me, but I can't read his thoughts.

'ASAP.' Is all he says.

*

It's a lovely drive out to Hill Vale. The sun is still high in the sky though it's already late August, the verges listing with an over-abundance of dark green hedgerow lowering down onto yellow dried-up grass and weeds. I search for some music and sing along... La mer, da didi da... I need to put aside my own troubles for a while. Sam needs me to help her over the coming months and who knows, maybe beyond that. I wonder if I could manage to let her and the baby stay with me for a while – we'd be crowded, but... I haven't heard from Paul since he left but, somehow, I feel sure that I will quite soon. Things will take their course.

Maybe it's time for me to accept I will never be the one to solve the mysteries surrounding Albert Terrace. Maybe it's time to move on, to set it aside and let Naomi and P.O. Morgan do their work. I hope they are still working on the case. I should phone and try to find out.

I turn into Hill Vale and once again slow down, looking out for number eight. I can roughly remember how far along it is. There's no sign of the man with the dog today. I reach the house and turn into the drive. There's a slight incline on the gravel slope up to the house, so I park half way under a tree and walk the rest. The sun is still high and feeling warm. I remove my jacket, slinging it over my arm. The property is double-fronted and probably dates from the 1920s. When I put the key in the lock, it turns smoothly and the hallway is immediately filled with shadowy light from outside. A large dusty cobweb wafts over my head in the unexpected breeze. Fortunately, there's no sign of the spider. The usual junk mail and flyers litter the hallway. There is a stuffy, unused smell and it's obvious the place has been empty for some time. I leave the door ajar to let in some air. The once beautiful parquet floors are covered with indifferent looking bits of carpet that look like off-cuts. I turn right into the first downstairs room and immediately understand why Charlie is so keen to get his hands on this one. The room is a huge square, with high ceilings and cornices. A fireplace, unused for years, sits along one wall, its wooden surround carved with fruit and vines. The hearth is a mess of feathers and twigs where a bird once made its nest in the chimney. The leaded windows let in shafts of light. Dust motes, startled by the intrusion, hover uncertainly in the air and it's evident everything could do with a good clean, better still, a coat of paint. We need to suggest this to the owner and arrange something before we book any viewings. I think an open day would be perfect for this house. Ideally, it's the kind of place you want to find properly furnished with leather sofas, velvety cushions, and faded rugs. An enviable, old fashioned house where in the kitchen, mother is making jam from blackcurrants that father tends in the garden when he gets home from the city. Thoughts of Paul come unaccountably into my head. Two children, a boy and a girl, the boy a little older and taller plays with his aeroplane running in and out of the rooms, while the little girl, I think her name is Maisie, is dressing her dolls. The kitchen at the back of the house has hardly changed from the day it was built. No modern extension, no conservatory. A dark oak dresser stands against the wall, just waiting for jars of sugar and flour. I think mother has help from the village, a friendly soul who comes in daily with advice about white vinegar and a chat about local dark practices.

My daydreams are interrupted by a scuffling noise coming from overhead. I tiptoe up the wide, uncarpeted staircase. Glancing into the bathroom, I see that very little has been altered. The big old bath tub, still in decent condition, has a blue streaked water stain running down to the drain. The deep hand basin with its brass taps sits stately on its pedestal, thick square tiles cover the walls, the grouting worn to a dull grey. I hear a scratching sound coming from somewhere – perhaps mice have got in, it wouldn't be surprising, or squirrels in the loft, but when I walk into the first bedroom I see a black cat, in the corner, crouching terrified on bare boards. There's no obvious smell of cat piss, so he can't have been here long. It's wearing a red collar but I can't get close enough to read it.

'Come on, puss,' I say, reaching out my hand. He hisses as I approach. I make a little clucking sound. 'Are you hungry?' The cat stares back with its big yellow eyes then after a bit more clucking, cautiously pads towards me. 'How did you get in, then?' The cat, anticipating salvation, lets me pick it up. Underneath the crouching and the hissing, it's quite tame. From the collar I see his name is Freddie and there is a telephone number. 'We'll put you outside, shall we. Somebody will be missing you.'

The cat is now pushing its nose upwards towards my face. Its whiskers tickle my throat. I'm wondering how he got in. I hope there's no broken window. Still carrying him I go downstairs and make my way through the kitchen to the garden door. It's locked and there's no obvious sign of a key. I must make a note of that. Through the scullery window, I glimpse a decent sized garden with a pond at the bottom with a statue and a fountain. I walk back through the hall and carefully let go of the cat. He runs quickly out of the open front door and away across the gravel into the bushes. I go back through each room in turn, methodically taking measurements and making note of any original features, trying to imagine the lives of the people who once lived here, or of those to come. But like the cat, they slip away. I take a number of photos on my phone before leaving.

I haven't been home long before there's a ring at the bell. Mrs Baxter-Sellers is standing there. I still haven't heard from Paul, and I long to know if he's contacted his father, and whether there is any news of his return.

'Come in,' I say, opening the door wide. 'I was just about to make a cup of tea.'

'I don't want to be any trouble, dear, I know you've had a hard day at work, and please call me Elaine.'

I reflect on my afternoon up at Hill Vale. How could anybody think of that as hard work? I brush my hand over my forehead as though removing sweat caused by exhaustion. Elaine has already stepped inside.

'Don't bother about the tea, dear, I'll be cooking Jack's supper soon.'

What a lucky man is Jack, I think. Fallen right on his feet.

'I've come to let you know Jack and I are putting the flat back on the market. We've decided to move.'

'Oh.' I reply. Since their marriage, I'd expected them to stay put forever. 'How nice,' I say at last. 'Where are you planning to go?'

'We haven't made any decisions yet, but Jack wants to find somewhere with a garden, for Bobby, you know.'

Ah, yes. The dog. 'Well, this is a surprise. Would you like Fortunes to help?'

'Well, that's why I came to you first.'

Jack must have hidden resources, I think, if he thinks they can buy a bigger place with a garden on the sale of the flat upstairs. But then, perhaps he has savings from the sale of his former life.

'I'll tell Charlie first thing in the morning,' I say. 'Then I'll make a proper appointment to come up and talk to you both. I'll be sorry to see you go.' It's almost an afterthought, and although it sounds automatic, I realise I shall miss her.

'Have you heard from Paul?' I ask. She looks a bit surprised. I wonder how much she and Jack know about Paul and me.

'I'm not sure if Jack has spoken to him since he left.'

'Oh?'

'Well, you know how men are.'

I wonder what she means. I fumble around for the right response. 'Do you expect him back soon?'

She is looking at me now, questioning. As though for the first time, 'You'd have to ask Jack.'

I look away, wanting her to think it's just a routine, friendly enquiry. Trying not to show my heart might break. She must have noticed my face turn red.

'I'll phone you tomorrow,' I say. 'About the flat.'

'Thank you, dear. By the way, I meant to tell you, that young man with the bicycle has been looking for you.' She's frowning.

Man with the bicycle. She must mean Rob. 'He's just a friend,' I say, 'there's nothing…'

'How lovely for you to be so young and carefree,' she says, getting up and walking to the door.

I could spit. Why does Rob keep turning up in this

way? Mrs Baxter-Sellers is shrewd. If she knows I've been seeing Paul, she probably thinks I'm two-timing him.

'Goodbye, dear, I'll hear from you tomorrow, then.'

In the silence that follows, I hear faint footfall overhead, followed by something dropped, and the banging of a cupboard door. No doubt Elaine is already peeling potatoes for Jack's supper.

The thought makes me feel hungry. I look in the fridge wondering what I might find. I haven't planned anything and I haven't been shopping. There's some cheese, but no milk or bread. I pick up my purse, ready to go to the shop, when there is another ring at the doorbell. It must be Elaine come back. She's remembered news of Paul after all and she's come to let me know he's longing to see me and will be back very soon.

59

Rob stands at the door. He's carried his bicycle up to the landing and is fiddling with the padlock.

'Can't be too careful,' he says.

'What is it, Rob?'

'I was expecting you, you know, after we last spoke – you were supposed to come over.' He's obviously hoping to be invited in.

'I've been busy,' I say.

'Me too,' he replies.

It occurs to me that I have no idea what his day job is. Perhaps he's a courier, that's why his bike is so precious to him.

'I've been too busy to do any shopping. I was just about to…'

'I haven't eaten either. We could chat over a bite – if you want, of course.'

I think quickly. Anything would be better than asking him in. 'Well, it would have to be quick – I've got a lot of paper work to catch up on,' I lie.

'Do you mind if I leave my bike inside? It'll be safer.'

I'm already regretting agreeing to eat with him. I wait

on the landing while he manoeuvres the bike past me and props it against the wall.

'Got your key? He asks.

We walk down the street to the mall and go into the first place we see that's open.

*

'I think this is where we once had coffee,' he says. 'Somewhere near here, anyway.'

I give him only a brief smile, not caring to re-enforce any sense of past intimacies. It's early evening and there aren't many other diners. The waitress smiles and asks if we'd like something to drink. Rob orders a beer and, though I hadn't planned to, I hear myself ask for a glass of house white.

'What is it, Rob? What is it you wanted to tell me?'

The music is loud and I have to lean towards him to catch his mumbled reply. A plump girl wearing a checked apron brings the drinks. 'Ready to order food?' she asks.

'Give us a minute,' says Rob. He raises his glass. 'Here's to us,' he says. 'Here's to the truth.'

'What truth is that?' I ask.

The wine is very cold and rather delicious. A small gnat, black and drowning has fallen in. I try to fish it out with a spoon.

'I've wanted to talk to you for ages,' he says. 'Really talk, I mean.'

Rob is not really talking. He's only talking about talking. He wipes his mouth with his sleeve and leans over towards me. The couple of sips of wine have already reached my legs and I know I should eat something soon. The waitress returns, smiling patiently, waiting for us to order.

'I'll have the Niçoise,' I say.

'Same for me,' says Rob.

The waitress keeps smiling. She thinks we're a couple. I lean back in my seat and wonder why I'm here.

'Rob,' I say. 'Is this a pretext? Just a ploy to get me here?'

'Of course,' he replies. 'What else?'

I'm too tired to smile or even be angry. I realise that he has no intention of sharing any more information about Albert Terrace. I doubt he has anything new to say. I've hardly touched my wine, but somehow the glass is almost empty.

Rob waves at the waitress and holds his fingers up in the air. 'Two more,' I hear him say.

'Actually, Rob, I've had enough.'

The waitress arrives with the food and more drinks. The tuna sits fat and pink beside black-eyed olives and yellow wedges of egg, all balanced uneasily on unidentifiable leaves.

'This looks good,' says Rob. 'You should eat something,' he adds.

We stay silent for what feels like too long, chewing and avoiding eye contact.

'I expect you miss your friend.' he says at last.

How does he know about Paul? Has he been watching me? Taking photos?

'Your friend, Adele,' he says.

I wonder how long it is since I heard anybody speak her name.

'Yes,' I say, 'I miss her a lot.'

'You and she were close, I think.'

What a trite remark. What business has he to even mention her in this way. Then I recall the reason why I'm sitting here.

'You know something, don't you, Rob?'

He is carefully probing his tuna. It falls away tenderly from the knife, revealing its fleshy, undercooked heart.

'This is good', he says.

When I don't respond, he looks up and I ask again. 'What is it you want to tell me?'

He puts down his fork and wipes his lips on a paper napkin. A small morsel of fish is caught in his beard. As he speaks, it works loose before dropping into his lap. Without thinking, I take swift gulp from my glass before remembering I hadn't intended to.

'I should have said more at the start,' he says.

'Go on.'

'It's about the photograph.' he says at last.

I'm exasperated by his slow holding back which seems deliberate, but try not to show it.

'You're such a tease,' I say.

He laughs and waves his knife towards the waitress who is now busy with other early diners filling the empty tables.

He nods at my almost full wine glass. 'Isn't it any good?' He asks. 'Can I get you something else?'

'What I'd like, Rob, is for you to get to the point of why we're here.'

'Yes, of course. Well I think you already know, I did see Adele a couple of times in Albert Terrace. She always gave me a smile and we once said good morning or afternoon.

That was all really. But she is, was, a good-looking girl. People came and went from number three, then one day I saw her walking down the street with a man. It seemed more than just work.'

Luk, I'm thinking to myself. He'd seen Luk. He would be able to recognise him in a police line-up. I keep looking at him, wanting to encourage him to say more. I take a gulp from my glass and feel a slight twinge of dull ache start over my left eye.

'And?'

'I was a bit pissed, but thought no more about it. Then I heard voices, laughs, coming from the garden. I looked out of the upstairs window. They were sitting together on the garden seat. It didn't look like a normal viewing, not professional, and I suppose I felt angry, resentful, that she was giving all this attention to a stranger. I took their photo. I admit I took more than one. Whether I planned to show them to her boss or use it in some other way, I don't know. But anyway, I took it. Then I felt ashamed. That's why I told the police I knew nothing.'

Rob has finished the tuna, has given up on the salad and pushes it aside. His beer glass is empty.

'So?'

'Well, the thing is, I recognised the man she was with.'

My God. There is a buzzing in my head like a swarm of angry wasps. He knows Luk, is this what he's telling me? Is this confession going to lead to Luk?

'So, who was it?' I try to keep my voice calm, though I'd like to reach over, grab him by the collar and shake it out of him.

'The man's name was Batley. James Batley.'

I feel at once a let down. A strange mix of disappointment that he's not telling me anything I don't already know, but relief that he can corroborate James Batley's identity.

I sit back in the seat and finish my wine. Part of me can't wait to leave, but the other part doesn't want to miss any further revelations. I try to hide disappointment that his confession hasn't brought me any closer to Luk.

'How do you know James Batley? Is he a friend, or acquaintance of yours?'

'Nothing like that. I'm surprised you didn't recognise him yourself. It was in the papers. He'd not long been out of prison. Insider trading or something.'

Now why didn't that surprise me. I think of my recent visit to Riverside Apartments. It explained a lot.

'Did you ever see Adele with any other man, in the garden?' I try.

He looks surprised. 'I wasn't keeping notes. Wasn't that shifty bastard enough? I would have liked to warn her, but then it was too late."

'Do the police know?'

'What about?'

'Well, who you'd seen.'

'God no.'

'Don't you think you should say something?'

Despite the warmth of the restaurant and the laughter from the surrounding tables, I feel a cold shiver on the back of my neck. My thoughts turn now to getting home, with Rob at my side, and his bicycle in my hall. I tell myself not to worry. The twinge over my eye hasn't gone away. If anything, it is developing into a full-blown headache. Surely the police would have recognised Batley if he was as infamous as Rob said. I think he's waffling, not really trying to help at all.

'I'd like to go,' I say.

'Don't you want coffee?' he asks.

I shake my head. He probably hopes I'm going to invite him in when we get back to the flat.

'I'll need to collect my bike,' he says, unnecessarily.

We walk the short distance in silence. I lead the way up the stairs, planning to open the door and wait outside while he collects his bike. Paul is standing outside the flat, leaning against the door.

'I thought I heard footsteps,' says Paul. 'I hoped it was you.'

If Rob is surprised, he doesn't show it. He takes in the situation, nods an "all right?" in Paul's direction, carefully unlocks his bike and manoeuvres it onto the landing.

'Night, then,' he says, giving another nod before disappearing down the stairs.

'Just a work colleague,' I say, as we instinctively move closer together and our lips meet.

Much later, he tells me he is staying for another week, but will spend most of it in London where he has a round of interviews. He doesn't say what the interviews are for, or who with and I don't ask. I get this fantastical thought that he's some sort of international spy, caught up in a glamorous world of mystery and travel. When I voice this, he just laughs.

60

Next morning, I wake to the sound of pouring rain. Paul leaves early and, as I get into the shower, I know I ought to go into the office and bring Charlie up to date on the house at Hill Vale but I can't get thoughts of my conversation with Rob and his connection to James Batley out of my head. I find the card I'm looking for and pick up the phone.

'P.O. Morgan speaking.'

Even though I've dialled his number, I'm surprised to hear his voice. I try to remember when we last spoke. It must have been when he came to tell me about... when he came to interview me about... I've so successfully blotted out all memories of the woman with the hair extensions, I can hardly remember her name.

'Do you remember me, it's Hanna... Hanna Summers?'

'Hello, Hanna.'

His voice sounds just the same. He doesn't seem surprised to hear me. Now that I've got his attention, I can't quite remember what it is I want to say.

'How have you been keeping?' he asks.

'Very well. Well, well enough,' I say.

'Have you called for an update?' he asks.

I think quickly. That must be the reason I've called him.

'Have you got anything new?' I ask.

It's a comfort to be able to slip so easily into this conversation. It's as though he's been waiting for me to call and will know exactly what to tell me.

'We're still following several lines of enquiry,' he says.

I am disappointed at this reply. It sounds just like the sort of thing a policemen would say in a TV detective drama when he knows more than he wants to give away.

'That's what you said last time,' I reply.

P.O. Morgan laughs. A short laugh and I realise it's the first time I ever heard him do anything so normal.

'There's nothing new I can tell you, Hanna,' he says. 'But as soon as there are any new developments, I can assure you, you will be the first to hear. Did you phone for any special reason?'

This would be the moment to ask him if he knows about James Batley and his visit to Albert Terrace. To ask if he's spoken to Rob. If Rob has shown him the photograph of James Batley sitting with Adele on the garden bench.

'No special reason,' I say. 'But I'm glad to hear you're still working on the case.'

'You can be sure of that,' he says. 'The case will always be open until we have reason to close it.'

'A reason to close it?' I echo. 'What does that mean?'

'When we reach a conclusion, of course.'

The day passes slowly. I text Sam to ask how the meeting went with her parents and Dr Elliott. But she doesn't reply. I text again and say I'll phone her tomorrow.

Charlie wants me to check out something to do with planning permission at Hill Vale, but the clerk dealing with the property application is on holiday. I interview a young couple looking to buy a flat in the centre of town, but they are shocked at the prices. It's a familiar story. I forget to let Charlie know about Mrs Baxter-Sellers' flat.

At four-thirty I leave the office, telling Charlie I've got an appointment at the dentist. He tells me about Ed's titanium implants and how much they cost. I edge my way out of the door and get home to find a note on the mat. It's been typed, on a sheet of A4 paper.

Wanted to say more last night, but didn't want to intrude. Can we meet up – as it concerns Albert Terrace. Will you meet me at no.3 this evening? 6 o'clock.
Rob

I'm baffled, but at the same time rather excited. I feel I'm getting closer to unravelling the mysteries of Albert Terrace. It's obvious Rob knows more than he's told me. Wants to get something off his chest.

Despite having been recently painted, number three smells fusty from having been shut up for so long. I open the door and go inside. It's gone six but Rob hasn't shown up. I tell myself not to go looking for him, he'll see my car anyway, so I wait patiently. I don't want to look around or go anywhere in the house, so I sit on the stairs, looking through a local flyer for double glazing that's lying on the mat. I glance at my watch and realise it's already nearly six-thirty. Maddening man. Why should I expect anything more from him? I'm thinking of leaving, when the bell goes.

He enters quickly. 'I don't want that woman across the way to see me. She's always on the lookout.'

'Look, Rob. I think it's time you got whatever it is you want to say off your chest,' I say.

'I wish we could sit down somewhere,' he says, looking round at the empty rooms. 'We could go to mine…'

'It was your idea to meet here, Rob. There must have been a reason.'

'Yes.'

'Well.'

'Well, this is going to come as a shock to you. It did to me.'

'If it's about the photos, we did all that last night.'

'It's more than that.' He's not quite looking at me, focussing on imaginary phantoms behind me on the stairs. I force myself not to turn round.

'Have you remembered something else?'

'I think I know why Adele was murdered,' he blurts out.

'What are you talking about?' I think I must have misheard. But now he's looking at me, waiting for a response.

'She saw something.'

Despite the chill, I feel a prickle of sweat in my armpits. I lean back against the banister rail for support.

'She saw what happened to that woman.' He glances upstairs as he speaks.

'No,' I say, 'that's ridiculous. She would have gone to the police, said something straight away.' I try to pull myself upright and make for the door. But my legs don't seem to be working properly. I can hear a sound like a distant drill. Workmen must be digging up the road outside.

'Adele told me herself. I believed her. I promised I'd never say anything to anybody.'

'You must be mistaken,' I say coldly.

'No. She was a wonderful woman. I admired her. She offered to read my manuscript, you know, for my follow up to *Saturn XXX*…'

The drilling is getting louder which doesn't make sense, until I realise it's inside my own head.

'Rob, this is perfectly ridiculous,' I say. 'I want to go.'

It's already dark outside, shadows forming inside the hallway where we still stand. A damp chill seems to be creeping out of the walls.

'Please Hanna, listen. It's been on my mind. I can't work, can't think. Don't know what to do or say or who to talk to. I thought you'd understand.'

'How am I supposed to understand you talking nonsense,' I reply.

'I could show you what happened – what she told me happened – upstairs, in the back bedroom.'

I am not going upstairs to any bedroom with you, Rob, ever, I think.

'You can tell me here. That's if you've got anything else to tell me.'

'You don't believe me. Do you?'

'I find it hard to believe Adele had any part in that poor woman's death.'

'She thought it was an accident. Too many people came and went from this house, for months. She told me she had given some bloke a key. Luk or something.'

I look straight at Rob. This is what Adele had told me. It's the first time I've heard anybody mention his name.

'Go on.'

'She liked him. I could tell. I admit I was envious – wanted to catch sight of him – see what the competition was…' he laughs in his silly way. 'I think Luk let too many mates know about this place. Women were brought over – you know the sort of thing… I think Luk took a shine to one of them. One day Adele came and found them together, you know, and there was a fight. I don't think anyone was meant to get hurt. Adele said she came here one night and heard voices. She crept up the stairs and saw Luk and a young woman arguing. The woman fell, banged her head against the wall. It was an accident.'

The drilling noise inside my head has very suddenly ceased. 'Did Adele tell you this?'

'Yes. She was in a state. Didn't know what to do. She assumed the woman would recover, that the man would help her, but the next thing she heard, the woman had been found dead, and that the police are involved.'

'So, what happened to Luk?'

'That's the thing. Never saw him again. When the body was found, the house was boarded up. Adele was afraid – you can imagine… asked if she could stay at mine for a day or so. Then the police started doing door to doors. I tell you, I was in a right panic myself. In the end I told her she'd have to go for both our sakes. I felt bad, but…'

I thought back to the days after the discovery of the body, my late night phone call from her, then the silence.

'I had to ask her to go in the end. She said she'd be all right. I told her to go to the police, that they'd understand it was only an accident. Nothing to do with her. I suppose she thought she'd protect Luk by saying nothing.'

'So where did she go when she left you?'

'I have no idea. I assumed she had found out where Luk was and followed him somewhere. She told me she had a cousin living near Cambridge, perhaps she went there. I promise you, I asked her, pleaded with her, to go to the police, that she'd done nothing wrong. I think she got mixed up with the wrong crowd. I was devastated when they found her body.'

I don't know how long we've been standing there. The house is now almost in darkness and I'm finding it hard to breathe. My teeth won't stop chattering. It must be shock. I look for my torch, but it's in my other bag. I reach for my phone, as much for comfort, as anything else. I can't see enough to read Rob's expression. Can I trust what he's telling me? But why would he tell me all this if it wasn't true?

'I got a note,' I say, recalling the type-written one left for me at the office a hundred years ago when I was searching for the Christmas stuff in the basement.

'Asking you to meet Adele at nine…' he cuts in. 'Yes, it was me. I wanted to talk to you about what had happened, but your boss turned up, so I had to abandon the plan.'

I don't think I can bear to listen to any more of this. The urge to get away from this hateful place with its secrets and macabre history is overwhelming.

I manage to stutter, 'I have to go.'

'What are you going to do?' he asks.

This is the moment I should tell him, order him, to contact P.O. Morgan or D.I. Naomi – demand that he tell them what he's told me.

'I don't know,' I answer.

He doesn't react but moves towards the front door. I have the sudden fantasy that he is going to block my way, force me to go upstairs with him, determined to show me where it happened. But he opens the door and peers out.

'All clear,' he says.

The night sky is clear and cold, the early stars beginning to appear. Neither of us say anything as we prepare to go in our separate directions. I drive away, accelerating hard. How much of all this is true, and why hadn't he told the police, is the nagging thought that won't go away.

61

Mrs Baxter-Sellers rings the bell within minutes of my getting inside. 'Have you got any news for us yet?'

I haven't a clue what she means. Something to do with Paul? Rob's confession?

'News?' I feel exhausted. I need to lie down.

'About the flat – you know, putting it on the market?'

I've completely forgotten. Haven't given it any thought at all. 'It's all in hand, don't worry. I'll come up to see you and Mr Sellers tomorrow.'

'Call me Elaine, dear. I'll let Jack know, but he's getting a bit edgy. Said he thought we should talk to somebody else.'

Why don't you, I think. Please, just go away.

'No worries, Mrs… Elaine, I'll get back to you tomorrow.'

With that, I shut the door firmly, kick off my shoes, and go to lie down on the bed. I notice that someone has pushed a business card through the letterbox while I was out. Handwritten on the reverse is a note.

Hello, Hanna, Hope all OK with you. Could I drop round sometime for a chat? Sarah Fielding, freelance journalist

I don't know what to do with myself. I expect any time to hear from Paul, but my phone stays silent. I drag myself out of bed next morning; have to think hard to remember what day it is. I drive to the office, and exchange a few meaningless words with Charlie or Jason, though he doesn't seem to be around so much. I wonder if he's still got personal problems. I don't ask what they are.

Can I trust Rob? That is my main preoccupation. Shocking though his words were, the more I think about it, the more they seem to make sense. An accident. The first woman's death was an accident. Adele witnessed it. It's possible. That Adele sought help from Rob is also possible. I knew he was implicated, but in his version, all he did was to try to help her. But if it was only an accident, tragic and ghastly though it was, why would anybody need to murder Adele? I've been right all along to believe Luk was the perpetrator. Who else would have had a motive to see her dead?

'I've had a letter from James Batley. He's made a complaint.'

Charlie is standing over my desk, holding a sheet of paper. 'Do you know anything about this?'

He's waving a piece of paper around. What a worm, I'm thinking. I don't know whether to stay sitting or stand. What is the correct response to this new bit of ridiculousness thrown up by James Batley? I almost blurt out what James Batley knows about Adele and the photo

272

I've seen of him sitting next to her. And does Charlie know about his background of prison and fraud? And how did he fund the purchase of Riverside? But, I don't say any of it.

'We need to talk about this.'

'Good idea,' I mumble.

'What were you thinking, exactly?'

'I just went to see how he was settling in.'

'That's not what he's saying.'

'Well…'

'He's calling it harassment.'

'I only asked him one or two questions.'

'You seem to be taking things into your own hands, Hanna. Why on earth did you find it necessary to go there at all?'

I really have no answer.

'He's talking about speaking to his lawyer. What have you to say to that?'

I think it's unlikely, but I'm not ready to say it yet. In fact, I've nothing to say in reply, so say nothing.

'I'll try to fend him off but I want your word that this sort of thing will cease. We don't need any more complaints.'

'I'm sorry, Charlie.'

'What are your plans this morning?'

I think quickly. 'Mrs Baxter, you know, my neighbour, now Mrs Sellers. She and Mr Sellers want to move, sell up. She needs a valuation.'

'Better get on with it, then. I'll respond to Batley about his complaint and try not to involve yourself in any more cock-ups.'

Charlie disappears back into his office. Half an hour later, I leave the office to drive home.

*

On the way, I get a text from Sam. She wants to meet. I pull over and text *where are you now?* The reply comes back. *Blue Banana.*

She's sitting in the window, in the same spot where I last saw her on the day I'd gone there expecting to meet Luk. It seems so long ago, but I can't help glancing around, as if he might suddenly turn up too.

'Are you expecting someone else?'

She looks well, fuller and pinker in the cheeks, hair tidied back. A more mature look as befits a young woman three months pregnant.

'Shouldn't you be at work?' she asks.

'I could ask you the same about school, or have you given up altogether?'

'Mum's home-tutoring me now. She's in her element.'

'I can imagine.'

As though she's read my thoughts, she says, 'Dad's moved back in. I don't know how long for though.'

'Hmm. Did you want to see me for anything special?'

Sam asks the hovering waitress for a milkshake. 'Skinny,' she says. I order a cappuccino. 'Don't you think you drink too much coffee?' she asks. I almost laugh but ignore it and ask how she's been keeping.

'The doctors are pleased. Say the baby's healthy.' She reaches into her soft and scruffy cloth bag and pulls out a sheet of A4. 'See. It's a girl,' she says proudly. It's a fuzzy image, like a storm cloud, but she handles it tenderly as though it's the infant itself.

'I'm going to call her Jasmine.'

'Lovely,' I say.

We sit looking at our drinks, not quite meeting each other's eye.

'You were here that day, weren't you?' she says suddenly. 'Did that man ever show up? The one you were waiting for. Was he the one I saw at your flat?'

For some reason, I start to tell her about it. About Adele, about Luk, about Rob, about Paul. I make sure to tell her I met Paul after I'd broken up with her father. At least that's how I remember it.

'He was hot,' is all she says.

We lean back into the squashed cushions looking out at the street at people drifting past the window on a sunless afternoon under a disappointing sky.

'How are you getting home?' I ask

'Friend's picking me up.' She doesn't say who, but at least it's not her mother or father.

'Better go,' I say. 'Let me know if you need anything, or want to talk...'

My voice tails away. But she's finished her drink and picked up her bag.

'Sure,' is all she says.

There's a car I don't recognise parked in my usual spot, but I find a space nearby and make my way upstairs. I feel exhausted, though I seem to have done so little today. The woman standing outside my door is studying her phone as though it contains the secrets of something she desperately needs to know the secrets of.

'Hi,' she says, raising her head, tossing her hair and holding out her hand. 'Remember me? Did you get my note?'

Now I recognise her. It's Sarah Fielding, the journalist. 'What do you want?' I ask.

'I wondered if you'd had a chance to think about my offer?'

'Offer?' I struggle to remember. It's cold standing here on the landing. I long to go inside, get warm, lie down. Maybe find a message from Paul.

'Have you got a few minutes,' she goes on. 'For a chat?'

She's friendly. She smiles, tosses her hair again and talks with a low hoarse voice. It's quite an attractive voice and I wonder if it's natural or if she's getting a cold. I find my key and open the door. I'm wondering can we do it some other time, but she's followed me in and closed the door. I should ask her to leave, but don't as she's already entered the kitchen and put on the kettle.

'You look all-in, love. Would you like a cup of tea or what about something else?' She's looking round. There's an unopened bottle of pinot grigio in the fridge. Now she's mentioned it, it is a rather attractive thought.

'I think we should stick to tea.' I say.

'Good idea. Shall I make it?'

I slump down onto the sofa and lean back into the cushions. It's a long time since anybody offered to make me anything.

'Well…,' I say.

She's already setting out the cups and searching the fridge.

'There's no milk,' I say.

'Don't worry, I take it black,' she replies.

The bottle of Pinot is on view and, as she hovers by the open door, I tell her where to find the wine glasses.

'This is lovely,' she says, raising her glass towards me.

I find the words to say. 'I don't know why you're here.'

'Well, I have been thinking about you, wondering how you are. How you've been coping?'

'Not so well.' I say.

'Have the police got any further with their enquiries?'

'If they have, they're not saying. To me, anyway.' I breathe in the grassy, winey smell that promises so much and take a long sip.

'Hmm. Cheers. This is good,' she says. She puts down her glass and takes a notebook and biro out of her bag. It's a large, well-worn yellow leather bag, with gold fastenings. It sits wide open at her feet, filled with the sort of muddled detritus a busy woman like her carries around every day.

'What about you?' she asks, her voice deep. 'If you don't mind me saying, you look worn out love. Has it been a difficult day?'

I don't think I'm crying, but my eyes are running with water. I taste salt on my tongue as I lick it away.

'Here,' she says diving back into her bag, taking out a wodge of loose tissue. 'Let it out, honey.'

'I've been trying to find somebody,' I hear myself say. 'His name's Luk. He was Adele's boyfriend.'

'What can you tell me about him? Is he important to the investigation?'

I find myself telling her everything I don't know about Luk.

'What about the police? Can't they find him?'

'I think they've lost interest,' I say, taking another long gulp. The tingle has already started in my feet.

'Too bad. Well, I might have one or two avenues I could follow up. One or two contacts who owe me a favour.'

I tell her all I can remember. I ask her to cross her heart to keep it a secret. Tell her it's just... well anyway I think she understands. Night has fallen outside while we've been sitting. The room has grown dark but I haven't switched on the lamps. Our glasses are empty and so is the bottle.

'Make sure you eat properly,' she says. 'There's not a lot in your fridge. Do you want me to get you something?'

'No thanks,' I say, but I acknowledge her concern.

'There's a couple of eggs,' she says. 'Make yourself an omelette.'

'Yes,' I nod, childlike. I already know I've said too much. I want to retrieve the words. Want to snatch the notebook out of her hands but she's already stuffed it back into the yellow bag and zipped it up.

'Don't worry. I'll see what I can find out,' she says. And then she's picked up her bag and she's gone.

62

I don't expect to hear from Sarah Fielding in a hurry. She's probably one of those people who call themselves a professional but just likes worming their way into other people's lives and drinking their wine. So, when I get a ring on the doorbell a couple of nights later, I'm surprised to see her standing there.

'I've found him.' she says as soon as she steps inside the door. 'Well, more precisely, I've located him. Luk. You know, the man you were interested in?'

It's an odd way to express it, but I'm immediately taken aback and ask her to come in. This time it'll be just coffee, I say to myself.

'So where is –er, Luk?'

''Back in Romania. With his wife and three children. Cleaning windows.'

I am so shocked to hear this I have to sit down. 'How do you know?'

'Contacts,' she says, winking and touching her nose, 'like I told you…'

'But…'

'Oh, the police know all about Luk Berioskya. Ruled him out months ago.'

'What?'

'He was questioned right at the beginning. Had some hospital job at...'

She opens the bag, once more open at her feet and brings out a notebook. 'Whitefriars, wasn't it?'

'Yes, but...'

'They are satisfied he had nothing to do with any murder. Decent family man and all that.' She rolls her eyes.

'But I've heard...'

'What?'

She sharpens her eyes and points her pencil.

''He...'

'No, darling. He had nothing to do with any murder. I have it on best authority. From Jonny Morgan himself.'

'Jonny Morgan?'

'Yes. He interviewed you several times, I hear. Though don't let him know I said that.'

Does she actually mean P.O. Morgan? P.O. Morgan with the crisp white shirts.

'How do you know all this?'

'Well, it's hush-hush, between ourselves, but my sister and he were an item for a few months.'

She's continuing to talk but I can't take it any more. I can't believe he would have been so indiscreet to tell her all this. What's even more galling is the fact that I've wasted months, almost a year, trying to track Luk down, yet all the time the police knew about him and ruled him out of the picture.

'I...' I'm about to reveal the contents of Robs confession. But think better of it. 'I am so grateful to you Sarah,' I say instead. 'Thank you for finding him.'

She's running her hands through her hair as we speak. It's short, bobbed and red. I wonder how often she needs to go to a stylist to keep looking like a model for Modigliani.

'Well, darling. I want to help as much as I can. I hope that in turn you will be able to help me.'

I look at her, enquiringly.

'With my article. You know. For the women's press.'

'Oh, yes, of course. I'll give it some thought.'

'I can see you're tired. It's not a good idea to do this after work. What about one weekend? We can put our feet up and do it in a proper fashion.'

I nod and agree. 'Of course,' I say. 'Thank you for your help.'

'I'll be in touch,' she says, picking up her bag. 'I'll see myself out.'

63

It's Monday morning and I've rung Charlie to tell him I was held up on my way home from visiting Dad. He accepts my lie without comment. So now I feel bad twice over. Lying to Charlie, and also involving Dad. I feel especially bad about Dad. If I leave it any longer, it will be Christmas again. We've not spoken much on the phone lately and he must be missing Auntie Jean. I've washed my hair and I'm on my second cup of coffee when the doorbell rings. It's probably going to be Sarah Fielding again. I don't want to give her an interview. I'm sick of the whole business. But it's Elaine from upstairs on the doorstep. She's rather smartly dressed for a Monday morning in November and she's got Bobby sitting beside her in a travelling basket.

'I wanted you to know,' she starts. 'We've sold our flat. Julie helped us in the end.' She's not as smiley as she used to be and I wonder how things are going with Mr Sellers.

'Oh, that's good news,' I say. 'Will you be moving soon?'

'Well, dear, it's no thanks to you if we are,' she replies.

I've obviously offended her in some way. But I did go to her wedding, and never let on to anybody about the dog. As if agreeing with me, Bobby gives a low growl and a sharp bark.

'Jack wasn't pleased with Fortune Estates,' she goes on. 'All that time you had it on your books you never sent anybody round to view. Not one person. Still we must let bygones be bygones. Julie put us in touch with Challengers and the first person who came along made an offer. At the asking price too.' She turns on her heel. 'The removal van is coming Friday.'

I struggle to know what to say. I wonder who will be moving in. We both know she's been let down by me and by Fortune Estates.

'I never saw them but they want to buy the furniture too. That's fine with us because Jack wants us to make a fresh start. We're going down to Bournemouth, renting until we can find ourselves a nice little bungalow. Bobby will love the sea air.'

I realise she's still talking though I've tuned out her words. I ask, 'Shall I give you back your spare key…' but Bobby is growling again and drowns out my words. Elaine is trotting down the stairs. I shall always think of her as Mrs Baxter. I wonder where Mr Sellers is. Probably already down in Bournemouth, checking out the property market. No doubt in a year or two they'll be moving to Spain.

I haven't seen or heard from Paul. Surely he'd have told me if he was back from Saudi. No texts, emails, nothing. It must be over. Once again I've been a fool. If I'd been quicker I could have asked Elaine. Perhaps I'll be able to ask them on Friday before they move away altogether. I wonder what I can say to Charlie about the sale we've lost out on. It's probably best to say nothing.

I get to the office just before lunch. I'm rather surprised to see Jason sitting at his desk. It's such a rare occurrence, I remark on it.

'For somebody who turns up for work at midday you're a fine one to talk.'

Charlie must be out because the creep wouldn't have spoken to me like that in Charlie's hearing.

'Have you been very busy, then?' I ask, attempting nonchalance.

He ignores my question, goes back to his screen, then says, 'Remember that place at Hill Vale? I did a viewing at the weekend, while you were away, and they made an offer this morning.'

Of course, I remember Hill Vale. The supposed fake email, the two visits I made. Charlie must have passed it over to Jason. That's going to be a nice little commission for him that could have been mine. Once again, I realise how unfocussed I've been. I determine to pull up my socks, get back on the ball, try to do better. This would certainly not be the day to let them know we've lost the upstairs flat. I decide it's best to be generous, in the circumstances.

'Well,' I say, 'you've certainly earned your bonus.'

Jason doesn't reply, but can't resist a smile to himself as he turns back to his computer.

'By the way,' he says after a bit, 'remember James Batley?'

Of course I remember James Batley. He knows I remember James Batley.

'I don't think he's going to sue.'

'Sue? Why would he do that?'

'That unauthorised visit you made to him at Riverside.'

'I can assure you…'

'Don't bother. I just thought you'd be pleased to know it's going no further. I'm sure Charlie is.'

What an unpleasant man Jason has turned out to be. I look past him. The office looks sad in the afternoon gloom. I never did talk to Charlie about the lighting. I think I'll take some money out of petty cash and buy a new plant for the window sill. Again, it brings memories of Adele. She was always the one to take care of that sort of thing. I suppose now it will be mine unless Jason plans to take that over too.

64

It's Friday afternoon and I'm driving up to see Dad. Jason suggested I should take a different route to avoid the motorway traffic. I try to nod politely at his mansplaining. While looking at Google maps, the name of a place seems to draw my attention. At first, I can't think why but then I remember. Stamford. Isn't that where Adele's cousin Rosemary lived? I heard no more from her after the funeral, hadn't expected to, but wonder if it would be courteous, a friendly gesture in fact, to drop in to see her on my way up to Dad's. It would only mean a few miles out of my way. A coffee stop. Hardly any distance at all. I should really call or text her, but don't have any details like that, so put those thoughts out of my head. However, when I see Stamford writ large on a sign post, I make a sudden decision to pull off. It's a small, picturesque market town, bigger than I'd imagined. This is silly, I think. I've no idea where she lives. Minor roads lead off the centre square and the bridge over the river goes off in all directions. I park on a side road, phone Charlie and ask him for her address. I explain that she had told me to get in touch if ever I was in the area but I've mislaid the details. This isn't actually true, but Charlie manages to finds her details. 'Drive carefully,' he says. 'Give her my regards.'

Rosemary's address is an ex council house on a rather mean looking estate on the outskirts of town. Something about the uniformly grey pebble-dash frontage puts me in mind of Albert Terrace. The curtains are drawn and it doesn't look as if anyone's at home. I'm relieved, already wondering why I've come, and I'm about to walk away, when the door opens and a man leans out.

'Yes?'

He's wearing tracksuit bottoms and a sleeveless vest despite the chill in the air. There's some slogan written on the front in a language I don't recognise. I smile and reach out my hand.

'I've come to see Rosemary,' I say.

'She's out,' he replies and goes to close the door.

'I've come quite a way, especially to see her,' I lie.

'What did you say your name was?'

'I didn't. It's Hanna. She'll remember me. I'm a friend of her cousin, Adele.' Is it my imagination but does a small shadow flicker across the man's face. 'She said to call in, if I was passing.'

The man shrugs and goes to shut the door again. I push my hand against it. 'Hang on a minute,' I say, 'can you tell me when she'll be back?'

'No.'

'Can you take a message for me then?'

He doesn't get a chance to reply, as we both hear footsteps on the path behind me. The man turns his back, leaving me to greet Rosemary.

She's carrying shopping bags and wheeling a large

suitcase behind her. I don't think she recognises me. I hold out my hand again. 'Hello, Rosemary,' I say, 'Do you remember me? I worked with Adele. We met at her funeral.'

She gives me a blank stare.

'I hope you don't mind,' I go on. 'I was passing – on the way to visit my father actually. I thought I'd just call in… say hello…'

Rosemary's expression is hard to read. 'I've been shopping,' she says. 'I'm sorry but we're rather busy at the moment.' She squeezes past me and hauls the suitcase over the step.

'Can I help you with that?' I say.

"No, I can manage…'

But I've already grabbed hold of the other end. Despite its size the case is light and obviously brand new with the retailer's plastic bag wound round the handle. She's already through the front door, so I follow her into the house still holding my end of the case. We stand awkwardly in the hall until she nods for me to follow her inside.

'I expect you want some tea,' she says checking her watch. 'Why don't you wait in there.' She indicates the small front room.

What is immediately evident are several boxes leaning against the walls, shelves stripped of any ornaments or books. Somehow, the room doesn't quite match the woman I remembered meeting at Adele's funeral.

'Are you moving?' I ask, when she returns carrying two mugs. 'Decorating,' she replies. 'They're coming next week.'

'Always a big upheaval,' I say, sympathetically. There's no sign of the man who'd opened the door to me. Wherever he is, he's not going to join us for tea.

'Afraid there's no biscuits,' she says.

I perch on the edge of a tea-chest.

'Sorry there's no milk either. So, what's this about?' She asks.

It's an odd question and I struggle to reply. 'Adele was a good friend,' I say. 'I miss her. I expect you do too.'

'Of course,' she says. Then, after a pause, 'but life goes on, doesn't it?'

Silence hangs heavily between us. Each little sip of tea sounds too much like itself. The tea tastes bitter but I'm sure there's no sugar either.

'Are you still working?' I ask, struggling to remember what her job was.

'I've given up.'

Of course, Rosemary was sole heir to Adele's estate. She inherited a decent house in a decent part of a decent town. We had no part in the sale. I wonder if I dare ask if it sold. But I just say 'Of course.' I'm struggling to understand why this is so awkward. Far from being pleased to see a friend from her cousin's past, I feel unwelcome. I hear the sound of heavy footsteps thumping down the stairs and the front door slam.

'I hope I haven't sent him away,' I say, finishing as much of my tea as possible and putting the mug down on the floor.

'We're quite busy at the moment.'

'Yes, you said. Sorry if I've come at an awkward moment.'

'Awkward?'

'Well, inconvenient.'

I suppose I had hoped for a nice chat. A chance to talk to somebody close to Adele. To let her know how much I miss her, but there seems little likelihood of that. In fact, she's standing up, as though expecting me to go. I take the cue and follow her to the door.

'Good luck with the decorators,' I say. She looks at me blankly. 'Next week. The decorators.'

'Oh, yes. Thanks.'

Just as I'd thought. She was lying. Since when do you pack your goods away in t-chests for decorators. And buy a new suitcase. She closes the door behind me. I am as relieved to get out of the house as Rosemary clearly is to see the back of me.

I negotiate my way back out of the small neighbourhood streets and re-join the motorway. There was something very odd about what had just taken place. What surprised me was how little she wanted to talk about Adele. I think about it for some time, until I find myself back on the familiar road leading to Dad's.

*

I get there just after six o'clock. I wish I'd thought to bring a bottle or a box of chocolates. There's a warm smell of something cooking in the kitchen. Dad hurries to greet me, gives me a hug, then turning back to the kitchen says, 'I'll be with you in a sec.'

I peep into the dining room and I'm surprised to see a white cloth covering the table, a bowl of dark red chrysanthemums at the centre and a candle waiting to be lit.

'Oh, Dad, you needn't have gone to all this trouble,' I call out.

The words are hardly out of my mouth when a smiling woman in a pink cardigan enters the room.

'Aren't you going to introduce us, Jack?' asks the woman.

Dad steps in beside her, and lifts her hand. 'This is Thelma,' he says, smiling, a faint redness reaching his ears. 'I invited her along to meet you.'

Thelma's hand is very soft, with pink tipped nails. No rings I notice. I wonder what she's doing here, but I think I already know.

'You remember meeting my neighbours last Christmas? Thelma is Tom's mother. You'd never think it, would you?' He lifts her hand again. 'We met when they invited me to a barbecue.' He can't stop smiling. He's like a teenager introducing his first girlfriend to his mother.

'Why don't you both sit and get to know each other while I see what's going on in the kitchen.'

'Let me know if I can do anything,' says Thelma.

I think that should have been my line. She leads the way into the lounge. The fire is lit and the overhead light has been replaced with a string of small lights draped over the mantelpiece. There's a pot plant standing by the window and several bright cushions on the sofa. The wallpaper's different too. Dad never said anything to me about redecorating.

'He's such a lovely man, your dad,' says Thelma, sitting down and patting one of the new cushions.' We get on so well. We like the same things.'

I wonder what she means. Daily trips to the supermarket? Watching the news? *Cash in the Attic*?

'Jack tells me you've got a really good job.'

She's warm and friendly, and I find myself telling her

about Fortune Estates and I'm already into an anecdote about money laundering when Dad calls, "Dinner's ready."

He sits in his usual spot at the end of the table and Thelma places herself comfortably opposite. She lights the candle and serves the vegetables while Dad pours the wine. I sit between them feeling like a small child given permission to sit with the grown-ups. Later, when I excuse myself to go to the upstairs bathroom, I spot a basket of lavender guest soaps and a jar of fancy body lotion, not E45. Glancing into Dad's bedroom I see a fluffy pink dressing-gown lying across the bed. Downstairs, soft strains of music drift from the lounge. Thelma is obviously a fan of Lloyd Webber. It's no surprise when Dad tells me Thelma will be staying overnight rather than driving back in the dark. It's clearly not the first time and I wonder how long it will be before they announce she's moving in and they plan to marry. I should be pleased for him. In fact, when I think more about it, I am. But for the second time today, my expectations have been challenged and I've felt out-manoeuvred. I have been dwelling so long in the past I've failed to notice the changes right under my nose.

All this is going through my head as I drive home. Dad presses me to stay, but I give my excuses and tell him I have two viewings tomorrow. It's not true, but I feel exhausted and I'm ready to go anyway. Dad protests – 'you're tired, set off early in the morning. Traffic will be quiet and it will be daylight.' But I don't take any notice. I wish him and Thelma all the best, then set out. I should have listened to him. I am almost home when it happens. I don't remember anything about it. Don't remember seeing the truck coming round the curve until it's too late.

65

Adele is standing next to my bed, except it isn't my bed. There's a strange smell in the room that I can't identify and she's shining a torch into my eyes. She asks my name and I can't think what she means. She's cut her hair. I want to tell her it was a mistake, but somehow can't get the words out.

'I didn't know you were a nurse,' I say. At least I think that's what I say.

I'm not too sure she hears me because she asks my name again. 'Why, Madame Bovary, of course, you know that.' I want to ask her why she's taken up nursing. Is that why I haven't seen you in a while? And tell her the uniform doesn't suit her but my voice is slurred and I can't seem to get my words out. She offers me a drink of water.

'You've spoken to Rob, haven't you?' she says.

'Yes, but why didn't you tell me you knew him…?' My voice stumbles. I can't get the words out. There's a buzzing in my ears and my head hurts.

'I just need to take your temperature,' she says.

Why is she acting so formal? As if she doesn't know me. I want to tell her about Dad and Thelma. How I'm trying to be pleased for them.

'Try not to move,' says the nurse. 'I need to take your blood pressure.'

Fancy Adele having all this expertise. I struggle to lift myself off the pillow lean on my elbow, but can't. My arm is covered with thick white plaster and my chest hurts.

'What's happened to me?' I ask. But Adele has disappeared.

'It won't take long,' says the new nurse. 'I'll be back with your meds, then you can get back to sleep.'

I think of all the things I should have asked Adele but it will have to wait. She's sure to be back later.

There's a pain in my arm and in my shoulder. In fact, I realise I can hardly move my upper body at all.

'I'll give you something to help,' says the nurse. She proffers some tablets in a plastic cup, finishes her business and gives me a cheery smile as she manoeuvres her equipment trolley away from the bedside. 'I'll be back to check on your later,' she says.

I look around the room. I seem to be the only patient. I lean back with a sigh and know no more. I must sleep for a long time because when I wake it's dark outside.

P.O. Morgan is at my bedside. He's not in uniform which confuses me.

'Why are you here?' I ask.

'You've had an accident,' he replies.

I don't know what he's talking about, but I nod in agreement.

'You're in Whitefriars,' he says.

'Am I in trouble?' I ask him.

'Trouble,' he replies. 'Why would that be?'

'I spoke to Adele,' I say. 'She was here. She's a nurse now. I'll be able to find out what happened.'

P.O. Morgan is not looking at me. He's not writing anything in his note book either. I feel confused and lean back against the pillows. I tell P.O. Morgan I am going to have a little rest. Perhaps you can come back later, I say. I think how nice it would be if he and Adele could meet. But something's troubling me. I'm about to say something about it, but my eyes close again and I can say no more.

66

They keep me in hospital for five days, then send me home. I never see Adele again, or P.O. Morgan on the ward, so I suppose it's a sign I'm getting better. They replace the thick plaster with a lighter one and a splint. I was concussed, broke my left arm and cracked a rib in the collision. Could have been worse, says everybody. I think people will say that the day I die. It's still painful and I can only do things slowly. Dressing and washing take an age. Charlie and Ed come to see me, bring flowers and tell me they've topped up the fridge. I'm grateful. Even Jason sends a card. 'Come back when you're ready,' says Charlie. But I'm lost at home and miss the office.

At eight o'clock this morning, I hear Mrs Baxter-Sellers' removal van arrive. I go upstairs to say goodbye and she gave me a hug. Actually, we were both quite teary. I tell her I will miss her. She said they've notified the post office for sending on mail, but gives me her forwarding address.

'Where's Mr Sellers… Jack?' I ask.

'He's gone on ahead already. With Bobby.'

'Good luck, Elaine.'

'Thank you dear. I hope things work out for you, too.'

This is my chance to ask about Paul.

'Oh, he's working over here now.'

Already working. There's been no word from him, no contact. I try not to let myself feel too crushed.

'So, he won't be visiting here again, then?'

I hope I don't sound too wounded. Wish I hadn't said it. But Elaine has turned away and is telling the removal man to protect some dishes he's packing away in newspaper.

'Good luck, Elaine. Write when you're settled,' I say, going back downstairs.

P.O. Morgan is waiting outside my front door. 'Hanna, can you spare a couple of minutes?'

'I'm thinking of going into the office, actually.' It's a lie. I'm not supposed to drive for another week or two. My car's still in the garage for repair, but they've already delivered a white Clio in replacement.

'This won't take long.'

We are standing awkwardly in the way of the removal men who are trying to pass us with boxes and bits of furniture.

'You'd better come in,' I say. 'What do you want?'

'Only to ask a couple of questions.'

'Oh?'

'Hope you're feeling better now… after your accident.' So that's why he's here.

'My insurance company know all about it. Nobody died. There's no further action.'

'It's nothing to do with the accident. I understand you recently visited Adele's cousin, Rosemary – Rosemary Styles in Stamford.

'Who?'

'Adele's cousin, Rosemary, in Stamford. Can you confirm that you recently went to see her?'

'So what if I did?'

'Could you tell me the purpose of your visit?'

'Well…' I find myself struggling to remember exactly what was the purpose of my visit. What's it to him, anyway?

'I was just passing through. I remembered she lived in Stamford. I suppose I wanted to make some sort of connection.'

'Yes, quite natural in the circumstances.'

'Did I do something wrong, Officer?' I feel annoyed with P.O. Morgan. Who does he think he is? Is he checking up on me or something?

'Not at all, quite natural. How did you find her?'

I don't know where this is going. Despite his words, I feel as though I've somehow been rapped over the knuckles.

'Well, it went OK I suppose. She was getting the decorators in.'

What a stupid remark. P.O Morgan doesn't react. He's not taking any notes either. And how did he know I'd been to see Adele's cousin anyway.

'Have you been watching me, P.O. Morgan?' I look straight into his eyes as I say this. He holds my gaze for a few seconds, then looks away.

'We've had cause to put Rosemary Styles's house under surveillance.'

The news is somehow not as shocking as might be expected. 'But why?' I ask.

'I'm not at liberty to say, but it's part of an ongoing investigation.'

I don't like to think I've been linked with yet another ongoing investigation. 'Is it to do with Adele?' I ask.

'I'm not at liberty to say,' he repeats, 'but we'll keep you informed of any developments. Had you ever had any contact with Adele's cousin or her partner before?'

'Before what?'

P.O. Morgan doesn't answer but keeps looking at me. It occurs to me this is new. He always stuck to his notebook or stared out of the window when we talked before. I think back to Sarah Fielding's comments. Jonny Morgan, my sister's ex. It was an unexpected glimpse into his private life. I wish I knew more. Perhaps when I talk to Sarah again I will ask more about him.

'Are you here in your official capacity, Officer Morgan?'

'Was this your first visit to their home?'

'I'd never been there before.'

'Had you seen either of them at any other time? 'His questions are formal, with an edge. I'm not sure what he wants me to say. He repeats, 'Was this your first visit?

'Yes. It's not against the law, is it? You'll have to forgive me but I'm already late for work.'

'Hope you recover soon,' he replies, nodding at my plaster. 'I'll see myself out.'

I am bewildered and exhausted. I can't keep going over past events and coming to no conclusion for much longer. Nothing ever gets resolved and each new piece of information only delivers another question. I will have to let go for the sake of my health and sanity.

I look for the A4 print-out Rob gave me and tell myself I will either go to the police with everything I don't know or, more likely, just get on with my life. I adjust my reading glasses in order to take a better look at the picture. I don't want to keep it any more. Nothing about it seems to relate to the Adele I knew, or thought I knew. As I hold the flimsy paper up to the light, something flutters to the carpet. My rib-cage gives a sharp stab as I stoop to retrieve it.

Two sheets have somehow got stuck together. Rob probably didn't realise and I expect he's got a drawer full, the worm. I hold them both out at arms' length. Though at first they appear to be the same, one appears darker than the other. It's probably to do with the ink, or maybe he took them from his bathroom window at different times. The more I look the more it becomes evident that the two photos are not identical. While one shows Adele sitting beside James Batley in the garden of Albert Terrace, in the other, she's sitting next to a different man. I squint carefully and realise with a jolt that it's P.O. Morgan.

I stay looking at the two pictures for a long time. As my thoughts slowly clear, a glimmer of a plan begins to emerge. I pick up my keys and collect my bag. The car is a bit awkward to manoeuvre with my arm still in the sling and I try to put aside any memory of the last time I was behind the wheel. Out on the main road, I feel nervous amid the traffic, but soon find I can manage the familiar route without difficulty.

Charlie is surprised to see me. I tell him I was bored and wanted to find out what had been happening while I'd been away. After some small talk over a coffee, I ask if he minds me making a couple of photocopies on the office machine. He assumes it's something to do with the accident and I don't deny it.

'Of course,' he says. 'Take as many as you like.'

I need only two, and slipping them into my bag, I say goodbye and tell him I hope to be back at work very soon. Later I write a note.

Dear P.O. Morgan,
I think these pictures could be of help to you in your
investigation into Adele's death.
Hanna.

I put both copies into an envelope, stick on a first class stamp and catch the six o'clock post with a few minutes to spare. He should get it in the morning

67

I'm woken by my phone at eight o'clock. The unexpected voice brings a deep pang to my already sore rib-cage. I sit up, the better to hear his voice.

'I've missed you, Hanna,' he says. 'Sorry I haven't been in touch.' There is a silence as I try to collect my thoughts and rummage through my feelings. Trying to match what I say to what I feel.

'You're very quiet,' he says.

'What's been going on, Paul?'

'I've got a lot to tell you,' he says. 'If you'll let me.'

'Where are you now?' I ask.

'Nearby. Can I come over? I could bring breakfast.'

He hardly waits for a reply before the phone clicks off. I should get up, dash to the shower, freshen myself up, but instead I lean back against the pillow and wait. I hear the bell ring and go to answer it, wrapping myself in my dressing gown.

Paul arrives, carrying two take-away coffees and a bag of croissants.

'I remember how you like your coffee,' he says, finding plates and setting everything out on the table. He does this in a very calm and unhurried way, as though we do this every morning.

There's so little I know about him. So much I'd like to know.

He holds out a plate. 'Jam?'

'No thanks.'

'Just as well, because there isn't any.'

I take a sip of coffee, then, 'What have you been doing? Elaine said you were back in London.'

'Work has been hectic.'

'Why didn't you phone?' I say.

'I regret that,' he says. 'I've thought about you a lot, though.'

He's standing up, looking out of the window down at the street. He's not looking at me, but I think it's true.

'I've thought a lot about you, too,' I say.

He comes over and as if for the first time, notices the plaster on my arm.

'Does it hurt,' he says.

'It aches sometimes. But this comes off next week.'

He doesn't ask me how it happened. It's as if he already knows.

'Where are you living now?' I ask.

'London. But not for much longer.'

'Have you changed jobs, then?'

'I'm getting a new contract soon.'

'Will we see each other more often, then?'

'I hope so. Will it hurt if I give you a hug?'

I try to raise my arm but can't lift it far. 'Careful of my rib,' I say.

'Which part of you is safe to touch?' he asks, which makes us both laugh.

He gently brings me closer and kisses my lips.

'I'm going to stay in touch this time,' he says. 'That's if you'll let me.'

I don't need to answer. My response to his words and touch is obvious to us both.

'I can't stay long now. But I'll call you when things are clearer. And you've got my number now. Call me any time.'

Then he's gone, leaving behind the empty coffee cups and flaky crumbs. I get into the shower and smile to myself, quite certain that this time I will see Paul again soon. Later, I remember my letter to P.O. Morgan and wonder when I'll get a reply.

*

Five days later, my arm is freed from the plaster and it emerges pale and weak. A few strengthening exercises are advised and I'm told I can drive again. No excuses now not to go back to work, but I don't need any.

Charlie is pleased to see me and someone, surely not Jason, has put flowers on my desk. I open up my computer and try to think where I was before all this happened.

'We've had some new listings since you were here last,' says Charlie. 'And a number of enquiries. We'll have a meeting tomorrow morning, but take today to get back in your stride.'

'So, business has been good,' I say, remembering our worries of last year.

'Not bad. But we'll all need to pull together now.'

This is probably an oblique reference to any tensions he hopes won't be lingering between Jason and me.

'Of course, Charlie,' I say.

Sitting behind my desk, I really don't know where to start. I wish the meeting had been this morning so I could have had a clearer idea of what to do. I fiddle around, looking at old notes and try to raise some enthusiasm for bringing them up to date. The morning drags.

Around lunch-time, I glance up to see Sam waving at me through the window. She is heavily pregnant now, wearing a tight stretchy dress, proudly showing off her bump.

'Got time for a skinny milkshake?' she asks.

'Not today, I'm working. Perhaps tomorrow.'

She shrugs. 'How are you keeping?' I ask. 'Baby looks well. Must be due soon.'

'Six weeks.'

'Are you still going to call her Jasmine?'

'I like Sky now. But I might wait and ask her what she thinks when she gets older… let her decide.'

I smile at her naivety. Of all the decisions she is going to have to make this one is probably the easiest of all.

'What about the baby's father? Is he involved at all?'

'He's useless.'

What use would any sixteen-year-old boy be in this situation. He'd played his part. I wonder what Sky/Jasmine will make of him, or if they will ever meet.

'I've got a social worker now. She's good at helping me with benefits and stuff like that.'

'Brilliant,' I say.

'And what about Mum and Dad?'

'They're going to buy me a pram.'

'You'll be needing one of those.'

Sam's pregnancy has no doubt reunited Sam and Annie. I wonder how long it will last. I turn back into the office. 'I'll text.' I say.

She shrugs her cloth bag over her shoulder and walks away. My arm has started to ache.

'I think I'll leave early today,' I tell Charlie. 'But I'll make it up to you tomorrow.'

'No problem, says Charlie, as though he means it. I think he's glad I'm back.

I stop to buy milk on my way home and glance in the window of Challengers in the High Street. I do a double take when I see the apartment at Riverside is back on the market. From the photo and description, it's definitely the same apartment I sold to James Batley. Why is he planning to move so soon, I wonder? No doubt he didn't instruct Fortune Estates because of my unauthorised visit.

Five days have passed since I wrote the letter and sent the photocopies to P.O. Morgan. I would have expected a response by now. I was baffled by the picture of him with Adele. I wonder if he thinks he's going to get into trouble if the picture is made public. But I will be able to reassure him and let everyone who needs to know that he's always behaved in a perfectly respectful manner. I don't understand why Adele didn't tell me she'd met him, but she must have had so many other things on her mind. It would help if I'd known the date the photos were taken. I could find out, but that would mean talking to Rob again and I don't want to talk to Rob again.

That night, the doorbell rings, quite late and I rush to answer it, expecting it to be Paul.

'I got your letter,' says P.O. Morgan. 'With the photos.'

This is a strange time of night to call, I think, glancing at the clock, noticing it's ten thirty and that he's not in uniform. Does that mean he's off –duty?

'Is this an official visit?' I ask.

'We'd better sit down, Hanna.'

'Do you know James Batley is moving?' I say.

P.O. Morgan looks irritated by my question, brushes it aside.

'You must know I've seen that photo before,' he says.

'But it shows he was involved at three Albert Terrace, that he knew Adele…'

'Yes, yes, we are fully aware of that.'

'Well you never told me…'

He gives an exasperated snort. 'There is a lot about this case, Hanna, that you know nothing about. You seem to have appointed yourself Chief Investigator. Where did you get the photos?'

This is my chance to tell him everything I don't know.

'Rob Green took them… he didn't want to get involved. He gave me the pictures but I don't think he realised he'd given me two. You should be talking to him.'

P.C. Morgan is watching, waiting for me to continue.

'Why didn't you tell me you'd already met Adele when you came to interview me?' This comes blurting out, louder than I'd meant.

'When enquiries are ongoing, it's not always best policy to release all the information at our disposal.'

Why is he being so formal, using this stupid language. He seems to read my thoughts.

'Hanna, the police department was looking into

complaints about Albert Terrace well before the woman's body was found there. Information had come our way about alleged illegal activities taking place. The house and its occupants were under surveillance.'

'Why didn't the Agency know anything about it, then?' I sound triumphant, though I don't mean to be.

'For all we knew, Fortune Estates were involved,' he replies. 'That has been discounted now. Sometimes a complaint about one thing leads us to something else, and we didn't want to blow our chances of finding the bigger picture.'

Goodness. Did they think we were money laundering? How very exciting.

'Was it about money laundering?' I already know what he's going to say, but he says it anyway.

'I'm afraid I am unable to discuss an ongoing enquiry.'

'So have you interviewed James Batley yet?'

'All persons of interest will be interviewed as part of the ongoing investigation.'

'Did you know he was moving?' I ask again. 'He may have already gone.'

P.O. Morgan walks away across the room, then turns to me and says,

'Hanna, I'd like to give you a bit of advice. Let the police do their job. You're not helping.'

He's not going to say any more. He crosses the room and walks to the door. 'It's late. You should get some rest. I'll see myself out.'

I have a terrible night after he leaves. I cannot sleep and pictures of James Batley and Luk wander in and out of my waking dreams. They are in a garden, clinking glasses, pouring jugs of elderflower. Something stronger, shouts Luk. Rob wanders through with his camera. Gatsby did this, he says. And I've got money I want laundered. Where did the money come from asks P.O. Morgan. James Batley replies I've sold my house. We'll all be rich.

68

I've told Charlie I'd be in at the office by ten. I ring through and tell him I've forgotten an appointment with the physiotherapist and that I'll be in later. I feel guilty at telling him a lie, but I am hoping soon I won't have to lie to anyone any more. There are still too many missing pieces in the puzzle. I go into Challengers and ask to see details of Riverside. The man I speak to is not very helpful as he questions me about my budget and no doubt thinks it's outside my price range. I ask about its owner and why it's on the market.

'Business reasons,' says the man. 'He's moving abroad. Let me know if you want to view. I have other properties at our disposal you might be interested in.'

I drive up to Riverside and walk up the familiar stairs to the fourth floor where the blinds are pulled down and nobody answers the door. It looks as though Batley has already gone. It's as though I have come to the end of the road. I ought to heed P.O. Morgan's advice.

I drive down Albert Terrace and stop outside Rob's house. He won't recognise the white Clio so I'm not surprised when he doesn't rush out to greet me. Maybe

Rob was right all the time. The poor woman who died in Albert Terrace was the victim of an accident. Adele had witnessed it, then panicked and sought out Rob's help. But why was she murdered? It didn't make sense. I bang on the door, but Rob is out. Perhaps it's just as well. I don't know what I'd say to him, anyway. Nothing that he doesn't already know.

I'm back at home, thinking it's time I went into work, when I see someone has sent me a text. *Mind your business, for your own good*, it reads. It's not quite grammatically correct, I think initially. Some kind of scam; then the malice behind the words sinks in. My hands are shaking as I try to locate the card. It seems to take forever, but I find it at the bottom of my bag and dial P.O. Morgan's number.

'I'm scared.' I tell him. My voice seems to have disappeared and it comes out sounding like somebody else's, but P.O. Morgan picks up on the urgency.

'I'll send a car for you. Don't speak to anybody.' I wait for about twenty minutes, wishing Mrs Baxter Sellers was still upstairs. Her flat has been empty since they moved out and I've come to miss the sound of a dropped saucepan, and Bobby's occasional bark. It's an unmarked police vehicle that arrives and there are no sirens to shatter the quiet. I think of calling Paul, but remember what P.O. Morgan said about not talking to anyone.

It's the first time I've seen him sitting behind his desk. He looks very important. I show him the text.

'Do you have any idea who sent this?' he asks.

'No.' I point to the lack of grammar, as it must be a clue, but he doesn't seem that concerned.

'We should be able to trace it.'

He hands it to another female officer who has entered the room. I feel greatly relieved that I don't have to try to figure it out for myself. I wonder where Naomi is today and nearly ask, but don't.

'Now you're here, I can bring you up to date,' he replies. 'There have been some developments. A press release is imminent, so you'll find out tomorrow anyway. The woman found dead at Albert Terrace was identified as Sonja Kowski, a Romanian. Her brother, Marek, was already working here as a gardener. He was a well thought of young man, saving to bring his sister over to join him. It was Sonja's dream, but she was young and impatient and unbeknownst to him, had met a 'boyfriend' who promised her he could speed things up, help her find a new life, papers, work. She fell for it. After a rough journey overland in the back of a truck, she got here alright, but never got to see her brother and the only work she saw was lying on her back in Albert Terrace.'

I've never heard him say so much or talk this way before. It shows him in quite a different light. The same one 'my sister's ex' revealed. I wonder if he'd ever been a client at Albert Terrace, but shut the thought down quickly.

At this point D.I. Naomi walks briskly into the interview room. They have a brief word then she takes over. She must have been watching us on a screen, because she picks up the story exactly where P.O. Morgan left off.

'Marek doesn't hear from his sister and gets worried. Then he reads about the murder and sees her photo in the paper. Despite the shock, he comes forward. We were able to identify her and open up other lines of enquiry.'

'So where does James Batley fit into this?' I ask.

'He'd fallen in with criminal types when he was in prison; drug running, girl trafficking and general people exploitation. We think Batley needed money and agreed to be the coordinator this end. He was out of his depth. We believe Sonja tried to escape and asked one of the gang to help her. It's likely there was some sort of fight. We're still investigating. Her death may have been accidental, but Adele had witnessed everything that was going on and had to be silenced'.

It was Adele who was out of her depth, I thought. P.O. Morgan leant back, stretched his arms and took over. 'I'm sorry it's such grim news. But we've made several arrests; uncovered a number of illegal operations. Albert Terrace was just the tip of the iceberg.'

'So is James Batley under arrest now?

'James Batley has disappeared. There's a warrant out for his arrest. We'll catch up with him, you can bet your life.'

My life is not something I'd want to bet on, not at the moment. 'Do you think it was him that sent the text?' I ask

'Either him, or one of his criminal pals.'

'Why were you watching Rosemary's flat?' I ask. 'Is she part of it too?'

P.O. Morgan sits up and looks straight into my eyes. 'At the time, we believed Adele could be involved, and Fortune Estates too.'

'You'll hear this in the morning news,' goes on Naomi. 'In the meanwhile, go home, and try not to worry. We'll keep an eye on your flat.'

They don't look at each other as they get up and leave the office. The room feels very hot and stuffy and I desperately need to get out into the air.

As if to replace the worry I've carried around for the past year, I'm suddenly overcome by exhaustion.

I never told anybody about Adele giving Luk the key. I wonder if they know. I wonder if I should say something, but there's not a lot of point now. Nobody will ever need to know about her involvement. She and Luk are in the clear.

I'm driven home in the same unmarked car, and a plain-clothes officer sees me into the flat.

I fall asleep heavily until I'm woken by a ring at the doorbell at 2 a.m. It must be Paul, I think, sleepily. I'll have to give him a key if he's going to show up at all hours. I open the door, and feel the force of James Batley's hands as he roughly pushes me aside and enters the flat, kicking the door behind him.

69

'Sit down and shut up,' he orders. He paces to the window, flicks the curtains.

'What do you want?' I say. 'The police already know all about you.'

' 'First of all, a little chat, then the keys to your car.'

'Just take the keys and let's forget about the chat,' I say. The words stick in my throat. He looks as crumpled as his coat and I wonder where he's hiding the duct tape and the knife.

'You know the police are watching the flat, don't you?'

'So your detective work paid off, didn't it?' he jeers.

Is he here for revenge? Is he here to rape me and slit my throat?

'Did you kill Adele?' I ask.

His laugh is coarse and mirthless. 'Still playing detective, are we?

I look at him and think no, he hasn't got it in him.

'Where's your car,' he asks abruptly. 'I didn't see it outside.'

I pick up my keys and throw them, hoping to strike him on the face, but he catches them.

'It's the white Clio.'

He looks uncertain, sits down heavily beside me.

'If I thought you were having me on…'

I inch away from him. 'Just take them, just go.'

'I've got a better idea. You can drive me.'

'Where to?'

'We'll talk about that on way.'

He must know it's all over. I'm wondering how he managed to get in here – what happened to the police protection? Perhaps he has no intention of leaving. He's just going to sit here until the police show up.

'You could come with me.'

'I don't really think that would help, do you, James?' I say it softly and he seems startled by the use of his name. For a moment he looks at me as though to answer, then he's at the window again, checking out the dark night.

'In another life, I might have fancied you,' he says.

With no further word, he goes to the front door. I hear it slam. I hear the police car sirens.

I hear them throughout the night, long after the police have taken him away, and their shrill call has ceased.

EPILOGUE

Three years later.

Luk Berioskya sits in his back garden smoking a cigarette and looks with pride at his vegetable garden. How green and lush everything looks. The tomatoes already reddening and soon ready for eating. His gaze takes in his raspberry canes. Soon they too will be ripe and Onya will be picking them and turning them into jam. This year, Elena, their eldest, now 12, will be able to help her mother.

As he looks at his labours with pride, her sister, Maria, dances out into the garden, 'Dada can we go to the park'. Later, he replies, when your brother gets home from school. 'Where's Mama, asks Maria.' Still at work, he replies. We'll wait for them both. Luk smiles indulgently as he thinks of his family. How beautiful they are. How close. He will never let anything threaten their security again. And soon Mama will be giving up work. Another little one will soon join their family. He secretly hopes for another boy, but will not mind if it's a girl. He takes out his phone and makes a call to Stefan. The window cleaning business never stops, particularly since so many hi-rise flats have been built in the city of Statisova. They specialise and now employ over nine men and have three vans at their disposal. Soon he will have made enough to buy a small house in the country, or perhaps by the sea, for the family to escape to in the holidays.

It's not often that Luk has to get his hands dirty, not any more. But sometimes, when one of his workers is sick, or needs time off for a personal issue, for Luk is a compassionate employer, his thoughts are drawn back to the time he travelled across the UK to find work. He remembers a chance meeting at a hospital, a woman with dark curly hair, a willing smile. It could have worked out so well. It was sad the way things ended. He warned Stefan not to get close to the girls, but Adele knew too much. She had to be silenced. Stefan will have to work many years now to repay Luk's silence, probably the rest of his life.

Maria interrupts his thoughts, 'Dada, Mama's coming. Can we go to the park now?'

He sweeps the little girl towards him. How soft she feels in his arms.

'Of course, my darling,' he replies. 'Let's go.'

About the Author

Born London, studied Social Sciences at Manchester College Oxford and LSE. Has worked in the BBC, Social Services and developed her own fashion business.

M.S. Clary has won several prizes for short fiction and her first novel A Spell in France, a psychological thriller, is available as an ebook.

Married, with two sons, lives in Oxfordshire.

www.msclary.co.uk